Four Months Basqued

By: Bradley Basker

I0566666

Copyright © 2016 Bradley Basker

Published by: Griffin Collective

Griffin Collective

ISBN-13: 978-0692800478
ISBN-10: 0692800476

DEDICATION
To the vagabonds
To the lovers, heartbroken, romantics, and dreamers
To the people I met during my travels in Basque Country
To Cafe Agora - Houston, TX

For Erin - 03.14.15

CONTENTS

ACKNOWLEDGMENTS

Much thanks to Erica Babino (editor) and Jerusha Rogers (editor) for helping me bring this story to life.

Other titles:

The Meeting Place (2014)

It's Particular (2013)

Prologue: Somewhere in Between

Two months after Summer 1

Nothing can truly end when we don't know where to begin. There are defining moments, instances in life, where we can distinctly say, "That was when my life changed." However, to say something ended has a certain definitive ring to it. Finality has its way of defining every aspect of life. If you love someone, you let them go. If they come back, then it's meant to be. People fail to mention the other element of that expression, which is if they don't come back you sit in your bed hours on end lamenting the last year you spent waiting on their phone call, while thinking of all those seemingly wonderful partners you passed up because you believed some idiotic expression.

Saying that a period of one's life has come to an end implies a certain degree of devotion to the actions and decisions needed to begin something new. Anything new requires commitment and a certain conviction which I completely lack. I committed to moving to France, knowing that it would mean the 'end' of my relationship with her. I thought I understood finality, and that I was even its master. A couple of months into my life in La Roche-Sur-Yon, it became clear that I was neither as unaffected or decisive about ending the relationship. I had carried Derlenzistda in my heart; the heart which I thought I never had. I still loved her.

At first, I calmly searched my inboxes for her messages. There were none. So, I searched in the streets for someone similar, only to find many others. Instead, I fell into the arms of lovers at bars and discos and only found love for lease, with no option to buy. Each time I awoke to a cold empty bed. The warmth was as fleeting as their feet which tiptoed from my apartment during my slumber. To this day I can hardly remember all their names and it seems I've forgotten my own, or even my purpose in this life.

1

I've returned to the United States with life's mileage on my face and in my heart. My more than extended sejour in France has 'ended' but it doesn't feel that way. No. While I've lived a life worth writing about, I can hardly describe the delicacies I've tasted, or the wines that passionately educated my palate. I tell old friends and family of the places I've been and the people I've met. I paint a picture of the globetrotter's glorious luxury, all the while leaving out the finer details. Unlike a visa pasted in my passport or a fresh cut of ossau iraty cheese from the morning markets in La Roche, my experience has no expiration date. I doubt anyone understands, so I don't talk about her or many of the things I've done. However, that doesn't mean I don't remember. I can no more change the moments which make me nostalgic than I can the instances which made them memories.

After two months stateside, I've officially stopped trying to figure out my life. I head to the cafe, just like I had done each day before my life of cold beers and colder beds. The cafe gave me solace back then. Even in my most difficult of moments I could always come here for a warm cortado. It's home and history for me. It's also where I met her.

I enter through its old creaky doors wondering if I will see her; that one who I'd searched for in the streets of La Roche-Sur-Yon. However, I know I won't. She doesn't come around these parts anymore.

The sun shines brilliantly through the large cafe windows. Sunlight glistens off the glossy wooden floor. I pause for a moment at the entrance to admire the decor. There is always a new painting of Greek ruins or some classical scene of arguing philosophers blazoned across each of its four walls. I'm scanning the room when a sunbeam warmly strikes my face. I smile for a moment, as I remember the days I spent walking along beaches in the south of France, and even how the summer sunlight would rest upon me during afternoon siestas. I approach the bar, still smiling.

"Teo! I knew I'd see you here," says Jess from behind the counter as she finishes wiping off a wine glass. She reaches up to place it with the others which hang upside down above the bar.

"Where else would you see me? I don't go anywhere else," I say.

"And here I was thinking that because you had a nice smile on your face that there would be words to match."

"I've got some nice words, Jess," I say, smiling again. "I'm just not sure where I left them."

"Well do you have enough to say what you want to drink? The usual?"

"He'll take a cortado. Just make sure it's not too hot," says a familiar voice. It's Kevin, one of those faces from the old days, that I don't mind seeing these days. "My treat, *menino*."

"I'm not known for turning down free coffee. Sounds good," I reply.

Since I've returned from my journey, Kevin and I have become pretty frequent cafe buddies. I didn't recognize too many faces when I first returned. A lot of the usual crowd had moved on with their lives, and some aren't even in the country anymore. However, he's still around, and has been a pretty good friend when I need one.

We take a seat on the terrace. The sun greets me again seeping through the foliage, but I resist the temptation to daydream. We sit at one of the round metal tables. He chats briefly about some business endeavors, of which I'm always interested to hear.

"I've just come back from a convention," he says.

"Rubbing shoulders? Shaking hands?"

"You know all too well how these things go."

"Yeah."

"How are book sales going?" he asks.

"Slow. Steady. Have you had a chance to read it yet?" I ask. He pauses and looks away. "Really man? You begged me for a copy two months ago and you still haven't read it?"

"I'm super busy, Teo. You know this. Besides I don't like to read two books at once, and I haven't finished the one I was reading before I bought yours."

"Do you know the author personally as well? What prick wrote this one?" I ask.

"I would have loved to have met him, but he's dead. It's Hemingway," he says almost proudly.

"Oh," I say feeling a bit ashamed for having called great author outside of name. "Well, the dead ones seem to be the great ones. At least that's what I'm told."

"I don't think you have to be dead to be great. You just have to be great."

"Fair enough, I suppose. Perhaps, we'll see. What book is it?"

3

He pulls out a copy of *As the Sun Also Rises* and tries to hand it to me. I don't take it from him. My smile fades. I retreat once more into my thoughts, lips pursed, brows furrowed.

"I know it," I say, as I motion for him to put it down. I pull out a copy of the same book from my tattered green satchel. "I know it well."

"Whoa! What a coincidence! What do you think of the story?" he asks excitedly.

"I've been holding on to this copy for some time now," I begin. "That region of France, Basque Country, is exquisite. It's as if France and Spain collided bringing the best of their cultures with them. Needless to say, Hemingway had a lot to be inspired by."

"Didn't you live there?"

"No. Well. Yes. I was there for two months this past summer for work after La Roche-Sur-Yon. I was in Biarritz," I say. Even to utter its name fills me with a summer's emotions. "Haha. It's funny. I was thinking that today's sunlight reminds me of that place."

"Memories?" he asks.

"You have no idea."

"You don't talk about it much. Your adventures, I mean. Sure, you rambled about Portugal, your weekends in Paris, and it sounds amazing. But this, this, Biarritz? Almost never. You were gone a long time, so I know there's gotta be some crazy tales worth mentioning."

"Too many."

"You gotta start somewhere. Right?" he says, taking a sip of his coffee.

He's right. Absolutely correct. If I ever want finality, if I truly want to reconcile with my past, I've got to begin something new. Right?

"Ok. This could be a while," I say.

"I've got the time."

"It's worth knowing that I carried this book for almost two years without turning a page. I only finished it around the time I came back to the U.S." I take a nice sip of my cortado. "She gave it to me."

"Derlenzistda?"

I pause at the mention of that name. I take a deep breath and continue.

"Yes. She knew I loved to travel. She had to read the book for a class and thought I'd enjoy it. I didn't read it. She mentioned the Basque Country, and even Biarritz, but it passed clean through my thoughts. I didn't realize it was the same place until I was on a train to the south of France. I thought I fully understood how I messed up, but in that moment, I was sure. I missed out."

"On a good book?"

"On a good woman," I say expressionlessly. "But it was too late by that point. I was already having a Basque experience of my own."

"That's a good thing, right?"

"I'm not sure yet, but it is a *thing*. Look Kev, you've got to understand something about my time away...It wasn't like how things are here. After a while, I wasn't the same either. Here, I sheltered myself on the terrace, at this very cafe. I kept to myself, I didn't want be involved, but couldn't help it. Derlenzistda changed that."

"What did she change? I mean, how does she even fit in?" he asks.

"Because I didn't know I wanted only one woman until I had been in the arms of several. By the time I moved to Biarritz I'd lost sight of that and everything I stood for."

"So what happened? You can't leave me hanging on that."

"*Euskadi*," I say with a smile. "*Euskadi,* happened. Grab me a beer and I'll tell you all about it."

5

Summer 1

Chapter 1: *Le Pays Basque*

The journey from La Roche-Sur-Yon to Biarritz is six hours by TGV. It is far from the lengthiest trek I've ever made, but these days I measure distance in moments, not miles. Still, there is a lot of time to think. The life I knew in my home country is long gone. La Roche is my new home. I learned to walk its streets as if they had always been my own, collecting friendships, and frequenting a slew of restaurants, cafes, and bars where I became known by name and reputation. I partied all too often, almost never turning down an invitation. The wine filled glasses, the language filled my dreams, and my tiny apartment was never lacking for good company. I leave that reputation behind this morning. All I've got are 3 bags of clothes, a guitar, and a mind packed with anxiety and excitement.

I don't know much about *Le Pays Basque*. All my friends say how jealous they are that I'm spending a summer in Biarritz, the surf capital of France, but I don't understand their envy. All I can think of is the several hundred euros needed to take me across the Atlantic, and not getting into too much trouble. So yes; anxious and excited. I'm anxious to start getting paid so I can finally afford a flight back to the U.S., but excited about living in a hostel with food, accommodation, and salary, in an envy worthy city.

Biarritz is one of the last destinations before reaching the Spanish frontier. The idea of crossing into Spain becomes increasingly tempting as the train nears the station. Any other day I would roll the dice and see where the wind takes me, but that philosophy is what has me in this position in the first place.

Broke.

I have to be on time and in good form to meet a man named Bernard, with whom I'm supposed to work with for the entire summer managing a recreational center for tourists. I certainly won't make a good first impression by going rogue into Spanish Basque Country. The train comes to a stop at *Gare de Biarritz*. I hesitate for a second, but finally gather my things.

The wind encircles me as I step off the train. For a moment, the Basque breeze makes me forget that I'm here to work. The hint of salt spices in every gust let me know that the ocean is nearby. The sun is brilliant and blazing. Bernard probably doesn't have time for my wandering musings about the climate, so I snap out of it and quickly move to the station's exit. He must have seen a photo of me, because upon exiting I see a tall man leaning on a small silver Renault, with a cigarette in mouth, a stubbly beard, long straight brown hair, and his hand waving in the air.

"Ciao! Teo!"

"Bernard?"

"*Oui*!"

"Awesome to meet you!"

"Welcome to Biarritz, Teo. Did you have an ok journey?"

"Yes. A bit long, but quite nice. I'm ready to get to work."

"*Ouais, Ouais.* Yeah," he says with a quick puff of his cigarette. "You want to take something? A beer?"

"Right now?"

"Yeah. Right there. There is a bar here. Come on, it is fine. Don't hurry," he says as he points to the entrance on the left side of the station. A Carlsberg sign clearly marks where we can find a glass of golden goodness.

"Um. Well, sure," I respond.

We order two pints and take a seat outside on the terrace. The weather is even more pleasant with a cold glass in hand. Still, I can't seem to let go of my purpose for being here.

"So, has the team arrived?" I ask.

"Yes, but relax. You've had a long trip. Your French is pretty good for an American. You have come from the mid-west? Yes?"

"Thank you, and yes. I was in La Roche-Sur-Yon, in La Vendée."

"Ah ok," he says, nodding as if he understands something profound. "We do things a bit differently here."

"How so?" I ask while looking around at the people passing by. Some are loading luggage into their small cars, while others wait at the bus stop. There are several people eating at a restaurant across the street called *La Station.* They all look normal to me.

"We are Basque. *Hil arteraino bizi, han arte ez izi.* This means, 'Live until you die, and until then don't panic' in *Euskara.* Yes, it is good to live this way, I think."

"I love the sound of that," I respond finally loosening up a bit. "I guess I just thought we'd be getting to work right away."

"No worries, Teo. The season can be long. There are many people who will come for our services, and you are the one who will be mainly responsible for that," he says, pausing for a puff of his cigarette. "It is good to take in the moment, just as we are now. There is much work to do, this I promise, but we have much to see here as well."

He raises his glass and smiles.

"*Santé.*"

"*Santé,*" I reply as we clink our glasses together.

It takes a couple minutes to finish the last sips of beers. With my gear loaded in the car, we drive just a few minutes from the station descending through winding hills, whizzing past the quaint homes and their *orangish* clay rooftops. Another salty breeze slips through the open window space as we continue past trees and steep roads. We level out at the bottom. It's the first time I set eyes on the hostel. There are palm trees, Mediterranean roofing, large windows, which probably means there is no central heating, and trees. Trees, forest, and foliage surrounding everything. Through its huge windows I can see into the lobby, the hallways, and even into a small office.

Bernard pulls into the hostel's backside parking lot. He helps me out with my luggage, and we enter through glass doors. The first person I see is a tall, deeply bronzed man with wavy hair down his back. I expect a big booming voice to ring at any moment, but am quite surprised when he opens his mouth.

"What's up, B. It is the guy?" he asks in interesting island voice. I've never heard one like that in French before.

"Yes, it is *the* guy."

"The big boss?"

"Oh yeah. Biggest." replies Bernard.

"Cool. Super cool. Hey boss, my name is Hamza," he says switching to English.

"Hi, nice to meet you."

"Oh great. You speak French?"

"*Bah, oui.*"

"Phew, thank God. We are gonna be friends, my man."

He's a gentle giant. There's really no other way to put it. After talking a bit more I come to find out that Hamza worked as a bouncer. However, his heart is for the water, the beach, and the sun. He traded in the stressful worries of disco-security for a receptionist/hostel Renaissance man gig a long time ago. He never looked back, and now works four days a week before surfing for the next three. Basically, he's living the dream.

We are in the middle of a nice meet and greet when I hear two voices battling for dominance. At first it seems like they're arguing, but after listening a bit more the conversation seems perfectly normal.

"Aude! Aude! Did you send the document?!" belts out a man's voice.

"Greg! What?!"

"Shit! The document! It arrived before 16:00? Yes?!"

"No! I talked to them! There was an issue with their computers, so it is fine to send it tomorrow!"

"Shit! Ok. Thank you!"

I stand there wide eyed looking at Bernard and Hamza; half curious as to **who these folks are** and half ready to reach for my blade in the event that a fight breaks out. One of culprits emerges from behind the reception area offices. She's a short woman with peppered hair and glasses. Meanwhile, an equally pepper haired man descends from an upstairs office, still yelling a bit, but this time into his cell phone headset.

"*Salut*," says the woman who has suddenly become sweet as a *galette de rois*. "You are the Program Manager for this summer? I am Aude."

"Oh, yes. Hi. I'm Teo. Pleasure to meet you."

"Is that alcohol I smell?" she asks.

"Um..."

"Yes. It is," chimes in Bernard. "I treated him to a beer at the train station. He had a long trip you know?"

"Ah, really? He has just arrived and you have taken him for a siesta?" Bernard shrugs, and changes the subject.

"Aude is the Assistant Director for the hostel. This is her brother, Greg. He is the Director for this hostel and others in the city," says

Bernard. He points to the man who has just reached the bottom of the stairs, still on his phone. He pauses from his conversation.

"Who is this?" he asks angrily.

"I'm, Teo. I'm the Program Manager for this summer."

"Great! *Enchanté*. I'm Greg. Wait, what?!" he yells as he clutches his earpiece again. "No! Shit. Wait. I am getting on my scooter now! I will be there in 15 minutes. Don't touch a damn thing!"

And with that he walks outside. He straps his brown satchel around his chest against his pink dress shirt, plops down on his scooter, and speeds off. Aude bids us a good evening and walks out the door. I'm pleasantly overwhelmed by the variety of characters I've met in just minutes, and I haven't even gone to my room yet. Just as I am preparing to ask about me key, a short man with thinning black hair and tanned skin exits from the behind the reception glass. He's beat boxing while tapping on his chest, and stops in his tracks when he sees me.

"Hamza, who's this?"

"It's Teo. He's the boss man for the recreation program this summer. Teo, this is Guillaume, but we call him Gil."

"What's up, Teo. You play the guitar?" he asks enthusiastically eyeing my bag with his green eyes.

"Yeah, man."

"*Putain, c'est cool ça.* I play the bass," he says motioning with his hands in the form of an upright bass. "We will need to jam, yeah?"

"Right on. Count me in!" I say. He sticks out his hand for a fist bump. We bump, and he retreats to the office thumping his chest and humming.

Hamza and Bernard guide me to my room and leave me to settle in. Hermann, the Founder and Program Director from Germany, will come tomorrow to brief the team and I, but for now we have the night off. I come down to bid good evening to Bernard who heads to his car, cigarette in hand. Hamza guides me to a bar within the hostel to find my teammates. We pass by a small kitchen window, entering through double doors where two petite ladies are sitting and smiling at a table.

"Hello again, Katia, Shoshana. Teo has just arrived," says Hamza, ducking his head as we pass under the doors. I had met them once before during some training sessions in England, but we haven't spoken much since then. They stand to greet me; Katia, Russian, quaint and classy, sporting stylish shoes and handbag with an alluring scent to

11

match. Shoshana, German, blonde, just as quaint, but sporty and enthusiastic, and ready to take on any challenge.

"Teo! It is great to see you again!" says Katia, as she greets me with kisses.

"You too, darlin! Hey there, Shoshana! You ready for the summer?" I say, as I lean for kisses to each cheek.

"I've been waiting months to be here! Yes! I am ready to work, and I've got tons of ideas planned out!"

"Brilliant!"

"I will leave you all," says Hamza. "I am supposed to be at the reception. Haha."

"*Merci bien!*" says Katia. Hamza retreats back towards the reception area again ducking under the doors.

"Have you seen the lake?" asks Shoshana excitedly.

"What lake?"

"C'mon!" she says, as she darts towards the door motioning for us to come along. Just beyond the parking lot is a forest with trails suitable for running and riding bikes. We're surrounded by trees within the first moments of strolling on the path. We walk just minutes until we reach a small wooden dock which juts out onto the water. "Look at it! Isn't it beautiful?"

It's *Lac Mouriscot*. Shoshana tells me it's a natural site preserved by the European Union and I can see exactly why. It's shaped in an oval surrounded by dense trees. Its blue hue is a background to wildlife. There are some birds congregating in the middle. There are even a few lake houses along the way, and one has a family cooking outside. The sun shines down onto the water. Its reflection almost seems to be reaching out towards us as a beam of light stretches from the horizon, all the way to where we're standing on the edge of the dock.

"So, Teo? What do you think?" asks Katia.

"Live until you die," I say with a smile. "Until then don't panic."

Chapter 2: Hermann the German

Two incredible events take place simultaneously the next morning. The first is that I wake up for the first time to a Biarritz sunrise shining through my window. The second is the fact that I wake up in the morning at all. It's **7:30am**, and despite all the relaxing and easy going people I met yesterday, getting to work is still at the forefront of my thoughts. Hermann will **be** meeting us at **9:00am**. During training we were told that he is a man very **set in his ways**, and likes to stick to what he knows works. He is also quite discriminating with whom he chooses to work during the summer, so not just anyone is chosen to work here. Plus, there are all the German stereotypes about being on time and well organized, which in most of my experiences have proven to be true more often than not.

After a quick breakfast, Katia, Shoshana and I gather in the space that will be our office. It isn't much to look at and has nothing more than a couple of tables and two book**cases, surrounded** by glass walls. It's through the ones facing the opposite side of the hostel where I see a blue Volkswagen pass every parking space to pull into the grass just by our windows. Out steps a tall slim man wearing jeans, a short sleeve plaid button up **shirt,** and glasses. His facial hair is scruffy and his slightly thinned gray and black hair dances a bit as he moves around rigidly. He sticks his hand up and nods while opening his car's hatchback, which is full of boxes. He grabs two of them, and we watch as he enters the door into the hallway leading to our office.

"Good morning, team!" he says. We all stand to greet him. "So, **which** one of you is, Teo?! Hahahaha!"

"Haha. It's the short Russian one wearing red lipstick," I say.

"Opp la! I thought he was a tall black man!" he says, continuing to laugh and clap his hands loudly. His voice bellows like Barry White. A German, French speaking, Barry White. "Hermann Haase."

"Teo," I say, as I reach my hand out to receive his almost bone shattering handshake.

"And you, girls. Katia and Shoshana. How do we always get the prettiest girls working here?" He asks, letting out a laugh while giving them equally bone crushing handshakes. The girls laugh it off, while grabbing their hands in pain.

"The recruiters had to send only the most handsome and beautiful people to do this job," begins Katia smiling through her bright red lipstick. "After all, Biarritz is a city of luxury and glamour."

"Of course, Katia. We will need that enthusiasm for when we organize tours and excursions for our clients. Relax yourselves," he says.

He officially welcomes us to Biarritz and gives us the whole story. He founded a recreational program called Summers by the Seaside over 25 years ago, which means he's been in the business since before we were born. It began with French language courses for young adults and has grown to include surf schools, city tours of both French and Spanish Basque Regions, and a variety of recreational events like sporting competitions, game nights, etc. He joined SBS with a business partner 10 years ago to expand it to other regions, which is why we had our trainings in England with people from recreational programs across Europe.

"I know I am not a typical German," he begins. "It is because I have lived in this region since before you were born. I also know the training you received, which is good. However, here in Biarritz, we do things a bit differently."

At that moment, I finally let my guard down. It's one thing when Bernard, Hamza, and others say that things are done 'differently' here, but the director saying it is completely different; even if I don't exactly know what it means yet. He explains like the others that the summer is long, and will be very difficult during high tourism season. He then insists that we must be willing to take time to relax. There is a good deal of discussion about things that the three of us already knew. Katia is in charge of tours, social hours, and artistic events. Shoshana is responsible for tours as well and sporting events. I am responsible for organizing the recreational team in addition to a large collection of busy work like accounting, accommodation, meal planning, client relations, etc.

"The work can be very stressful at times, but I chose you all based on your profiles and have much confidence in you. Teo and I will work closely together. Refer to him if there is a need, and lastly to me for any issues out of his control. There will be others who will come in high season to help with the program, but we will get to that as the time comes. Any questions?"

There are none.

Katia and Shoshana start setting up computers, supplies, and decorations, while I help Hermann carry in the rest of the boxes. Soon most of the glass walls are covered with cork boards, calendars, and posters. We have office supplies, medical kits, sporting equipment, and even a fridge which we fetch from a nearby shed. With it in place, it seems our little office is taking shape. The only thing left in Hermann's trunk is a large cooler. He says, *"C'est l'heure."* which means literally that, 'It's the hour." He then hands me a cube of rosé. I stand next to him in amazement when I see he has two more cubes inside the cooler. It's not even noon.

"I have rosé stashed in a few places around this region. This one is for the office here," he says looking at me over his glasses. "You thirsty?"

"Oh yes. I should probably drink something to cool down a bit," I respond with a smile.

"Les filles! Do you have a little thirst?"

"Oh...Not much. But, ok," yells Shoshana through one of our sliding windows. Hermann and I walk back into the office, where he takes some glasses from one of the book cases.

"Just a little for me," says Katia. He pours four glasses; two full, two half full.

"To a great season, team!" he exclaims, as we toast to the summer.

Hermann takes us out for lunch. It's my first time really seeing any of the city, and it's luxurious just as Katia said. We cruise in the Volkswagen with windows down on Queen Victoria Avenue, and pass The Hotel Palais. Katia, staying true to her position, chimes in explaining how it was built by Napoleon III in 1855 as a summer villa for the Empress Eugenie. We arrive in Anglet, which along with Bayonne, make up the principal cities of the region, and even host the same airport since they're only minutes apart from each other. We grab a bite to eat at *La Station*, which is the same appropriately named restaurant across the street from the train station where I arrived. It's amazing to watch Hermann in action. He enters to a string of 'bonjours' from the workers. He jokes the entire time as he introduces us to the owners and suggests what we should eat for our first dinner in *Euskadi*.

We have to head back to the hostel quickly, because I have a meeting with Gil to plan for the arrival of our program participants. After such an interesting combination of work and play, it's hard to imagine that the meeting would be much different. Hermann stays with the Katia and Shoshana to explain a bit more about their jobs and to help them get organized, while I go for my first weekly meeting of the summer.

I enter his office. There are faint sounds of reggae coming from his computer as he makes the same tapping and beatboxing sounds from the day before. In the corner is an upright bass. Shit. He's really not messing around about this music thing.

"*Salut*, Teo. *Putain.* I didn't see you there."

"*Pas de problem, mec.* I see you have your bass?"

"Of course, I'm always ready. Hey, check this out," he says as he points to the video playing on his computer. He makes me an espresso while rocking his head back and forth. "Do you hear it? *Putain, c'est enorme.*"

This musical exchange continues for about five minutes as he explains that he's in a band called David-Carol, and he tours often around France. Finally, he shuts the music off and opens up a large spreadsheet. It's one thing to speak in French about music and good vibes, but when he starts explaining room assignments, prices, and meal planning I am completely lost.

"Do you understand?" he asks.

"Nope! Could you slow down a bit?" I ask. He tries to explain in English which is a disaster. I ask him just to take me step by step again in French. Eventually, I get the hang of it. Every week we will meet to discuss how many people are coming to be in the program. It's my job to bring him the numbers and duration of their stay so we can create room and meal planning, which eventually turns into an invoice. It's pretty mind numbing in any language, especially for two musicians. It doesn't take long before he changes topics.

"So. Katia?"

"What about her?"

"She's hot, yeah?"

"Oh, well, yes. She's super cute."

"Think she has a boyfriend?"

"Um. I don't know, man."

"*Quoi!?* You didn't ask yet? *Mec,* I would be all over that," he says exhaling and shaking his head.

"I don't know. We work together. Company policy is against it, of course. Besides, there's got to be plenty of women who come to stay here during the summer."

He pauses and looks at me intensely.

"You have no idea," he says shaking his head. "There are already the *meufs* who come for your program, but then there are regular hostel clients. All of this, and we haven't even mentioned the city center. I've been here for several years, and have seen it. This is a beach city, Teo. People come here to tan, party, and screw, for their holiday."

"Really?"

"You have no idea. You have all of this in a normal summer, but during *les ferias* it is even crazier!"

"What are *les ferias*?"

"Every city has a festival period in Basque Country. During this time people come from all over France, and even the world, to party. The streets are filled with people wearing red and white and drinking sangria."

"You're serious?"

"I am always serious about *les ferias.* They're even organized from city to city. You could go from city to city for weeks celebrating in the streets. It is in France and Spain, but perhaps *La Fête de Bayonne* will be your chance."

"Wow. Maybe I'll check it out."

"Trust me. *Les belles meufs* everywhere," he says nodding his head and putting some music back on. Just then Hermann comes into the office.

"Oh la la! Look at the two hard workers!"

"Come on, Hermann! You know me well enough. It's your fault for hiring a musician to work this summer!" says Gil as he winks at me.

"Well if the season goes to hell we will at least have a soundtrack. Teo, is everything clear?"

17

I say yes, because I'm almost certain he's asking about my job and not *les ferias*. Otherwise, I have no idea what to think.

The evening calms everything down. The winds are cooler. Work stops for the day. The summer season is just beginning so there are only a few travelers at the hostel bar. Katia and Shoshana turn in for the night, and rightfully so. Our first group of clients arrive tomorrow and it's a big group. I can't sleep. I sit at the bar. An intern named James from Leeds, England is the only person I talk to as he sells me beer.

"You get staff pricing, mate," he says.

"I didn't know. That's pretty awesome."

"You party a bit?"

"I've had a few nights turn into mornings," I say. "We'll see how long before I find one here."

He laughs a bit before getting back to work. There are some travelers playing drinking games at a table behind me. They're German, and talk loudly and joyfully. I try to imagine what it will be like to have groups of people like them from all over the world passing through here night by night. I'll know it by experience soon enough, but I can't help to wonder of my place in all this. A very pretty blonde comes up to the bar. She sits on the stool next to me and orders another round wine for the table.

"Hey! Don't drink alone, guy! Do you wanna join us?!" she asks. I turn to look at her. She smiles so brilliantly contrasted against her newly tanned skin. My first impulse is to say 'yes'. I have every intention to keep drinking, and she's much easier on the eyes than James. It'd be perfect, but something's just not right. My memories hover over me like a conflicting cloud. I think about all those nights in La Roche. I'd down no less than a bottle of port wine or a six-pack of 1664 before I was ready to go to the bar. If my wallet was full, I'd stay out until 6:00am, and go to work at 8:00am. If I met a '*meuf*' like the one currently waiting for my response, we'd leave the disco at 2:00am with the possibility of me calling in sick. I can't start this summer, the way those nights ended.

"Sorry. I have work in the morning."

"Aw! It's really so sad! Another time, guy."

James looks at me with an expression that if put into words would be, "What the fuck, man?", so I down my beer like I don't notice it. I tell him I'll see him tomorrow, and head to my room.

In the silence of the evening a familiar sensation sets in. Twilights are for the pensive, so I begin to think. To reflect. To ponder and lament. I sit on the edge of the bed and look at my green satchel, which is placed on the desk against the wall. Inside is a book I've never read.

I think back to a lifetime past. I close my eyes as I lie down. I try to imagine a very specific face, one that I've long tried to forget. Derlenzistda. I can only hold it in my mind for a moment before others appear. Each one counts like a thousand more miles I'm away from her and decades more since we've spoken. All I can see are flashes of their faces, my lovers and lusters, in ecstasy; bodies thriving in the moonlight. I try to move past them all to less provocative memories, but now I can only see that blonde girl's smile.

"Damn book," I say to myself. My eyes reopen and I sit once again on the edge of my bed. I reach into my armoire and pull out a bottle of Bordeaux. I fill a glass and quickly remind it of how empty it can be, gulping down the red richness. I pour another and repeat until the bottle is just a bottle.

I pass out.

Chapter 3: *La Fête de la Musique*

The next morning goes smoother than any of us anticipate. After a quick breakfast, we immediately take our places in the office. The best way to describe the workflow is like an airport traffic tower. I'm at the helm delegating and informing while Katia and Shoshana fly around carrying out tasks. Today's agenda requires a lot of logistics for arrivals as our clients come by train, plane, and even car. It's our job to make the transition as smooth possible, which means meeting them at the airport or train station and accompanying them to the hostel for check-in.

Summer tends to bring out the most interesting sorts of people, especially in a city like Biarritz. There's an elderly couple from Holland who've come to take some French lessons and tour the region, while a rowdy group of co-eds from Italy are here to see how bronze they can get from sunbathing at *La Grande Plage*, the most popular beach in the city. Hermann, despite not being required to, shows up to help with transportation.

"*Imagine un peu*, Teo. If you three had to be in four places at once," he says. I do imagine a little, as he suggests.

"It takes 15 minutes to get to the airport from here. It can become complicated fast with late flights and missing luggage. Also, we have a couple of groups arriving at the train station today. Our budget for taxis will run out fast," I say.

"Exactly. I love to help. *Je suis un homme qui rende service.*"

I think I understand what he means. He likes to be active and help out. If there is a service to be "rendered" he is willing to do it. Perhaps, that has a lot to do with how smooth the day is going.

The girls are out meeting people, and to be honest there isn't much for me to do. I stroll around the hostel before walking behind the reception to chat with Hamza a bit. A group of hostel clients arrive. Three ladies full of excitement for their summer vacation approach the reception. From the look of their bronzed skin it's obvious they're not strangers to the beach life. I watch Hamza as he speaks Spanish to them while taking their information.

"I am Hamza. If you have any questions let me know. Also, this is Teo," he says giving me a slight wink. "He knows the city well so feel free to bother him if you see him around too."

"*Hola*," I say with a slightly bashful smile. I'm tempted to capitalize on Hamza's introduction, but fight back the urge to flirt. After a couple of moments, they say thank you, smile, and rush off down the corridor with loud Spanish rumblings. "Is it always like this? All summer?"

"It is Biarritz, Teo. We have the beach," he says smiling that gentle giant smile.

"That is true. Maybe I'll have to help out at the reception when things get busy."

All of our clients have arrived by the late afternoon, which means it's time to hold our first welcome meeting. We gather everyone in the bar area with Hermann, Katia, Shoshana and I at the center. Hermann gives a speech in French introducing us all, while I follow up in English. We pass out itineraries for their perspective activities. The elderly couple, adorable as can be, snuggle up as they read about their hands-on French course. A group of long haired English surfers let out a yell during Shoshana's speech about how the surfing courses are organized, which adds a nice touch of humor to the room. Katia has a final word about the day's festivities, which fortunately for everyone falls on a very special day.

"Perhaps, you have noticed there is music everywhere. This is because today, June 21, is *La Fête de La Musique*. Musical events will take place all over the world, and in France every city is filled with concerts and performances for the entire day! In an hour, we will go for a city tour, if you're interested. We can explain how to use your bus passes and I will give some details about Biarritz history. After, this there are no plans for any of your programs, so there is plenty of time to explore the music," she says, very vibrantly. I almost forget I'm supposed to give the closing remarks as what Gil said about her during our meeting pops in my mind. I shake it off.

"Thank you very much, Katia," I begin. "Ok folks! That's all for now. If you have any questions about your programs for tomorrow, feel free to ask any of us. Otherwise, *bienvenue a Biarritz!*"

They give a hefty applause and even a few whistles. I look to the team and am happy to see smiles on their faces. It seems like we may be on the right track. We're even happier when every client shows up to take the city tour.

Hermann retires for the evening saying we've done well, which is exactly the type of start I'd hoped to make. We shepherd everyone onto the public buses and into the city center. Katia, with delicate command, leads us through the streets. *La Grande Plage* is buzzing with life, and people are filling the streets to hear everything from a single guitarist on the street corner, to full productions by the beach.

Despite all the excitement, Katia captivates the group with her stories about Biarritz's history. She is notably enthusiastic when discussing Russia's close ties with the city.

"The Russian aristocracy was here so often that in the 19th century the Russian Orthodox Church was constructed. Do you see its famous blue dome? It is beautiful, yes?"

Oh, it's beautiful alright, and looks even better from where I'm standing. I'm not sure I'd noticed her before, but watching her in action showed me exactly what Gil was talking about. She finishes the tour and the group disperses for the evening to do whatever they feel like, while we have a team meeting at *Les Colonnes* just across the street from *Casino Barrière Biarritz*

"What do you ladies think?" I ask. "It seemed pretty smooth to me."

"Yes, it was quite exciting!" adds Shoshana.

"I'm really happy with the tour, Teo. Tomorrow we will see, because it is really our first day for activities," says Katia.

"True, true. Anyway. There is music all over the city. Let's go check it out."

"I'm tired. I think I'll call it a night and get ready for tomorrow," says Shoshana.

"Really?! But it is *La Fête*!" says Katia.

"Yes, sorry! I want to get some more work done so things are perfect."

"Ok, ok!" says Katia. "Teo and I will just enjoy the festivities."

Shoshana bids us a good evening and walks into the distance, leaving Katia and me alone.

Katia is full of stories. We walk slowly through the streets as she tells me about her home in St. Petersburg, Russia. Her reasons for coming to *Pays Basque* are a bit different than mine, despite the fact that we both came to make money.

"My degree focuses on the Russian presence in France. My dissertation will be all about how the aristocracy influenced this city. I get to research in my spare time, to live in a beautiful place, and have a French work visa so I can go Paris after this. It is perfect! What about you, Teo? You have come from even further to be here. What is the story?"

"It does seem a bit bizarre, doesn't it? It's not even my field," I begin. "I've been living in France for a while now. I was doing an internship and even teaching a bit of English, but writing is really what I love to do. At least, it's what I used to love to do. To make a long story short, I spent all of my money on tickets exploring Europe, and a pretty busy social life. So much that I didn't have enough for a return ticket!"

"Ohhhhhh, Teo! Haha!"

"I know, I know. Not the best plan ever. In La Roche-Sur-Yon I was always finding something to do. Always going out, making new friends, finding new lovers, and just having a good time. If I could have found a gig there I would have stayed, but this was the only thing available with good pay," I say. I look down from the Casino's stairs at how the people fill the streets for a huge beachside concert. The lights flash as they dance, while the Biarritz Lighthouse gives us glimpses of the night ocean. I turn to her and smile. "I guess it's not too bad to be here."

"Not bad at all," she says smiling back. We look at each other for just moment before she continues. "So, Teo. What is your type? There are many beautiful women here."

"No, no, no, Katushka! You asked the last question. It's my turn. You tell me yours," I say, hoping to ultimately avoid answering anything. Her smile fades a bit, and she seems slightly worried.

"It is not so simple, I suppose," she begins. "Things can be complicated with my boyfriend. We both are very career focused, but he doesn't want to make his home in France like I desire. I am never sure if we are together or not, and it makes it difficult. Men always try to flirt with me. You men are like sharks. You can smell the scent of a single, or even almost single, woman like a predator does prey!"

"Haha. Yeah. For some it wouldn't even matter if you were married."

"No, Teo! You are like this?"

"No. Not at all. This shark has lost his appetite," I say with a smirk.

"What are your ideas then? Your situation, I mean."

"I'm a reluctant lover...I'd almost prefer to be in your shoes, but even that's not possible these days."

"You have someone special?"

"Maybe. I'm not even sure anymore," I say. I pause for a moment thinking on my 'maybe'. It's a lie. 'Maybe' is for the hopeful. "Actually, no. There was someone. That was another life, another journey. In any case, it was a long time ago."

"Ouf! Don't be so dramatic, Mr. Program Manager. We are in Biarritz. There is a sea of people just like the waters of Biscay. 'Maybe' you will find someone here! I will look out for you. *Da* or no?!"

"*Da*, Katia. *Da*," I say laughing. "And I will do the same for you."

Chapter 4: The Service and Bar Gorriti

The initial enthusiasm passes after a week or so. Those same entertaining clients have the tendency to become a customer service nightmare when things don't go their way. It doesn't matter who's wrong or right. It's all in the argument. That's my job.

"So, I can't get my money back?"

"No, and I apologize for that. The surfing package you booked was prepaid with our partnered surf school in Anglet. It's not the surf school's problem that you have a hangover and couldn't make the lesson," I say.

"This is just shitty! I wasn't hungover!" says the same guy who cried for joy inciting laughter during our welcome meeting.

"So that wasn't you on the security cameras vomiting outside your room?"

".....," he doesn't say. "Fine!"

You'd think we had kids on our hands, so thank God that I've seen none booked to come in on the schedule for our new arrivals. There is no such thing as nine-to-five in this world. Sure, people are free to do as they want, but if they have a question, or get in trouble, I am the source for all information on how to solve it. If the emergency phone rings at night, I've got to answer it. I'd like to complain but the rest of the team is busy as well. Sure, I have to deal with issues and paperwork, but they actually have to deal with people. Last week a group going to Hendaye was two hours late coming back because some guy was trying to pick up ladies at the beach. Katia had to call me to approve extra funding for tickets, because it cost five euros more per person to change the tickets. The same group of surfers keep trying to sneak in stragglers they meet at the beach into the surf lessons. Shoshana has had the hardest time explaining that they have register with the school if they want to join. On top of that, no one shows up for volleyball tournament she's organized, which they unanimously voted to have after surfing courses.

There seems to be very little sympathy in the summer, so I'm quickly learning how to do things 'differently'. I've done the accounting, met with Gil, and have all things updated for Monday. I crack open our office fridge, and pop the top of an icy bottle of Leffe Blonde. I pour it into a cup so no one knows my secret and sit at my desk. A few moments later Hermann pulls onto the grass, bypassing every parking spot until he's right by the office. This seems to be his personal parking space. He sees me, and raises his hand before getting out of the car and entering the office.

"Hello, Program Manager."

"Hello, Program Director," I respond as he delivers his customary bone crushing handshake, but by now I've learned to tighten my face muscles so he doesn't see the pain.

"What are you doing here?" he says as he opens the fridge and begins to pour himself some rosé.

"Looking at some of this accounting. You know. Administration."

"Haha. *Administratif.* Ok. You want a little?" he asks as he turns his head to fill a glass in anticipation of my response. I down the rest of my beer.

"Sure. *Cough, cough.*"

He hands me the half full glass. He downs his in one gulp and I do the same a minute or two later. After a few minutes of silence at our computers he speaks up again.

"Come on. Let's go."

"Where?"

"San Sebastian. The girls are there leading a tour right now. There's no work for you to do."

He hardly has to open his mouth before I'm shutting down the computer. With so much work being done I'd almost forgotten how much I had wanted to cross the Spanish border.

San Sebastian, or in its Basque name, *Donostia*, is just a 40-minute drive from Biarritz; 30 with Hermann behind the wheel. However, even he slows down a bit as we pass through the mountain ranges. The expressways are tranquil as the surrounding rigid beauty.

"Have you seen this route before, Teo?"

"No, never. It's gorgeous," I say. "I've never been in this part of Spain."

"It never gets old. I've lived here for longer than I can remember. Sure. I am German, but after so much time here I've taken to the way of life."

"I can see why. I don't think anyone could resist this," I say as we pass by fields filled with sheep, horses, and other livestock. Perhaps, they have just as much stress as we do at work, but from here behind the car windows everything looks like a countryside utopia.

"What do you do back home?" Hermann asks. My eyes don't leave the landscape.

"Not exactly sure, these days. I was working up to be a writer before moving to France some time ago. I actually wrote a book, but even that seems like a memory. I suppose we will see after the summer is over."

"That's great. You know," he begins. I turn to look at him, as he looks out ahead into the distance now with the same expression that I had upon seeing the countryside for the first time. "I have had an idea to write a book one day. I've got a lot of stories."

He lets out a loud laugh, and his bright white teeth shine from behind his stubbly beard. I wonder what stories lie behind that smile.

Most of the time when French people think of going to the United States it's either to New York or Los Angeles. Alternatively, when coming to France people dream of Paris. If they're thirsty perhaps Bordeaux, and if they're hungry, it must be Lyon. With Spain, I've heard so much about Barcelona or Madrid, with no mention of San Sebastian. With a couple of weeks passed in Biarritz, and mere moments in *Donostia*, I cannot understand why these places aren't itching and scratching at the minds of every traveler. Two of the world's top ten restaurants can be found here, and it's in second place for the city with the most Michelin Star restaurants in the world. Considering all of this makes me excited that we're here for lunch.

We arrive in the city center and park in one of the underground parking garages near the stunning Hotel Maria Cristina. We walk up to street level, sunglasses intact.

"It's an exquisite hotel," I say.

"Yes, of course. Sometimes I stop in to take a drink or use the bathroom," he responds with his customary hearty laugh and a slap to my back. We continue to walk the streets blending in with the bustling tourist life. Street performers dance while the youths sit in front of the

McDonald's with cigarettes. We bypass all of that chaos for a different type of colloquial commotion. There are many options of where to go, as sunny days tend to attract glamorous people to terraces, but Hermann passes all of this for a joint called Bar Gorriti. In a space that occupies no more than the corner of a building, people are standing, smiling, drinking, and of course eating a variety of available tapas.

"What is this place?" I ask.

"Welcome to *chez* Gorriti," he says with a laugh. "Come."

He sticks his hand up and one of the barmen acknowledges him. He wedges himself at the bar between the clusters of patrons. Just before him is an extensive spread of tapas. He motions for me to wedge in next to him. Without even asking, the barman places a wine glass on the bar and raises a bottle over his head. He begins to pour white wine into the glass without spilling a drop or looking. He hands it to Hermann, and looks at me.

"Oh. A beer, please," I say in conjuring up some Spanish.

"Size?"

"Umm. A pint. A *pinto*?"

"Sure. *Un canon*," he says as he pours the pint from the tap also without looking. I say thank you, and turn to Hermann.

"This place is awesome. Do you come here often?"

"No. Not at all. Maybe twice a year, but every time they remember who I am and greet me. I adore that," he says smiling and gulping his drink. "It is the service."

He's used that phrase in the past. Before I can ask him to elaborate I see him reach for a plate and begin grabbing tapas. He doesn't even seem to be paying for them.

"Go ahead, Teo. Take what you want."

"Don't I need to tell them?"

"No. You see there is a system. Look," he says pointing towards the register. I see several stacks of different sized coins. "They see everything here. The coins represent different tapa sizes. Just show the tapas as you take them. If they haven't already seen it, they'll add a coin."

I begin reaching for everything in sight. Tapas with scrambled egg and bacon, skewered sausages, fried fish, fresh fish, and more. The bar man looks at me and nods, while adding coins to a stack. I bite into the first one and my mouth explodes like I've tasted for the first time. I devour every morsel, leaving only the small square papers I used when grabbing the tapas.

"Where is the trash can?" I ask Hermann. He smiles still chewing his food. He crumples one of the papers in his hand and tosses it to the ground. I look down to see the floor is filled with little crumpled papers. Soon, I carelessly toss it to the ground, as if I had done it every day.

"What do you think?" asks Hermann.

"I could get used to this," I say as a second round of tapas finds its way into my possession.

I already knew that Spain was one more cost effective countries in Europe, but the price we paid for several drinks, and even more tapas, feels like a steal. We had eaten like kings, so it only made sense that we relaxed in the same fashion. At Hermann's suggestion we enter the Maria Cristina's luxurious lobby. We pass the doorman with a confidence that only a hotel guest would have and waltz into the bar, waving at the concierge's desk as if we are returning clients.

"Let's wait here," he says as we take a seat near the bar. "There is sure to be traffic on the road."

The crystal chandeliers light the brilliant marble floor patterns. I sink symbolically into the plush chair as a waitress comes to greet us. We order a couple of beers. She's damn beautiful.

"You see something like?" asks Hermann.

"What? Oh. Haha. Yes, I do. It's the hotel. The decorations are so..."

"Oppp! Don't feed me that salad!" he says. "She is a very beautiful girl. A bit too young for me though."

It's a relaxing day. We finish our drinks, use the bathroom, and hit the road. We arrive back at the hostel and take our places in the office to check some e-mails. Hermann says the next weeks will become very busy, which makes me feel glad that I had a leisurely day.

"Bar Gorriti was amazing," I say.

"Yes, it is. It doesn't matter how long it has been, they know me. I can walk in at any time, eat, drink, and be on my way. It is respect. That is the service. That's who I am, Teo. I am a man who renders service. Before I came by here today I was at *La Station* for a coffee. I overheard two young men debating the prices for a train from here to Irun. I asked how much the tickets were, and they said ninety euros. I offered to take them for fifty, and we were on our way. It is not even an hour to go and come back. Money in the hand," he says while smacking his hands together.

"I think I understand. It's all about making oneself available."

"Sure."

"Well, what about those the ladies there," I say with a sly grin pointing out of our office windows to a group of women wrestling with their large bags. "Do you render your services to women?"

"Opp la! Teo. What do you think?!" he says looking at my very angrily.

"Yes?" I say a bit uncertain of if he's really upset. He smiles and looks outside.

"Ohh la la. The young ladies. What are they doing there? They may be in need of our services," he says as he stands up and walks outside. I hear his voice bellow *'Salut, les filles!'*, as he begins to help them. I sit in the office laughing at the entire spectacle. Suddenly, being a man who renders services seems interesting.

Chapter 5: High Season

The trip to San Sebastian and one-on-one lessons about 'the service' were much needed. Even while Hermann and I were tasting the delicacies of Donostia, the coming week lingered in the back of my mind like a dark cloud at the beach. There's no way to avoid it, no way to out run it. I just have to deal with it.

High season is here. The number of clientele will double this Sunday, and will linger at the same amount for the next few weeks. We will be responsible for attending to the needs of some eighty persons who are under the impression they've paid for our undivided attention. If that wasn't enough, we'll be responsible for a group of teenagers coming for a two-week language holiday. Adult-sitting is one thing. You just need to be professional, have the answers to questions, and leave them to their own devices. Teenage-sitting will require being professional, answering questions, and making sure they're *not* left to their own devices.

The corporate office knows this and in tandem with the increase of clients already planned to send another team member. I am thrilled to learn that Jean-Pierre, a French-man of about my same age who we all trained with in England, will be joining us. I'm expecting him to be the boost that myself and the overworked Katia and Shoshana desperately need. Hermann tells me that he will be staying in my room in order to save money, which I'm not particularly happy about. I've gotten pretty used to having my own room, even if there is an unused bed. However, he could be a good deterrent. Lately, I've felt my resolve weakening, and I don't know what to make of it. I imagine that I appear to be composed and focused to Hermann and the team, but every day is inner dialogue of indecision. There have been several moments where I wanted to invite someone up to my room, and occasionally I feel that I even *need* to do so. However, I know that habit all too well, and it only seems to bury my problems deeper; not solve them. It didn't work in La Roche, so why should it work here?

However, summer doesn't care about my efforts. It's high season for all of Biarritz, so the city, and especially our little hostel, are full of potential '*meufs*'. I find myself lingering more and more around the reception at the exact moment groups of beautiful women arrive. I begin to think it's only a matter of time before I make Gil proud, but having a roommate will make that difficult. Also, drinking myself to sleep will be complicated to do with Jean-Pierre sleeping five feet away.

It's early Sunday evening. The new clients have all arrived and Katia and Shoshana have successfully led two separate city tours. Jean-Pierre arrived earlier in the day. He's tall, with short blonde hair and brown eyes. He was an amateur soccer player, so his physique is quite noticeable. Hermann and I give him an orientation after the tour before helping him get settled into *our* room.

"Teo, thanks for everything. I am excited to be here," he says as he places his duffle bag down.

"Don't mention it. It's great to have you here. As Hermann said, we definitely could use the help. I'm gonna go down to the bar and have a drink. Want to join?"

"No, thank you. I will just stay here and get settled in."

I leave the room and shuffle down to the bar. By now I've been around so much that I simply walk behind it through the back door and get my own drinks. Having staff pricing on drinks and a key to almost every door does have its benefits.

"Oh, Teo. It's you. I should have known you'd be here," says James lifting his head up from the computer.

"Well there are not too many places I could be."

"You, haven't tried going out in the city center?"

"Not really. I'm quite busy," I say while taking a sip of Desperados. "Besides, look at this place. It's full just like a real bar would be."

"True, very true. High season, mate."

"Yep. High season."

James is in a particular position as he has to juggle bar responsibilities and any late check-ins that arrive. A group of backpackers come into the bar asking if they can get their room keys and check-in, so James asks if I can watch the cash box and help out. He tosses another Desperados my way, so I oblige to help. I sell to a few people and honestly it's kind of fun. They come from all over the world, so I'm never sure what accent I'll hear or what language they'll speak. I am equally intrigued when a red-headed woman approaches. She has green eyes and a ridiculously infectious smile.

"Hi! Do you work here?"

"Not exactly. Just keeping an eye on things."

"Oh, ok. Well, I am Izabela. You can call me, Iza," she says smiling brilliantly.

"I'm Teo," I say becoming a bit nervous. Most people don't just linger like this. She just keeps looking at me and smiling, not saying anything. "Would you like something?"

"Oh. Of course! Um. A glass of red wine please."

I grab the bottle and exchange a shy glance and smirk at her. She's cute, but it's her oozing enthusiasm that's pulling at me.

"Where are you from?" I ask, cracking under the flirtatious pressure.

"I am from a small city outside of Budapest, in Hungary. Do you know it?"

"No, not yet. I've always wanted to go. Maybe you can…," I'm saying when James returns.

"Phew! Crazy ass clients! They ask if dinner is still being served and I told them no. It's almost midnight! They got mad at me like I'm the one who works the bloody cooker! It's a bunch of bollocks, yeah?"

"Um. Yeah. Those bastards," I reply.

"Oh, it will be ok. They will be calm after a good night's sleep," adds Iza. Why does she have to be damn nice when we're all content with complaining? I have to stop for a moment and really think. Am I annoyed that she's optimistic, or am I annoyed that her optimism attracts me? I don't give myself the pleasure of answering that one. I tell them I'm turning in for the night.

"So soon?" begins Iza. "Well, I will be staying here while looking for a summer job. Maybe I will see you again, yes?"

"Maybe," I say slipping out the back door.

I remember that Jean-Pierre is in the room, and happily so. Another hour or so of that smile I would have surely made a move. There's no way I could invite her up with him there. The hostel is completely booked, so I know there is no space for romance in her room either. It's comforting and frustrating at the same time. I gently open the room door thinking that Jean-Pierre will be asleep, but am surprised to find him wide awake in his bed.

"Oh hey, man. You're still awake?"

"It seems I am a bit restless. I found this book of yours and figured I would practice on my English," he says. I didn't notice it at first, but Jean-Pierre is sitting upright on his bed with *the* book; with *her* book in his hands. "It is not so bad. Did you know it is about *Pays-Basque*?"

"Where did you get that?"

"It was sitting on the table. Well, it was sitting on top of your bag on the table. I hope it is no problem, I was just quite bored."

I think back to the moment where Derlenzistda gave it to me. She had so much optimism. Even more than Iza. She was so excited to think that she would be able to influence me and my vagabond heart in some way. I told her, 'Ok. I'll take a look at it," and placed the book next to my computer. My eyes never left the screen, so I don't recall how she responded. Derlenzistda. I can't see her face. I don't even remember what I was working on that was so important as to ignore her.

"Teo?!"

"*Quoi?*" I say snapping back to the moment. "It really is a personal item, Jean. Um. I'd prefer you not read it."

"Sure, sure. No problem," he says as he hands it back. I place it in the bag. I go into the bathroom to shower before bed. When I exit, the lights are off and he's fast asleep. I lie down on my bed, looking up to the ceiling. I close my eyes and try again to remember those moments with her and am taken back to the first time we sat down at the cafe. I didn't get any work done that night. How could I when she was so captivating. I fall asleep. Finally.

"Teo!" yells out Jean-Pierre.

"What? What's wrong?"

"You're snoring!"

"Well, I don't know that I'm doing it. I'm sleeping," I say trying to keep as much composure as possible. "I'll try not to."

I try sleeping on my back, stomach, and sides. I bury my head in my pillow, and try to keep my mouth closed, but eventually I begin to *ronfler* again, and he's sure to let me know every time it bothers him. I have a feeling that things aren't going to work out with him, but at least I find a funny piece of peace. Perhaps, it wasn't for a lack of love or romance that resulted in waking to cold beds so often. Maybe all those women left during the night because I snore.

I would like to say that the troubles involving Jean-Pierre stay confined to our room and that they consist solely of snoring and violation of personal belongings, but that's hardly the case. The first few days are just fine. He seems to be acclimating and has no complaints about the work load. By the weekend he asks if he can have a meeting with me and, like any good manager, I agree.

"I quit."

"What?"

"I can't do it anymore. I mean this job just is not what I thought it was going to be."

"Look, I know how it goes. We've been here longer than you, so we understand the weight. Imagine my position. Sure, you have to deal with issues with people, but your issues are my issues, as well as Katia's, Shoshana's, and everyone else involved. Relax a little bit. We're having a movie night here at the hostel. I'll talk to Katia to see if she will be willing to take your spot organizing the outdoor activities so you can stay here."

He gives me his most earnest thanks and is able to spend the evening in the comforts of the hostel instead of out in the city. I talk with Hermann, who says that Jean-Pierre had even come to him about leaving.

"Teo, I told him as you did. Wait it out. Pace yourself. The season is long," he begins. "But I have a feeling about him. Something is up."

Hermann, the man's man, the odd-job aficionado, and renderer of all things *servicewise* who has been in this business before we were born, is telling me that something is not right. I am officially concerned.

Jean-Pierre asks if he can have the morning off to take care of some personal things, and I say it's not a problem thinking that he could use the break. I am terribly surprised when returns later that afternoon with a note in hand.

"What's this?"

"I went to the doctor this morning. He says I am suffering from fatigue."

35

"What the hell does that mean?"

"The work has been too much. He says I need to take off for two days and then return to him to see if I can work again."

"Ok," I say.

He walks out of the office. I send a message to Katia and Shoshana that we need to all meet before dinner tonight. A couple of hours later they come walking in having completed a tour of St. Jean de Luz and a bike ride along the coastline. I can see the fatigue of high season on their faces, but somehow they're still smiling.

"Do we wait for Jean?" asks Katia.

"No, he won't be joining us."

"Why so?" asks Shoshana.

"The doctor says he is suffering from...fatigue...He is not allowed to work for two days at which point he will see if the doctor will release him to work again."

"Haha! That's hardly a good joke, Teo!" says Shoshana.

"Because it's not one."

"Oh."

"*Putain*," adds Katia.

Their smiles fade. Sure, I have my personal problems, but that's for me. My responsibility is this team and this program. We all knew the season would be long and hard. No one hid that from us. However, this is something else. The book and snoring ordeal, and even my itching libido, are secondary to seeing my hard-working team demoralized.

"What the hell are we gonna do?" says Shoshana. "I mean, seriously. I've mapped out the schedule of events and who is working what for the entire week, and now we're a man down for at least two days? I call bullshit, Teo."

"I agree with Shoshana. Look at us, Teo. We are in the sun everyday doing our jobs. He is supposed be some athlete, and he is fatigued? We are fatigued!"

"I know, I know. I am too. Don't worry. It's just two days. I will fill in for him everywhere I can. Don't worry."

It seems they at least take confidence in my words, but none of this regulates the tension throughout the hostel. The three of us still have to get up early every morning. I have to wake up to a blissfully, non-snoring, Jean-Pierre. Even with his extra sleep he still insists on interrupting me to tell me stop snoring again. I respond '*ta gueule*' which more or less means for him to shut his fucking mouth. He shuts it.

High season is not just about the work volumes, but also about the temperature. We're baking in the sunlight every single day, and even I have had to make trips to the beach. I *never* make trips to the beach. I return to the room after working sport activities, more bronzed than my already brown skin and sticky from all the dried sweat, to find Jean-Pierre napping.

"Oh hey, Teo," he says with his hands locked behind his head. "How's it going out there?"

All I can think about is that he has two days of salary, free meals, and two free nights in a hostel during his fatigue break.

"It's ok. You feeling better?"

"A little bit. Let me know if you guys need something."

"Don't worry. We've got it. Get your rest."

I leave the room and call Hermann. He tells me to relax a bit, and that everything will be alright. I tell him it's difficult to do that when my team member is having a holiday during high season. He agrees and tells me he's been thinking about who could fill the place in the event that Jean-Pierre's 'fatigue' persists. I tell him I will think about it as well.

The next afternoon Jean-Pierre shows up saying that the fatigue has not left him. The doctor's orders are to no longer work, and that he will leave us tomorrow.

"You know, I just need to get better, Teo."

"Well. If the doctor says so, who am I to say otherwise?" I respond. At that moment, Iza sticks her head through the office door smiling as usual.

"Hello! Are you busy, Teo?"

"Yes. I can't talk now," I reply quite coldly.

"Oh, ok," she says disappointedly before going back down the hallway.

Jean-Pierre apologizes again and leaves to prepare his things. It's colder than a woman leaving your bed after a passionate evening. Hermann calls soon after to tell me the news, but I say I already know. To my dismay he has no prospects to take Jean's place, and it will be weeks before our client numbers start to go down. He asks if I know anyone. I have already thought of the one person who would do it. However, the only thing I'm thinking about is if I can rely on a man who, despite having the perfect resume, is even more prone to *les meufs* than I am. We passed night after night in the streets, bars, and discos of La Roche-Sur-Yon. There was hardly a day without a drink or party that I missed in those days. All of that, and I was the milder one of us. I think of Katia and Shoshana's tired faces, and I realize there is no other option. We need help. We need Reda Tj.

Chapter 6: The Full Reda

The first time I met Reda was at a disco called *Le Castel*. He found out I was American, and proceeded to lecture me about Dr. Martin Luther King. I told myself I would be fine if I never saw him again. A week later a woman called out to me from the top floor of a building in the city center after seeing me pass on the street. I, not known to turn down a pretty lady, went up to her apartment after she told me there was a party. I walked in to see Reda. He and his friends yelled with excitement, and said 'motherfucker' more times during the next two hours than I'd ever heard before. That night, while we were all migrating to *Le Castel*, he and his friends jumped on top of a bus stop screaming the lyrics to a rap song, which was also *motherfuckerlaiden*. The last time I saw him was no less spectacular. I was walking down the street holding hands with a lover en route to my apartment. We'd just gone for a drink or two, and hadn't been able to keep our hands off each other. In the serenity of the night my phone rang with his name on the ID. "Teo! Is that you!? I can see you!", he asked. I turned and squinted my eyes to see Reda's head in the tiniest window of the top floor. He asked if was going to 'fuck her'. I told him it was none of his business.

Every encounter in between these encounters was equally as impressive, and I knew I could always count on him to give me a "Reda moment". If there was nothing else about him, I knew that he was always on level 100, "The Full Reda", whether or not anyone was ready for it. The only reason I've considered him for the position is that he had asked to see if there were openings before I moved to Biarritz. At the time, I thought I would never refer him, but Jean-Pierre's departure has called for desperate actions. Despite every Reda moment, and there are certainly plenty, he has the perfect resume for the job. He's already worked for several camps and centers in different countries, and speaks 6 languages. Basically, he is the perfect candidate.

I give his resume to Hermann. Hermann immediately calls him, and says it's a go. We gave him the news on a Friday. He was on the road by

Sunday morning. The entire scene with Jean-Pierre left a bad taste in my mouth with everything to do with Biarritz, so walking to the train station knowing that I would see a familiar face is a refreshing concept. That and we almost always communicate in English, which will be a nice break from speaking French all day. I arrive to find him sitting curbside with a huge bag and guitar case. He stands to greet me.

"What's up boss!?" he says, greeting me with two kisses, which is always funny considering how short he is by comparison. He almost has to be on the tip of his toes to reach me. He has short buzzed black hair, hazel eyes, and pale skin. It's obvious that he hasn't been in the sun, like most people just arriving to Biarritz.

"Reda Tj. I'd never thought I'd see you here."

"Well, I'm here now! Shit!"

"Haha. Thanks for coming, man. You ready to go?"

"No, man. Stand here with me. I've been in a fucking car for 7 hours straight and I couldn't smoke. I need some nicotine and a second to adjust," he says pulling out his pack. He lights one and takes a puff and looks at me. "So, what's the situation?"

I fill him in on everything that's happened. I let him know what we have ahead of us, and he assures me he's the man for the job, and after he finishes his cigarette we begin the descent to the hostel. I introduce him to the team and have an introductory meeting with Hermann, who takes the lead to let him know what he can expect.

"I see. I see. Well, we can do it. I'll be on top of everything. Just let me know and I'll get it done. I'll take extra shifts, whatever we need."

"That's good to hear, but take your time. We've lost one worker to the season already. Make sure you get some rest when possible," says Hermann as he renders his usual handshake. Reda winces slightly. "Glad to have you aboard."

With Jean's old room key in hand, he heads off to get settled in. Hermann opens the fridge and pours two glasses of wine. He hands one to me.

"He's strong," he begins while leaning back in his chair and crossing his arms. "I like strong personalities. I have a strong persona, and so do you. He does as well. I think we will work fine, but pay attention. He seems like he could get a little wild."

"No worries. I know Reda. I'll keep an eye out. You sure have an eye for the wild side, Program Director."

"Of course I do, Program Manager!" he says with a wink.

Reda is great. He loves to talk, so he has no problem organizing the group of surfers in the morning, which is just in time to give Shoshana a much-needed day off. He moves with a certain social poise that I'd only seen before in the bars. Aude smiles during the first time meeting him, and calls him a charmer. He and Gil spy a group of biking tourist *meufs* and discuss which one they would like most to sleep with. It all sounds brilliant, but I am waiting for it. He will eventually give me one of those famous moments.

One day Reda has the morning off in place of working the evening for Katia. Just before noon he comes to the office and sits in his chair at the computer.

"So boss, what do we have for lunch today?"

"I'm not sure. I've been thinking about dipping into the staff catering budget."

"That exists?"

"I can make it exist," I say with a smile. He pats me on the back.

"Order *La Boîte à Pizza*! It's fucking great!" he says.

I pull up the website to order as he walks outside. At the same time a tall brunette exits the back door of the hostel. They exchange a few words, kiss on the lips, and she heads on her way towards the hill which leads to the bus stop. I think nothing of it. I order the pizza, and decide to go to the room to change into some shorts. I am surprised to find a woman's luggage sitting in the center of the room. There are hair products and perfume in the bathroom. I try to think nothing of it, and walk back to the office to find Reda there singing and playing on his computer. I sit down at my desk, and pretend to do some work.

"You got that pizza, Boss?" he asks.

"Yeah."

"Hell yeah. I'm hungry as shit."

"Yeah, me too," I say. "So. What's that bag doing in the room?"

"Oh, it's Marie's. Remember her? She was chatting with me at the bar last night."

"Yeah, yeah. I remember...Why are her things in our room?"

41

"Oh. Well she needed a place to leave her stuff, otherwise the hostel would make her pay for another night. She doesn't need a room for the night, so I said she could leave her stuff until she has to catch her train."

"Ah, ok," I say, fully knowing that we all have keys to the luggage room and that he could have locked her things up there. "What about the things in the bathroom?"

"Oh. She needed a shower."

"A shower?" I say finally turning in my chair to him.

"Sigh...I fucked her, man."

"What the hell, Reda?"

"Don't worry! I didn't get anything on your bed!"

"I'm not worried, not about that. You've been here a few days and you've already had someone in the room!"

I laugh hilariously. I knew he would give me a moment.

"Man, what's the deal with you? I'm surprised. You mean you haven't been racking up some ladies around here? Katia, Shoshana?"

"Nah, man. I haven't thought much of it. Been laying low since La Roche," I say. "There is this one girl. She's Hungarian, a red head."

"Oh yeah, I've seen her around here. What's up with that?"

"She's really sweet. Really cute. She's been flirting with me like crazy."

"Man you need to get on that, Teo. It's high season. You're gonna explode around here if you keep taking the summer seriously."

Even at the tail end of a Reda Moment, he somehow makes sense. A delivery scooter speeds unto the grass just in front of our office window, with our pizza in tow. I pay the man and Reda and I head to the bar area to feast. As we pass through the lobby Iza comes walking in wearing nothing but her bathing suit, using her towel to dry her hair and not much else.

"Teo! How is your day?"

"Um. It's great! What about you?"

"It's such a beautiful day. I went swimming in the lake. Hi, Reda! Nice to see you too!"

"Sup, Iza?!"

"What will you guys do tonight?"

"We don't know," pipes up Reda, while looking my way. "What about you?"

42

"Not sure. I'd maybe like to make some type of party at the beach. We should all go, yes?"

"I don't know," begins Reda as he turns towards me. "Should we, T?"

Iza look at me with those green eyes. She's standing so close that I can feel her breath on my face.

"Sure. Why not? I'll buy some drinks for us."

"Oh perfect!" she says. "I will meet you here at the reception at 10:00pm."

"See you then!" says Reda giving a thumb up. Iza walks away. Aude steps from behind the reception to chastise her about walking around wet and that she needs some clothes on, but from where we stand she can do no wrong.

"Yo, T. She wants it man. I know these things. You gonna hit that?"

"I don't know. Why do you ask?"

"Because if you don't, I will."

Chapter 7: The Sand

I empty the office fridge of every alcohol I can find and place it all in my green satchel. The collection is already enough for a small soiree considering that Hermann and I keep it stocked pretty consistently with beers and wine. I buy another bottle of rosé from the hostel bar just in case we need it, and pack it into the stuffed bag with some plastic cups.

As requested, Reda and I meet Iza at the reception at 10:00pm. Another ten minutes by bus and we're walking into the cool night air of Biarritz. The city center is filled with people young and old, drinks, cameras, and lovers in hand. Almost as soon as we exit the bus, it begins to pour down rain. We run down the staircase leading to the beach and take shelter under the casino's canopy which stretches the length of *la Grande Plage.* In most cases weather like this would be a clear sign to call it quits, but we, along with several others, take shelter under the canopy, completely soaked from the couple of minutes it took to get there.

The three of us pick a spot along the wall. I open my bag and hand Reda a beer, while pouring a glass of wine for myself and Iza. We touch the plastic cups together and get the party started. A very exciting aspect about our situation is the solidarity of everyone hiding from the rain. There is a line from end to end of people who would not let a little rain ruin a night of their Basque summer. It becomes almost a makeshift community, as people are open to making friends and sharing drinks, and it's not too long before our trio becomes a proper group.

"Do you want a beer?" asks Reda to a guy he just met. "Teo, can we get this man a beer, please?! He is dying of thirst out here, brutha!"

I laugh, because , as in typical Reda fashion, he has taken over the soiree. I hand him an opened beer, while Iza smiles at me.

"Is he always like this?" she asks.

"You have no idea. Haha. More wine?" I ask. I'm pouring into her glass before she can even respond. "So you were telling me what you're doing here in Biarritz? I don't think heard it all."

"Ah yes! Well, I am just staying at the hostel until I can find some type of job and apartment for the summer. It's quite difficult because many people come to do the same thing."

"I see. Well what about when you're not in *Pays Basque*. What does Iza do in Hungary?"

"I am a student of environmental sciences. I love nature, especially the seas. Biarritz is simply the perfect place for me to be."

"Yes. I can imagine," I say while sipping my wine. I look off to Reda as if to find some escape from the continuing dialogue, but she won't let me.

"And you? What brings you here? A love for recreational programs?"

"Haha. Nope! Not at all," I begin. "I'm a traveler. A writer. I've just come to Biarritz to make money to go home."

"Ah ok. So, you have work there?"

"Not really."

"Oh. Family? A girlfriend?"

"Yes. No," I respond. "Reda do you need a drink?"

I officially duck out of this line of questioning, because I know where it's leading. At least, I think I do. Reda plops on the ground next to me, while two of his new friends sit next to Iza. I pour them all drinks, and watch as these Frenchmen try to flirt with her. She doesn't speak much French, and their English is horrible. Reda ends up doing a bit of translating, which starts well until they're asking if she wants to come back to their place.

"What did they say?" asks Iza.

"Oh. Um. Nothing," responds Reda. "Hey, Teo is that Katia? Let's go see."

I know Katia isn't here, because it's not her type of scene. Still I agree to go with him to see if it's her. We stand to our feet and walk over just beyond the end of the casino. He turns and looks at me.

"Man, what the fuck are you doing?"

"Drinking, man! What's wrong?"

"Aside from the fact that there's an army of horny ass dudes and a few girls, and you're ignoring one that wants to screw you?"

"Dammit," I say grabbing at my hair. "You think so?"

"Are you kidding me? She wants it, T. She's been wanting it."

"I know, I know."

"Well do something about it. Look. I'll run interference, so you can make your move."

45

I finally give in. I've been talking myself out of situations that I've created for weeks now, but the combination of booze and Reda are too much. I stop trying to fight it. This is who I am.

We walk back and Reda immediately dives into some immigration debate with the guys. Iza, looking somewhat relieved, moves closer to me as I sit down.

"Was it her?"

"Who?"

"Katia?"

"Oh no. I think he just wanted to flirt with some girl," I say. I see her cup is empty and pour a glass of wine for both of us. "A lot guys flirting with you this summer?"

"Haha. Yes, actually. It's so silly. I know exactly what they want, but they never say it. It's like a child's game!"

"Yeah. I think I know how that goes. Do you know what you want?"

"Sexually?" she asks.

"I meant in general, but sure. Sex is included."

"Oh, I am simple. I love life and adventure. I want to experience new things and meet new people, for whatever that means," she says. She takes a smooth assuring sip of her wine. "I suppose that means sexually also."

Up until this point there was a coyness about our body language. We had spoken while looking around, or even at the ground. However, her response has an intent behind it; the same intent I had when asking. Her eyes are filled with sensual optimism. I no longer see hope, but certainty; an assurance as if she no longer wants me to ask her to take a walk in the sand. She knows I will.

"Have you ever seen the way the lighthouse dances on the ocean's water at night?"

"Not at all. Should we go?" she asks. I stand to my feet and reach my hand out. She grabs it firmly as I lift her to her feet. We stroll off without a word. Reda looks me in the eyes with a proud smile on his face and nods. It doesn't take long for us to disappear in the night's darkness. The sand is gently wet, and persistently clinging, building up more and more with each step we take. We stop just behind a sand dune.

"This lighthouse was built in 1834," I say.

"Oh, that's amazing. Do you know something else?"

"It's 74 meters tall, and has 248 step until the top. Also, it's the northernmost point in the city," I say while turning to her with a smile. I chuckle a bit. "I guess know a few things after watching so many city tours."

"Well go on. You have all my attentions," she says. I can still see the glimmer of her green eyes in the moonlight as I grab her by the waist and pull her towards me. An instant later tongues tie, so tight that the only breaths allowed are the exhales from our noses.

We disconnect as if to come up from the waters for air, and in that fast breath we smile. Our shirts flutter clumsily as we kick off our jeans and shorts with a fury of sand. Her bra is unnecessary, so she loses it. We attempt to lie on top of our clothes, but the rolling fury of our lust leads us onto cool wet sand. She's wild. Expressive. Explorative. It's as if her red hair was a caution sign which I'd ignored, and now it dances passionately below my waste.

I look to the moon in a state of ecstasy, when I hear a whisper. It's the condom calling from my jean pocket. My arm reaches for it, and she is filled with even more passion as she sees me opening it. She takes it and slips it on for me. I enter her warmth. She tenaciously drives me deeper into the sand. She kisses me as best she can between her cries, which wail into the night sky. We turn and twist, taking as many forms as the sand will allow. Our breaths are lost in the night's breeze. Our bodies lost within each other, until there is no more. Only climax. Two smiles. She kisses me gently, a deceptive second to her furious sexuality. She stands and walks into the water for a swim. I lay in the sand.

Chapter 8: *Les Quatre Fantastiques*

I've broken my sexual barrier. A part of me, that I've been trying to hide for last few weeks, has emerged, and it's more potent than ever. The easy way out would be to simply say it's Reda's fault. He has few issues with bedding down a lady, and was kind enough to provoke me into doing the same. One could even say that it's Iza's fault. After all, she knew what she was doing, always stopping by the office and wearing bathing suits in public. The temptress!

No. Those perspectives are far too shallow. Perhaps I've searched for a way back to a day where even the most beautiful woman couldn't tempt me, but those days are over. If there is one thing I've learned from lovers, which there is definitely more than one, it's that everyone makes a decision. So, if there was even a way to place Reda or Iza as instigators of my sexual reawakening, it could only be done with implicating me, because I knew what both of them were about and still made my choice. My only claim to innocence is that fact that I didn't know I wanted, and perhaps needed, a roll in the sand. That is until I was covered in it.

I linger around the reception more often than not these days. There isn't a pretty face that passes through these walls that escapes Reda's, Gil's, or my attention. Pretty ladies in need of locking up their luggage during siesta hours?

Well, I don't really work here, but I have a key to the luggage room. I guess, I can help you out. Let me know if you need anything else.

A group of dudes in need of locking up their luggage during siesta hours?

Sorry bro, don't work here. You'll have to wait until the reception reopens at 5:00pm.

If that's not enough, meetings with Gil become exceedingly longer and less focused. There is always some discussion on music, and we do eventually get work done. However, after my sandy evening I am quite open to discuss his favorite subject.

"I'm telling you, Gil. There are *meufs* everywhere. This city is crazy."

"I told you how it would be. Doesn't matter though, you're not doing anything about it."

"Well..."

"*Putain,* who? Wait, do you want a coffee? We need a coffee for this," he says completely turning his eyes from his computer to look at me. He whips up two espressos on his machine, hands one to me and sits back down. "Ok. *Allez* go!"

"The redhead. The Hungarian."

"No! *Putain.* She's hot, *mec*! Details, please."

"At *la Grande Plage*."

"Ufff! You're an asshole! It was wild? I know it was wild," he says slowly nodding his head.

"It was pretty intense, man."

"Hey! Is this what you two do? Sit around and talk about women during your meetings?" yells Aude from the adjacent office.

"What, we're talking about the number of women clients versus males," says Gil, while winking at me.

"That's garbage. Gil you're the worst! Teo, you're a *bartineur*!"

"A what?"

"A flirt!" she says switching momentarily to English.

She's right on both accounts, and it's probably good that she broke up our meeting to help us focus. Between bottles and beaches my life seems to be already full, so much so that I forget I'm here to do a job. Furthermore, it's a job that's about to become a lot more difficult.

Reda has proven to be the force we needed to keep the program running, but nothing has prepared us for this week. We have a group of teenagers coming from different European countries. Until now we've only had to point our adult clients in the right direction and they can do their activities as they want. The teenagers are here specifically to take French classes in the morning and do activities in the afternoon. Someone has to be with them from the moment they wake up until the time we say lights out. We all have some experience working with youths, but this is not the same. Those experiences were not during high season in Biarritz.

Four Spanish girls arrive at the hostel each with their parents following closely behind and bags big enough for a year's stay when they're only scheduled for fourteen days. Miri, Ester, Clara, and Sandra are their names and I can already tell they're going to be an interesting bunch. I'm not sure if they coordinated their appearances, but they're all wearing short jean shorts. They all have really long dark hair except for Clara who's blonde. To make their presentation even more lively, Miri has her phone connected to a small speaker playing some bachata music. I talk to their mothers and finish all the documents for their deposits and room keys. Apparently, Miri has been here before, so there isn't that much need for explanation. Everything seems to be flowing smoothly, when she asks a very strange request.

"Oh, we're on the second floor?"

"Yes, why do you ask?"

"Is it possible to be on the first floor? We'll be tired from walking up the stairs all the time."

"Oh, ok. I will talk to the hostel and see if there is a place to move you to."

"You're the best, Teo!" she says. The girls and their parents head off to check on their rooms, when I see Hermann pull up in his customary parking spot in the grass. He brings in a cube of rosé to place in the fridge.

"Hello, Program Manager."

"Hello, Program Director," I respond. He crushes my hand.

"How go the arrivals?"

"Pretty solid, I think. Actually, there is this one named Miri. She has asked to be on the first floor. Is that possible?"

"Miri? Spanish?"

"Yes."

"I remember her. Look out, Teo. This is a different game."

"What do you mean?"

"It's high season. *La Fête de Bayonne* is next week and four Spanish teenagers ask to be placed on the first floor where they can open the window. Imagine a little, Teo. She asks so they can sneak out easier at night," he says pointing his index finger to his head. I pause for a moment.

"*Merde*. She almost had me," I say. At that moment Miri's mother comes back to the office.

"Yes, Teo. Can I have a word with you?"

"Sure thing."

"Well as you know, these are young teenage girls, and I know there are some boys in the program as well. They're good girls. They're really sweet, fun, and pretty, but you know what teenagers think of in the summer, yes?"

"Teenagers?" I say, considering from experience that teenagers aren't the only ones thinking of summer activities. "Oh yeah, I was once a teen. I know how it goes."

"Good, good. So, can you," she says stopping mid-sentence and pulling at her eye with her index finger. "You know?"

"I'll do just that," I say pulling at my eye in complete understanding that she's asking me to pay extra attention.

We hold a separate orientation meeting for the youths where we explain the rules. Despite my concerns for sneaking out and babysitting, it's immediately an interesting situation. Even if there are hormones raging, Spanish, Dutch, German, Swedish, Russian, Italian, and others are mingling, and exchanging languages and ideas. It's a brilliant cultural clash. The task, I suppose, is to keep them from exchanging bodily fluids and partying, which at this point seems a bit hypocritical.

We give them a tour of the city, and make sure they're all in their rooms by 10:00pm. It seems like a simple task, and we think the night is over. Reda and I run into a group of female travelers drinking on one of the picnic tables in front of our office. We grab a few beers from the fridge and join them outside. It turns out they're Italian and it's pretty easy to open the lines of communication as both of us speak a little of the language. They're immediately intrigued by our attempts and it's not long before we're all laughing together. It's close to midnight when Reda and I spot pairs of long tanned legs running down the stairs.

"Boss! You see that right?!"

"Sigh," I say sipping my beer one more time. "Yes. I see it. Excuse us, ladies."

Reda and I set our beers down and bolt through the back-hostel doors moving through the lobby. Miri, Ester, Clara, and Sandra, are joined by a Swede named Lans, another Spanish girl named Carlota, and Spanish boys Miguel and Borja.

"Hey! Where do you all think you're going?!" yells Reda. Ester steps forward smiling. She stands almost 6 feet tall which is several inches more than Reda.

"Hi, guys! We're actually just hungry and going to the vending machine," she says with a twinkle in her eyes.

"I call B.S. on that one, boss," he responds looking to me.

"Why were you running then? I know you four girls are in a room together, but the boys aren't and neither is Carlota. You sure you're not trying to sneak out?" I ask.

"No, no, Teo," begins Miri. "We're just really hungry. The dinner wasn't enough for us."

"You're not supposed to be out of your rooms. If you need something to eat you can get it, but you have to go right back to your rooms."

"Yahhh! Thank you, Teo. You're the best!" says Ester. They rush over to the vending machines while Reda and I try to talk about a strategy. I can see Clara stepping timidly towards us.

"Um excuse me," she begins. "I was um, wondering, like if I could stay in the hallways by our room because I need the Wi-Fi to call my boyfriend. There is no internet in the room."

"No, it's not possible."

"But we are in love. It's so hard to be away from him. I promise. I just need 10 minutes and I will be in my room. Pretty please!" she says. She tosses her blonde hair and looks up at me as angelic as can be with blue eyes waiting with hope of my words.

"I will be up in ten minutes. We will have issues if you're still there, Clara."

"Oh, Teo! I love you! Thank you!" she says as she runs with her phone back upstairs.

"You're a big ol' softy," says Reda.

"I know, I know. That's why I have you here though, right?"

"Damn straight!"

We wait for them all to walk back upstairs before going outside. The picnic table is empty. Our Italian beauties have left, and taken the rest of our brew with them. It's probably for the best because these 'hungry' teens have us on red alert. We decide it's not a good idea to drink too much. Reda stays in the office and I head upstairs. Clara is nowhere to be found, and I can hear Miri's music coming from the girl's room. I knock on the door and tell them to keep it down, before going to my room at the end of the hallway.

I am finally alone for the first time today. All of my wine is in the office, so for the first time in weeks I'm even somewhat sober. I open the window, and sit on the edge of my bed. I think of Iza. I hadn't had much time to speak with her because of all the work we've had to do, but I do know that she has found an apartment and job in the city. It's better that way, because I know she wants to see me after all that happened. The sex as wild and beautiful, but not enough to satisfy me. I feel just like I did back in La Roche; alone and confused. As usual my mind tries to think back to Derlenzistda. Now Iza's face is one that I must sort through with all the others. I reach for my bag. The book is still inside. I didn't even bother to remove it for our visit to the beach. I pull it out and open to the first page, when I hear whispers from outside my window. I stand up and look into the night just in time to see legs running around the corner. I rush out of the room down the hallway, and notice the music is no longer playing. I turn left and exit on the terrace to see a group running in the distance from the hostel. I can see that Katia is sitting near the reception on her phone, while Reda is in the office tapping his feet at his computer and drinking a beer. I call him on his phone and he rushes outside.

"Which way did they go!? Did you see who it was?" he yells.

"Up the hill towards the bus stop! I have no idea!"

He runs in that direction. I come downstairs bypassing an unknowing Katia, and take my seat in the office. He comes back a couple of minutes later panting and sweating.

"Sorry. Not a person in sight, boss!"

"Shit," I say. I take a beer out of the fridge. "Staff meeting tomorrow. We've got to prepare for this game."

"Hell yeah," he says.

I head back upstairs to the terrace and take a seat. Maybe there will be some other escapees. I don't know who it was. These kids were lighting fast. However, I have a pretty good idea that somehow Miri, Ester, Clara, and Sandra are involved. Hermann, and even Miri's mother, tried to warn me. If there is one involved, they all are. That's how a team works, and certainly these four are in a league of their own.

Chapter 9: *La Fête de Bayonne*

La Fête de Bayonne is a series of festivals and parties lasting five days from the last Wednesday of July leading into August. It began as a way that the people of Bayonne could have their versions of the *ferias* in Pamplona, and has been a tradition ever since. The city is electric with festive energy, as people can be seen wearing their white clothes, red belts, and scarves throughout the streets. Daytime is more family oriented and even the smallest children have on their *feria* gear. However, the night is an affair for the reveler.

A group of teenagers has tried to sneak out every night since they've arrived, which has been stressful enough without the presence of *les ferias*. The evening streets are already filled with people dancing and drinking on a normal basis, and everyone wearing the same outfit makes it easy to lose someone. To think something would happen to any of our youth is increasingly stressful, as they seem intent on tasting the Biarritz nightlife.

Last night Reda and I caught *Les Quatre Fantastiques*, Miguel, and Lans pulling up the hostel fencing to sneak out on the side of the hostel opposite to our office. They must have realized that we were staying up to keep them from sneaking out and adapted their game. I admit almost fun figuring out how to catch them, but *la Fête de Bayonne* is no child's affair. In fact, it's hardly even an adult's affair.

None of this stops Reda and me from buying our party gear. We're borderline hypocrites as we tell the teens they're not allowed to go to festival at night, while making plans of our own. But we're adults. We can handle it. Right?

I'm lingering around the reception, as is habit, when two women are walking up the path to the hostel door. One is tall, with long dark hair. Her toned, pale skin complements her brown eyes. She's quite young, but looks a bit older than any of our youth clients. They enter and walk to the reception where Hamza and I are sitting, and begin to speak French with him. It turns out they're German and here for holiday, and of course *les ferias*.

"Here are your keys. You said you will go Bayonne. Yes?" Hamza asks.

"Yes, we're so excited. We don't know much about it."

"Well you should meet, Teo," he says while pointing to me. "He loves the *ferias* and I'm sure he would go along with you?"

"Really!?" says the tall brunette, flashing those doe eyes in my direction. I hesitate a bit, but respond as coolly as possible.

"Yes, for sure. I'm actually going tonight. You're welcome to join my party if you like. I'm Teo," I say while sticking my hand out to shake theirs. Her friend is named Anna, but she, she is named Justine.

Reda, Justine, Anna, and three Austrian girls named Carmen, Veronika, and Liz, and myself rendezvous in the office that night. We look amazing in our matching outfits, and have jugs of sangria to go along with it. We take some photos, and walk up the hill towards the bus stop. This time of year, there are night buses devoted solely to people going from Biarritz to Bayonne. The trip lasts about forty minutes as a bus full of people dance, pound on the walls, drink, and sing French songs. It's like no party I've ever seen, and by the time we arrive in Bayonne I am ready to revel.

We step off the bus and mix in with the crowds. We are but drops in an ocean of white and red. We quickly run out of sangria, which is no problem as street vendors are selling jugs for two euros. We arrive to what would normally be a plaza near the city center, to find instead a huge stage, where Dj's and dancers play the *feria's* soundtrack. We quickly join the mass of dancers. Reda jumps around furiously, while Anna seems to have found some shirtless Brazilian man. They're ravaging each other's faces, as she sticks her hand down his shorts. I polish off the last bottle and look to Justine, who's dancing alone. I grab her by the hand and begin to spin her around. She smiles felicity. Maybe it's her youth that makes the moment innocent in this field of debauchery, but she reminds me of dancing with Derlenzistda. She takes me to a time that seems so long ago, and that leads me to a place in my mind that I should not go. She's not Derlenzistda. This is just some woman I met, and if it's dancing, it should be just that. Keep it in context.

56

However, I feel my thoughts slipping into romanticism. I release her from my arms, and move closer to Reda. She looks confused, but is distracted when Carmen says we should go to the bathroom at a bar. We make a chain holding each other's hands so no one gets lost and make our way to a nearby pub. Reda and I buy some more sangria, while the girls take turns in the bathroom. Justine comes out and looks at me. She grabs me by the hands and starts dancing. Tucked away in a dark intimate corner, we kiss. My hands explore her waist, and large breasts. She drives her tongue deeper into my mouth. We're poised to go further, but whistles and laughter from the group break up the moment. We disconnect bashfully. Reda gives me a high five, while Justine giggles amongst the girls in German. We all head back to the stage.

It's so late, that it's early. Drunken definitively. In just moments after entering the crowd, I find Justine once more. In each other's arms, kissing for everything that it's worth. I gently kiss her chest as she grabs at my hair. Around us is a rage. People crowd surf, mosh, drink, and pass out, but we're in our own moment, devoid of the chaos. Carmen pulls us apart. When I look around Reda is nowhere to be seen, and neither is Veronika, Liz, or Anna. We go back to the bus stop hand in hand as if we were a proper couple. It's 5:00am and we sit on the bus, which is now quiet, and mostly empty. We're arm in arm, kissing gently and laughing. We arrive at the hostel where I walk her to her door.

"You mind if I come in?" I ask. She checks the inside.

"Shit. It is not possible. The other two people are sleeping and I don't know when Anna will come back."

"No problem," I say as I pull her closer. "You're here for some more days, right?"

"Yeah," she says with a smile. "We can try again another night."

We kiss once more. She walks into her door holding onto my hand until the last possible moment. I return to the reception and find Reda smoking a cigarette outside. I exit the hostel.

"Hey! Where did you go, man?"

"I got lost. What's up with you and Justine? I saw you, man!"

"Oh," I laugh bashfully. "She's incredible. She has roommates, but is hanging around here for a few days. I think we will get there."

"You want me to take a walk and leave the room to you?"

"Nah. It's cool. She's already in her room," I say. "What happened to you? I looked up and you were gone."

"I wasn't really lost. I was getting a blowjob in an alley, Teo."

"I expect nothing less my friend."

I try to keep my mind from going to that sappy place, but it does. My new habit of denying my true thoughts seems to have completely crumbled in the last weeks. Iza infectious smile provoked my wandering lusts, and now Justine, in her budding youth and beauty, has given me a glimmer of completely irrational hope. I begin to ponder on the possibility of Justine being more than a fling.

When I first realized how much I missed Derlenzistda, I tried dating. I tried to replace her, but this game doesn't work that way. I fell fast, pained often, and learned to despise my perhaps natural taste for romance. It's been over a year since I've fallen for anything, but this sudden rush of romanticism is reminiscent of those old days and it seems like I'm poised for trouble.

Sundays are by far our busiest days, but my mind is busy running through scenarios of how I could possibly have a relationship with Justine. I know it's wrong to think. It's even shallow. However, I can't help it. Just the idea of having a connection remotely close to what I had with Derlenzistda makes me feel nice. I don't feel that way often. I'm smiling more, and it shows.

"Teo, what has happened to you? Did you meet some girl?" asks Katia.

"Haha. I met a girl," I say. At that moment Justine and Anna exit the hostel with their beach gear. Justine waves in my direction and smiles. "That's her."

"Ohhhhh, Teo! Good Job!"

"I know. I know. It's nothing. Really. We just had a couple of sparks fly it seems."

"It takes sparks to make a fire," says Reda.

"Yeah, and with my luck I'll be the wood that gets burned up!"

"Well at least *les ferias* are ending," adds Katia. "You will have less to worry about kids being in Bayonne, and more time to focus on not burning up," she says laughingly. Reda gets up from his seat to give her a high five and even Shoshana chuckles a bit at her computer. I don't think any of it's funny.

"Ok. Ok. Team SBS. We will see who's pulling night duty on the schedule this week."

"But seriously, Teo," begins Katia. "Do you really think there is something with this girl? You don't know her."

"Damn, Katia. Let the man dream a little," begins Reda. "I've seen my man handle tougher situations than this."

"It's ok, Reda. Katia is just looking out for me, and I guess you are too," I say. There is some rosé in the fridge. I take it and pour a glass for myself and the both of them. "I don't know what I'm doing, but I know it's summer. The worse that could happen is that she leaves and a never see her again. Right?"

They nod their heads in agreement, and we all drink. After everything that has happened, even the worse doesn't seem so bad.

It's the last day of the *fête*, which is a good thing. It signals the end of the high season, and my worries about students going to Bayonne. However, it's still a terribly busy day. I have accounting, a new welcome meeting, and a thousand other things on my list. I'm in the office, and in the zone, when Lans comes by. He's wearing all white clothes.

"Hey, Teo! What's up, man?" he says. I respond dryly wondering why this seventeen-year-old think it's ok to call me, 'man'. "Do you have a red scarf I can use?"

"Get out of my office! Are you crazy?!" I say firmly. He scurries away. Did he think I would say yes? Why is he even at the hostel? I had him transferred to a host family in the city a few days ago after Greg caught him trying to cover up a security camera. I try think nothing of it, and continue my work which runs into the night.

I eventually head to the bar where I find Reda already waiting for me. We sit at the bar talking about the crazy weekend. We're still recovering from the *fêtes*, so it feels good to have a mellow evening. Strangely enough he keeps receiving text messages, and I grow suspicious as he begins to smile at them.

"What the hell is that?"

"What, boss?"

"That silly smile on your face. Who are you texting?"

"Oh. It's just this girl. The one from the alley way."

"No."

"She's really cool, man. She's Swedish and in town to learn some French. She keeps messaging me."

"Could it be? *The* Reda Tj is having feelings?"

"Hell nah! Pftt. You know that's not my style. I'll leave that to you and Justine," he says with a wink. "You don't *really* care about her, do you? I mean. You just met her."

"I probably don't, but I guess it's the idea that has me open. The idea that I could care is nice."

"Yeah. Maybe. Take it easy though. I didn't want to say anything but, I remember the last time you were like this. You went on a three-day drinking binge after leaving Agathe crying in the middle of the dance floor."

"I remember. I remember all of it," I say. I pause and look down into my almost empty glass of beer. For all of his insanities Reda has always shot me straight, perhaps even more than I'm willing to do for myself. However, silly possibilities have a way of clouding even the soundest of advice and the cruelest of lessons. "I also remember when I thought love at first sight was a real thing; that every story had a happy ending. I know now it's all bullshit, but if I can have even a piece of that silly shit in my life it could be worth the effort. Yeah?"

"Ok, T. Ok. Just stay sharp man."

"I will," I say.

Optimism carries into the morning. Katia and Shoshana go about their duties taking the students to school, and leading expeditions for the other clients. I take a late breakfast. I sit down at my computer and sip my coffee, as I do every morning. I begin to open some emails when I see Lans burst out of the hostel door in a sprint. He's wearing the same white clothes from the night before, except now they're covered in filth and handwriting. I quickly slide open my window.

"Lans! What the hell are you doing?!"

"I'm going to class," he says with fear in his eyes.

"Yeah, I can see that. You're late, and from the looks of it you went to Bayonne last night after stopping by my office!"

"I'm sorry! I'm sorry. It was a long night; I was with this girl and..."

"Wait! What?!" I say. I imagine him with one of the *Quatre Fantastiques* and think I've failed Miri's mother who asked only one thing of me. "Are you screwing one of my students?"

"No! No, sir! Not at all. It's a girl from the hostel."

"Who?!"

"You don't know her."

"Try me."

"Um. Her name is Justine. She's a German girl."

His words though spoken timidly, cut unrelentingly though every part of me; body, spirit and soul. I look at his lips, and then realize that those lips have been locked with ones I was with just nights before. He's standing waiting for a response wondering possibly what angry rant will come next, but I have nothing left.

"Go to school. We will talk," I say staring at him. He runs off, but I'm still standing, staring at nothing for a few moments before sitting down. I put my hands up to the computer, but decide not to type. I reach for my coffee, but decide not to drink. I would decide not to sit, if I wasn't already sitting.

I hear singing in the hallway. Reda enters eating a croissant and drinking coffee.

"Sup, boss!? Good morning!"

"Sit down."

"What?"

"You're gonna wanna sit down for this one, mate," I say. I turn to him in my chair as he places his breakfast on his desk.

"Ok. Lay it on me."

"Lans slept with Justine."

"What the fuck are you talking about, Teo? Wait. Our Lans? Youth program Lans?"

"Our Lans. Youth program Lans."

I explain to him the whole scene and even tell him about how he stopped by the office the night before. I was already going to meet with him, but this takes things to another level. Reda knowing how I am, steps up.

"You want me to handle it?"

"No, no it's fine. I'll talk to Hermann. We'll figure something out," I say. I grab a beer from the fridge. This time I don't even bother with putting in a plastic cup. "It's my fault. I'll handle it."

"You need something?"

"Think I'm going to take the day off. Can you take the emergency phone, and hang around the office for a while?"

"Take all the time you need, Boss. I got this."

I shuffle out of the office. It's a slow shuffle. Hamza is sitting at the reception with Gil. He yells out to me.

"Teo! I get no 'good morning' or what?"

"Oh. Sorry. I'm a bit tired."

"It's because he's been hooking up for the *ferias*," says Gil proudly nodding his head.

"Yeah. Something like that."

Chapter 10: They Don't See a Thing

I've fooled myself once again into thinking I am built for this game, or at least that it's possible to have a heart and be a whore. Wait. No. From the moment I arrived here, I've heard the disclaimers. *It's Biarritz. It's Pays Basque and here things are done differently. It's summer. It's high season. The ferias will be absolutely insane, and I'll be with many women.* It's all true. In all my travels, I've never seen such a place beautifully and stubbornly ingrained in their culture and traditions. The Basque language is everywhere, even though you'll hardly find it anywhere else in the world. The attitude and pace of life is as desirable as the local dishes and vista. No one ever said to have feelings. No one said to construct a fleeting future on a moment's fancy. I did that, again. It appears that while things are done differently here, I am still the same. I've learned nothing.

I'm lounging in bed, looking up at the ceiling. The window is open and at least there is a reassuring breeze to slightly dry the sweat on my skin. It'd be a perfect hour for a siesta, but a siesta is what one does to unwind. I've coiled myself tightly around my indiscretions and sins. I'm so lost in thought that I don't realize there is a knock at the door. Reda enters a few moments after that, clutching my phone in his hands.

"Teo!" he says firmly. I snap out of my self-loathing trance.

"Huh?"

"It's Greg, on the phone. He's pissed off. "

"He's always pissed off," I say as I reach for the phone, still lying on the bed. "*Bonjour, Greg. C'est, Teo.*"

"I have had it, Teo! These kids are shitty. Listen to me! I know the season is long, it is tough here. That is why I have to be tough. You are the one in charge? Yes?!"

"*Oui, Greg. Oui.*"

"Well then I need you to get control of these damn kids! They've damaged the fence sneaking out again last night! I hear they jump out of the windows at night to sneak into town. We already got rid of the Swedish boy! If I hear one more complaint about this, I don't care who it is, where they're from, or how much money their parents have, I will personally kick them out of the here! You understand?!"

"*Oui, Greg. Oui.* I will handle it."

"Good. Thank you, Teo. How are you, by the way?" he asks suddenly switching his tone.

"I'm brilliant. Never been better," I reply sarcastically.

"Good. Me too. *Ciao!*"

I sit up, resting on the edge of the bed.

"Should I take the phone back?" asks Reda.

"No. I might as well just get back to it."

"Drinks on me tonight."

Reda leaves. As the door closes I can hear a familiar music coming from down the hallway. I grab my things, and shuffle out of the room. *Les Quatre Fantastiques* are sitting on benches just at the end of the hallway on their phones laughing.

"Girls, what are you doing here? I thought you had surfing today?"

"Yes, but Teo. It's too hot! We're so tired," says Ester.

"Yeah, because you were out at *la Fête de Bayonne* all night?!"

"What!? No, no, Teo. It's not true," says Clara. "We did not sneak out last night! Other nights yes of course, but not last night, Teo!"

"So you don't know anything about Lans or the broken fence? I just got a call, and the next person caught doing anything is getting sent home."

"No, no, Teo. It was not us this time. I mean, c'mon. We've been out every night, but last night we did not," says Miri.

I look at them emotionless. I sigh, turn, walk out to the terrace and sit down in the chair, looking off into sunlit nothing. The girls go quiet in the hallway. They turn the music off and began to murmur in Spanish, still under the impression that I understand nothing. Clara, who they think I like the most, is told to come see what's wrong. She walks onto the terrace and sits next to me.

"What's up, Teo?"

"Nothing."

"C'mon, man. You look sad. Tired and sad. It's not good for you, Teo. It's summer," she says. "So tell me, guy. What's the problem?"

I don't know why, but I am somewhat honest with this 16-year-old.

"It's a woman. Well, I have women issues."

"You have a girlfriend?"

"No. I had one a long time ago. I think I made some mistakes, but now I'm still dealing with them. You know how that goes?"

"Oh yes, absolutely. Don't worry. You will find someone perfect, Teo!"

"Thanks," I say sarcastically. "How is your boyfriend?"

"Oh, he is just the best. I think we are truly in love, Teo! I cannot wait to see him," she says. I stop looking at nothing for a moment and fix my tired eyes to her. She looks like a Catalan angel with all that enthusiasm in her face. Her blonde hair, blue, eyes and even chipped tooth are just perfect. "It could be true love. Yeah? Do you think it could be something good?"

My first impulse is to unload years of painful wisdom on her. I'll tell her about Derlenzistda, my failed flings, and beach rendezvous. I'll tell her that love and romance are lies, and that the sooner she figures it out the better off she'll be. I'm about to say just that when I see the other *fantastiques* curiously looking out onto the terrace as well, waiting on my response. I look at them briefly, and then I look back at my angel. I remember when I was their age. I had that same hope.

"Something good? No. Clara. It can be something great, and don't you ever forget it," I say. It's as if my 16-year-old self somehow bursts through the years of adventures and dalliances for the sake of their romantic futures. Something about that innocence in her eyes inspires me. For at least that moment, it saves me. I smile from a deep place. "Besides, you're my angel. You only deserve the best."

A crackdown begins immediately. With Katia and Shoshana taking over all the adult client's programs, Reda and I focus on organizing the teens. The next day I ask Bernard to send Lans to the hostel once classes are over. Once he's in the office I unleash in a way that I didn't know I was capable of. I have Reda there to make sure I kept it professional, which means not mentioning that our lips kissed the same women during a weekend. The facts are plain in simple. He was completely disrespectful asking his Program Manager for *feria* attire. He confesses to damaging the fence at the hostel, along with some culprits who he gives up in a heartbeat. We punish him in the best way we could, which is to repair the fence, and sending a detailed letter to his parents.

He gets the picture.

I realize that the soon departure of our teenage students will be the end of high season. The decrease in clientele means a decrease in personnel, meaning the end of a need for Reda. With that in mind, we live every day on the cusp of breaking professional boundaries. I use the staff catering that night, and Reda has promised me drinks to help cope with my Justine incident. It certainly doesn't help that she's still around the hostel, and I've gone out of my way to avoid her. I see her walk into the bar. Reda and I are in the middle of a debate about drunk nothings, while James instigates the exchange. She and Anna take a seat next to us, but we hardly acknowledge their presence. After a while she gets that something is off and tries to speak with me, but I receive a text message. It's from Iza, and she wants to know if I'd like to meet her in the city center. I show it to Reda, and he nods.

"Excuse me. Duty calls." I say to everyone. "Good night."

"Oh. You're leaving?" asks Justine.

"Yeah," I say as I grab a bottle of wine and walk out of the bar.

I take the long walk up the hill towards the bus stop. It's a lot of time to think about what I am doing, and even on what I'm about to do. Justine left me hopeless when I was already so, while my angel reminded me of what hope could be. I'm not sure what to expect from a meeting with Iza. Well, no. I am sure what to expect, and I know it won't help my situation at all. Maybe I should stop lying to myself. The guy I was before Derlenzistda isn't here anymore, no matter how much I'd like him to be.

I arrive in the city center and stop by a shop to grab a couple of beers, having already finished the rest of the wine. Iza pulls up on her bike; beautiful in spite of her own beauty. You'd think a cute summer dress would do the trick, but that's simply not who she is. She wears her comfortable long pants and spaghetti strapped shirt with her hair pulled back in a bun.

"Teo!" she shouts. "It has been too long!"

"Hey there, Iza. One sec," I say as I turn to pay for the beers. "Yes it has! Where have you been?"

"So busy with this job. I'm glad I found one, but obviously, I was so much more carefree when I was just hanging around the hostel," she says as she greets me with two kisses.

"No worries on any of that now. I've been a bit busy myself, but let's leave that for work hours."

"Agreed."

We take a promenade through the city. Drinks in hand. She tells me of her dreams to go to Cambodia next year to do nonprofit work, and asks about mine. I'm in a sharing mood for some reason. Perhaps, cooperating socially would put off my impending sexual tasks so far as to not have to engage them.

"I want to come back to France. I don't know how or why, but I doubt I can blend in easily after so much time away. I haven't written in so long, and I don't have any job ideas. I'll find the way."

"I greatly like the sound of that," she says with a smile. I can see that she's gazing a bit at me, but I pay her no mind. If I look, if I give in, there is no turning back. I don't need to look into those green eyes to see them. "Hey! Have you been down there?"

She points to a set of stairs which leads down to a small secluded beach not far from the casino and *la Grande Plage*. The sea wall is rock and at least 20 feet high; with a bridge that extends out unto the water where it connects with huge boulders which stick out of the sea. Tourists walk along the way to get a gorgeous view of the ocean, and during the day the secluded beach is perfect for lovers. That is if a thousand others don't have the same idea. Tonight, Iza is the only one who has this idea.

Descending those stairs is like a return to blissful madness. Every step is closer to the sand, and deeper into perdition. We remove our sandals, leaving sand once again between our toes. However, this time she's the one leading the way.

"Let's sit over there!" she says as she walks to a shadowy spot, just below the bridge. We sit down, undoubtedly knowing what will happen. However, we go through the motions anyway. "Do you have another beer?"

"Sure," I say. I remove a Desperados from the plastic bag and hand it to her. I down the last of mine and open another for myself. "Good beer."

"Yes. It is ok. We have some good beer in Hungary. You must come one day so I can show you!"

"I think I'd like that. Hungary has always been a dream of mine."

She then goes on some monologue about how marvelous the city is and how there is so much to see there. I nod casually, taking bigger gulps of my drink than usual, which are already big enough. It seems even she's doing the same in between giving Hungarian factoids. Shit. She might as well be giving the history of a lighthouse with the way she's going on.

"Do you like the sand?" she asks. We're sitting with our legs crossed, facing each other. She takes her hands and plunges them into the beach. She begins to let it run through her fingers. "I love the way it feels to have the earth against my skin. Don't you?"

"I'm not sure," I respond. "Guess I've never thought about it."

"Give me your hands," she says. She takes them and piles sand on top of them. She begins rubbing into them and over them, piling more on as the majority falls to the ground. "Do you like it?"

"Actually, it feels pretty nice," I say. I didn't think I'd enjoy it so much, and fail to realize that I'm smiling. When I look up she's smiling back. She quickly leans forward and kisses me once. I pull back slightly, only enough to look into her eyes. They will tell me the story, and as long I know the plot I can handle it. It's nothing more than what it is. We're young. It's summer and our last rendezvous left so much more to be explored.

I take my large hands to her cheeks, leaving my lips in limbo just near hers. I breathe just hard enough to let her know that I'm alive, heart beating and blood pumping, before pulling her face to mine. She leaps on top of me knocking us both back on the sand. This time I have no illusions, no lighthouses to light my way, or personified condoms. I'm here for the thrill.

She removes my shirt, and I hers. Her body is newly bronzed, beautiful. This time she wears no useless bra.

"You've been in the sun."

"Yes. Soon I will be like you," she says jokingly as she begins to kiss my chest.

Each touch accurate, sensual, and sizzling at once. She quickly removes her pants tossing them to the side, and I being a bit too her slow for her taste, am intrigued as she hastily helps me remove mine. There is some laughter above on the bridge as occasional tourists take the walk out to sea. If they had a mind to look down into the shadows they would surely see us, but they never do. Not even when I disappear in her mouth do they notice us. It's exhilarating. The fear of being caught pulses throughout as she much more vigorously than before has her piece with my person. I have to urinate, but don't want her to stop. I hold off until I can no more.

"Hey, stop for a sec. I need to pee," I say. She responds with a muffled 'no', and keeps about her business. I have to say it a bit more directly. "No, I *really* need to pee."

She leans back, still with my penis in her hand. She pauses, then says 'Ok'. I walk just a couple of feet away to relieve myself, while she removes her panties. I walk back towards her. She resumes while I stand on my feet. I watch a group of people pass by on the bridge. They don't see a thing.

I sit on the ground, and she mounts me.

"Wait," I say.

"What's wrong?"

"Nothing, I just need a condom," I say while reaching for my pants. She looks almost impatient touching herself as I put it on, and as soon as it's strapped she mounts me completely. Grinding is for amateurs. Lubricated frictions, a healthy collision of our organs. Our bodies' rhythm begins surprisingly just as calm as the waves cascading into the small beach front, but eventually becomes something else entirely. It is as if the moon looks down upon us and calls the tides of lust to increase mercilessly. Her cries are endless and banshee-like, and if not for the melodic waves the passersby would surely discover our rendezvous.

"Do you think they can see us?" she says slowing down slightly.

"They can't, and if they do I don't care," I say, shocking even myself. Iza digs her nails into my back as easily as she had done to the sand. I ignite, tackling her onto her back. She laughs in delight as she becomes one with the sand, as I still one with her. She asks for more. I grant her request. Her screams are louder now, but the concept of being caught is an aphrodisiac, only scary enough to provoke us to take advantage. But even these things must end.

When the time is right. We do.

"Did you fuck her?!" asks Reda who's still drinking as I return the hostel bar. Thankfully, there is almost no one there except for him and James, but I'm sure he would have said it even if the place was full.

"Something like that."

"Teooooo! My man is on a roll, James!"

"Haha. For sure. Definitely seems like you're making the most of your time here!" replies James

"It's good you did too man. You should have seen it when you left. Justine was sitting here upset talking to Anna about it all. Shit. They thought I couldn't understand, but I did," he says with a wink. "She said something about wanting to talk to you. Gotta feel pretty good to have options, yeah?"

"I don't feel any different to be honest. A bit tired maybe," I say reaching behind the bar to grab a bottle of wine. James slides a glass my way and I fill it with red.

"What is it, T?" begins James. "I mean, I saw Iza. She's a catch, mate. That makes twice on the beach now, doesn't it? You gotta like those odds, even with girls like Justine running around."

"Gents, I can't lie to you. These moments with Iza are what a summer in Biarritz is made of. I can't say I've ever had such a wild time."

"And that's a bad thing?"

"It's not a bad thing. It's not a good thing. It's just a thing," I say. I drink the entire glass of wine, and fill it up again. "It's for that moment. It's for this summer. So, I can only take it for that. It's high season."

I stand up from the bar and take the wine bottle and glass with me. I walk past the reception, through the double doors, up the stairs. I walk down the hallway. There is no music from *Les Quatre Fantastiques* room, which means they've probably already snuck out for the night. I walk into my room, and place the bottle on the sink in front of the mirror; empty the glass into my body. I look into my eyes. I don't recognize that man.

"Are you there?" I say. Hoping to see some glimmer of that 16-year-old who believed in angels.

He's silent.

Chapter 11: Guns for San Sebastian

To say that you've passed a night of empty sex is supposed to be a two-way street. It's supposed to mean that your partner provided you with nothing more than a carnal experience, devoid of substance beyond physicality. However, it's worth mentioning that typically they're two people rolling in the sands and sheets.

"Don't say you've had empty sex, because that would imply that you're empty yourself," says a would-be sage assuming that they've made some profound statement, and perhaps even influenced someone to think more highly of themselves and others. However, most of the time when the would-be love doctor says that, they leave out the truly profound part; which could be found with a simple follow up question.

"Are you empty?"

If the 'philosopher' really cared about someone's emotional state they would have asked this from the beginning, instead of trying to sound enlightened, because what if someone is empty? What if they've nothing left? This talk of emptiness becomes pretty condescending, because there's no feeling like that void. When you, yourself, your person, becomes the calm eye surrounded by the storm that is your love life, or even your life in general. That's emptiness. The only thing you see in that eye is the abyss that once was love, or even the slightest most earnest of intentions, and you somehow fool yourself into thinking you can fill it with fleeting fancies. It's never enough.

I am empty. Wild romps with Iza, despite her actually being a nice girl, have left me fatigued, while this Justine business is a shit show on any day. I've been taking every backdoor I know of to avoid her during her final days at the hostel, while Lans does the same to avoid me. Word travels fast in these walls, so I am sure everyone knows by now. The youths whisper when I walk by. Clients go silent when I enter the bar. I'd love to let hate live in my heart, but it's simply not pragmatic. I brought this upon myself. Lans was just being a horny seventeen-year-old during high season. Can I really blame him for that? Justine is eighteen or nineteen, and neither of those ages are exactly the most responsible periods in anyone's life. I guess I thought I'd left those follies six years past where they belong. They both will leave Biarritz soon. It's easy to think that it's over, that this clusterfuck of mine can just pass, and I can finish the summer, but I can't. I'm not built that way.

I wake up and lie down with my thoughts knowing that my indiscretion has made them, and perhaps even Iza, a part of my story. I used to fantasize of some great love. Often as a child I'd have some dream of romance, and I'd write about it in my journals. Even when life began to show me otherwise, I still believed in it. That boy and his angels thought of it every day. He knew that it would be his story, but I? I have Justine, Iza, the in-betweeners, and of course Derlenzistda. I have sand in my clothes and crevices, and a hangover. If I could see me now. Perhaps, unlike my optimistic predecessor, I'm merely learned. I've lived, loved, and certainly lost, leaving me only to decide to be that hopeful romantic again only endowed with the wisdom of my indiscretions. But that's easier said than done.

Reda is somehow in a relationship. Neither of us have an idea how it happened aside from meeting a Swedish woman as crazy and sexually profound as himself in the chaos of Bayonne. It began with texting, and now he meets with her almost every night which typically means me taking a drink or four at the bar while he does what he does. It's only fair, as per our agreement, at least within reason. I'm sitting at the bar with James when Reda *and* his Swedish lover approach me almost timidly.

"Teo, I need a favor."

"Sure. Anything my man."

"Can Laura stay in the room tonight?"

"No. No. No."

"Teo, please!" she says. "It is my last night in Biarritz and I want to spend it with him! I promise we won't do anything!"

"Yeah, T! She's coming to visit me anyway later this year, and we could go a night without sex."

"...Dammit. Ok."

"Yahhh! You're the best!" she shouts as she reaches out to hug me.

"Don't touch me, "I say playfully knocking her hands away from me. They hold hands and walk down the corridor. While I head to the office to finish some work.

I walk in and see Katia with a guy sitting side by side, but pay it no mind. His name is Pierre, and he's been lingering around the hostel for days flirting with anything that moves. I go about my work as best I can with him trying to whisper bullshit to her. It's even more nauseating considering that he doesn't think I speak French.

"I'm not sure if I will be able to come to Paris, I don't have a place to stay," she says. Out of the corner of my eye I can see him take her hand and lean in.

"Don't worry, my dear. I have many connections in Paris. I am sure we can accommodate you," he says.

"Anyone want a coffee? I'm gonna take a cup of Joe," I shout, breaking up the moment.

"Oh, no," he begins. "We're good."

I leave the office and head towards the vending machine shaking my head. While he is trying to close the deal with my overworked colleague, I am trying to catch up on all the work I've been turning in late. I suppose it'd be different if I felt some sense of fulfillment, but no one wins being melancholy *and* behind on work. I shuffle back down the corridors and see a very unsettling scene as I arrive at the office. Pierre is leaning in trying to kiss her while she is leaning back, obviously trying not to be kissed. I throw my coffee to the floor.

"Get the fuck out!"

"What, what? What do you mean?" he responds while quickly pull his hands away from her.

"Get the fuck out of my office. You've been harassing my team for days."

"Oh! You speak French."

"Yeah, *connard.* Leave. This is a place of business and you're not welcomed here."

"You don't have to say it that way. I know you're not from here, but we are in France. You can speak politely," he says standing to his feet and gently putting his hand on my shoulders.

"Well, you'll have to forgive me, I'm not from here. No means no where I am come from. I'm not exactly domesticated either, so if you don't take your hands off of me I'll break them and your fucking face."

"She asked me here!" he yells while removing his hands.

"Katia, do you want him to go?"

"I want him to go, Teo." she responds while clasping her hands to her face.

"Get the fuck out," I say. He cusses quite gently as he throws his hands up and walks down the hallway. My heart is racing. I have to calm myself down. "Are you ok?"

"Yes," she says as she leans her head on her right hand. I look at the spilled coffee and grab a rag to clean it, but she stops me. "No, let me. Thank you, Teo."

"You want some wine?" I ask. "I don't think coffee will do anymore."

She agrees, so I take two glasses for the rosé. I fill mine to the top, hers halfway as usual.

"Maybe fill it up this time," she says laughing. "Thank you again, Teo. This guy, he just wouldn't stop."

"You're welcome," I begin. "Why are you even talking to him? He's flirted with every woman here. Well, I do my share of flirting too, I guess."

"I've had some issues with my boyfriend. We're not so stable, as you know. I guess this loneliness has gotten to me so I wanted someone to talk to," she says as she takes a sip. "Yes you flirt, Teo. But you wouldn't do something as he did."

"I guess not...I don't know what came over me, Katia. I, I can't remember the last time I spoke to someone like that," I say as gulp down the last of my wine, and refill the glass. "I just didn't like what I saw. I reacted. I've certainly got my ways, but that's not one of 'em."

"What is it with you, Teo? This Iza? I know you're always talking about the women with Gil and Reda, but you're not like this."

"I don't know that. Neither do you."

"Well it doesn't seem like the same guy I spoke with at the beginning of the summer. Teo, do I need to treat you like my grandson or something, and teach you the lessons of life?"

"Really, *babushka?* Maybe you do."

"You're a good guy. You just need to make a decision; you need to mature. You're not made for this promiscuous life, you have too much heart."

"Is that a compliment?"

74

"Yes, I think so. Seriously!" she says. "I never thought you were some guy to always sleep with different women when we first met, but I did think that you'd help someone if they needed it."

"I suppose that does count for something."

"It counts for everything. Don't be too hard on yourself. Take your time. You will see," she says.

We clink our glasses together. Katia doesn't finish her wine and turns in for the night. I sit a bit longer, drink a bit longer, and think a bit longer. Is it that obvious? I'm out of my element it seems, which makes sense I suppose. This lifestyle is a default, a coping mechanism. However, I'm not coping.

I shuffle to my room. A bit less sober than I planned to be, with a bit less work completed than I intended. I gently shut the door to the room, knowing that Reda and Laura *should* be asleep. Thank God I enter to silence and gentle snoring. I put on my shorts and sit on the edge of my bed. Just feet away is her bronzed nude rear exposed as her leg lays over his body. I look to my bag, and pull out the book. *As the Sun Also Rises*. The sun is really going to rise if I don't get some sleep. Still. I sit with it in my hands rubbing my fingers against its tattered cover. I place the book on top of my bag, not inside, and glance once more at the two sleeping kids. So, I'm not a guy who lets guys harass women. That's good a start. However, I am a guy who sleeps alone. Snoring or not, that's no way to be.

The road to San Sebastian is perhaps one of the only sure things these days. Rain or shine the frontier to Spain is beautiful, and never fails to invoke powerful emotions. It's almost like a mirror. The green hills, the towering trees, fields of livestock and southern European houses, show you more of who you are, because as they draw you into a day's dream there are no filters. You can't place it down like a phone to think about how to respond. No. It removes consciousness with its beauty, leaving me comfortable. Only I wish I was more at peace with things.

Hermann and I set out, much as we always do, just before noon. Reda and Katia have taken a small group for an excursion, and as it's Reda's last weekend. We're planning a 'team building" exercise at Bar

Gorriti. That is of course considering if I haven't spent all of the catering budget on ordering pizzas. I'm normally in overwhelmingly good spirits to be heading to Spain, but there is a weight lingering. Hermann, who has had so much confidence in me seems to know nothing about my activities, and it's eating away at me. For the sake of the service, I try to come clean halfway through the journey.

"You seem a bit quiet, Teo. That's not normal."

"You're right. I've had a lot on my mind. High season really took a lot out of me."

"I can tell. You know everyone has noticed. Your work, it's not as organized. It seems like you're spending as much time closing down the bar as you do in the office."

"I know, I know. My reports have been a bit late, but I still get them done."

"True, but you don't work for the hostel, do you?" he says. Hermann even when joking can be intimidating because of his booming voice, but this is no joke. "The season's not over yet. You've got to hold it together."

"I know. I'm a bit on the edge. I resisted as long as could, but before I knew it I was having sex on the beach. It couldn't be helped. Even *La Fête de Bayonne* was too much. I thought I'd go out and just taste the Basque summer," I begin. I think about my words carefully. "You should know though. I had thing with a woman who slept with one of the students."

"What?! You slept with a student?"

"No! No, no, no. She was a hostel client. She's not even in our program. I found out that Lans was with her the day I caught him going late to class."

"Oh, good," he begins. I can see him thinking about it, and he almost laughs when he realizes what that means. "Damn. That's a messed-up situation."

"Oh, I know. I realize I've been off my game. I, at least wanted to tell you that before it came to you in some twisted way."

"Don't worry, Teo. He is leaving tomorrow, and you have just over a week left," he says. "Thank you for telling me."

"You're welcome...You know. She was a German girl," I say. He laughs loudly and slaps his knee.

"You should have come to me for advice, of course."

76

By the time we arrive in San Sebastian I've dropped a bit of the weight off my mind. How can I be in the least bit downtrodden in such a beautiful place? We park in our usual garage just below the Hotel Maria Cristina. Hermann, as is tradition, makes a comment as we pass saying that perhaps we will need to stop by to check on our rooms. Perhaps we will, but for now we have a rendezvous.

The feeling I get when entering Bar Gorriti reminds of the cafe at home. When I walk in, I'm known. It's incredibly inviting as the barman, in the middle of pouring one of his famous no look glasses of wine, winks at us upon entering. Reda, Katia, and Shoshana, arrive shortly after making our team building exercise complete. We began filling our plates with tapas. Shoshana tries to hand them money, but I have to stop her and explain that things are done a bit differently here in San Sebastian. I feel like I do Hermann and 'the service' justice as I tell the team they must throw their trash on the floor. They all oblige, except for Shoshana who thinks it's a bit too messy.

"What's wrong with throwing trash?" asks Reda. "I guess some of those stereotypes about Germans being neat are true, yeah?"

"Whatever Reda! Hermann is German and he does it just fine," she responds.

"Hermann hasn't been German for years," I say jokingly. She doesn't think it's too funny, and soon after asks Katia to take a walk with her to do some shopping.

"You two are just a great team, aren't you?" says Hermann.

"We're the best! Ain't that right, boss?" responds Reda gleefully.

"I never thought I'd say it, Reda, but yeah. We are a pretty good team," I say looking at him with a smile.

"You know, Reda, Teo. Next summer will be my last as Program Director. I'd be nice to have you two back, if you're interested."

"I think it could be kick ass. We could do this again, and even better!"

"We will see," I begin. "I still have some time left here, you know?"

It's a nice notion. The three of us coming back next summer would be a walk in the park. We know how things work, so there will be no shock of teenagers or even the high season. However, I didn't come here for that, and at this point I can't think of a reason why I would ever need to return.

If we hadn't exceeded the staff catering budget before that day, we certainly did in that meal. Even with how cheap everything is the three of us continue to eat and drink like kings, which makes me wonder what type of state Hermann and I are in for our drive back to Biarritz. It's a good thing the Hotel Maria Cristina is in the cards.

Reda leaves us to meet up with the girls and the tour group while Hermann and I stroll to the hotel. We enter the lobby like we're staying in their most luxurious suite, while bidding a good afternoon to the doormen and receptionists. We head straight for the bar, immediately becoming one with the plush seats.

"Teo, do you want something to drink?"

"Sure."

"Yes, me too. It's the hour," he says as he calls over a waitress. He orders two Guinnesses, and I watch as the waitress walks away.

"So is that a woman who needs services rendered?"

"Oppp la! Teo!"

"What? Maybe she needs help carrying those drinks."

"And you're going to help her?"

"No. I'm quite tired from the sun. I think I've had enough adventures for now anyway," I say. The drinks arrive. We clink glasses. "What's your situation? I mean, I've never asked if you're married or have kids."

"I have a daughter. I was once married, but she passed."

"Oh, I'm sorry to hear that."

"Thank you. It's been a while though. Hah! I was young, even younger than you it seems. I was backpacking here in France. Today is nothing like those days. We were at the whim of the moment. No cellphones or internet. I remember. We were sitting down by the beach, a German friend and I. We saw these two beautiful women. We had some wine, but no bottle opener. They had a bottle opener, but no wine. We wanted to offer them as much wine as they wanted if they could open the bottles for us, but we could not speak to them. We only spoke German, and some poor English, while they only spoke French. However, we all spoke rosé."

"Seems you still speak it."

"Yes, fluently," he says laughing. "Anyway. We ended up drinking for the whole afternoon. We didn't have any hostels or societies like the one you're staying in. We had our bags, a small tent, and cooking supplies. In any case, we invited them to join us, and it seems they were doing the same as we were. Traveling. Living. Loving. That night we sat around our small campfire. My friend, Heinrich was a bit occupied with her friend, but I only had eyes for her. They did other things, but we, we talked. As best we could. I knew some French words, and had some old dictionary. Somehow we made it work that night. I knew I loved her at that moment. We were so young. That was a long time ago, I suppose."

"What a story," I say in awe. I think of not just this summer, but of my adventures in La Roche, and even Derlenzistda. Fleeting it all seems by comparison. "And now? I mean, are you with someone else?"

"Yes, of course. For some time now actually. After my wife passed, it took a while. I threw myself into my work. I worked with a lot of troubled young men. Eventually, I founded the recreation center. But you were just being born around that time."

"Yeah, I suppose I was. And look. Now I am here, in the Maria Cristina."

"Oh yes, you've really made it in life!"

We sip our drinks slowly. He asks about my plans for after the summer. I tell him about being excited to return to the cafe, and even mention everything that happened with Derlenzistda before I left. He laughs at me, and says in that deep voice, "Bah! You're still young. Don't be so dramatic! Talk to me next year and we'll see how you feel!"

I laugh freely, and with it leaves a bit of my burdens. We use the hotel's porcelain palace, and hit the road. This time, I look at those same hills and wilderness and see hope. How could anyone care about the past with such a picturesque present?

For the first time since arriving I try take things into perspective. What if Hermann is right about this being simply a phase of my life? If he's correct, then that would mean these aimless nights are just that, nights. Not days, weeks, months, and years. I should keep them that way, until they prove otherwise. It just took one day of needing a bottle opener for Hermann to meet his wife, and I'm certain he didn't imagine to be sitting in the hotel Maria Cristina telling me about the whole thing decades later. Vision. Scope. Time. They'll make or break you, but that's all down to decision.

Perspective is everything.

The ride back to Biarritz is as tranquil as can be. However, there's an inevitable situation awaits us all. The time has come for Reda, my right-hand man and friend, to leave. Hermann and I arrive before everyone at the hostel. He bids me adieu for the evening and I sit in the office waiting for Reda to arrive with the team. It's funny. I would have never imagined him as someone who could come to work with me this summer, but now I don't know how I'm going to function without him for end.

He struts into the office. I stand up and grab two San Miguels from the fridge, and hand him one. We are unusually quiet as we clink the bottles together. It's not until after we've each taken a hefty sip that I speak up.

"You sure you want to leave tonight? I've got the beer, if you've got the time."

"I wish, Boss. This fucking carpool is going to suck. I'm not even makin' it to Nantes until 1:00am," he says. He pauses to take another sip. "All of the train tickets are at best double the price I'm paying. I just got my direct deposit and don't want it blow it all getting back home, ya know?"

"Yeah. I know," I say. "Thank you. For everything."

"Thank you too, man. I know how I can be...So, it means a lot that you guys thought to have me down here. You know, coming back next summer might not be such a bad idea. I'm in, if you are."

"We will see, Reda. I still have a lot of things to figure out. I feel somewhat better than I did when this summer began, but I'm still in between."

"Between what?"

"Don't know."

"You'll figure it out, boss."

"You may be right, my friend."

We finish our beers. Reda fetches his luggage from the room and meets me in front of the hostel. He lights up a cigarette and exhales smoothly. He complains for a little bit about how the driver doesn't allow smoking in their car. We're reminiscing over the last few weeks

80

until a tiny blue Peugeot pulls up. Reda hastily puffs the last of his cigarette before flicking it into an ashtray.

"*A plus, mon ami*," he says as we exchange kisses to each cheek.

"*A plus, mon ami.*"

Chapter 12: Fritzi

I can feel the seasons shift. The inevitable end has been creeping into my mind for the last few days, but as I watch Reda ride off into the evening I know it's almost time for me to leave as well. *Les ferias* have come and gone, leaving bottles and even a few hungover bodies in the streets and beaches. Its aftermath signals the end of high season and the departure of our lovely group of teenagers. *Les Quatre Fantastiques* have grown on me, so much to a point where I've become protective. I'm a bit worried of having to look after them without Reda, but it's their last night. Tomorrow morning even they'll be on their way.

I hear the typical sound of Miri's music coming from the bar, and follow it so I can tell them and any of the other teenagers that it's bedtime (even though I know they'll try to sneak out eventually). As I enter, I see Miri dancing with one of the hostel clients, some 30-something year old man, and I immediately break it up.

"Hey! Stay away from these girls! If you want a woman, head into the city center!"

"Hey man! She wanted to dance. Who are you anyway?"

"I am her Program Manager, and she is one of my students. Touch her again and I'll have you kicked out of this hostel."

"Ok, ok! Shit," he says as he and his buddies leave the bar, leaving Miri and the rest of the *fantastiques* to bashfully look at the ground.

"You ok, girls?"

"Yes, Teo," says Miri. "I don't know who that guy was. He just came and started dancing with us. Thank you."

"Don't worry," I say, finally thinking that I had lived up to my promise to her mother. "It's my job."

"You should totally come party with us! It's our last night!" says Ester.

"Yes!" yells Clara.

"No. I don't party, and it's past your bedtime."

"You don't party? Then what's in your cup all the time?"

"Yeah. Every time we see you, you have a cup, and it smells pretty funny, Teo," says Miri putting her hands on her hips.

"It's, um. Juice."

"You drink juice like we stay in our rooms at night," says Ester as they all begin to laugh.

"That's actually pretty funny," I say with a smirk.

"Will you miss us?" asks Clara. I tighten my face.

"No. Time for bed ladies," I say motioning for them to move along. They look almost sad, which for some reason makes me a bit sad. "Ok, ok. Maybe a little.

"Yahhhh! We knew it!" says Ester.

I shepherd the girls to their room and come back to the bar. It's a strange to see it empty. I'm used to seeing Reda sitting on a barstool waiting on me with cold brew, but instead it's just James playing on his phone. I grab a bottle of red wine from behind the bar and toss a few coins to pay.

"Where is everyone?" I ask.

"High season's over, mate. There's a few stragglers around, but that's all," he says not even lifting his eyes from his phone. I leave him to his device and walk outside to take a seat at one of the terrace tables. The weather is nice and even without Reda to nudge me along, I'm still a bit thirsty.

At a table in the distance are two people speaking Spanish. They pause for a moment and ask me if I'd like to join them. I have nothing against it, and take a seat. After a bit of talking I discover that the man is from Mexico and is a traveling worker. He's much older than the girl, and she doesn't appear to be Mexican at all.

"My name is Fritzi," she says in broken English. "I am German, but I studied in Mexico."

"You two are traveling together?"

"No. I've just met Armando tonight actually. I am travelling with another German girl. She has gone to take more drinks."

"Tell her to wait," I begin. "Give me your money. I can get some bottles cheaper because I'm working in the hostel."

Everyone lights up at the concept of more booze for less bucks. Her friend returns and gives me the money and I fetch some more bottles. The four of us soon have a table full of wine and all the time in the world to drink it. It seems that Armando was flirting a bit with Fritzi before I arrived, so I focus on her friend Cathrin as to not interfere. As if the four of us carrying away isn't enough, three more Germans show up and ask if they can join our party. I extend the same offer of buying their bottles so that we can have more wine, and ideally a merry time.

Now seven strong we've become quite loud, and the hour is a bit later than allowed. Aude comes to lock the bar up for the night, and says that we can't stay after hours because it's too many people.

"Teo, drinking again?"

"Yes, yes I know. Aude."

"Not tonight. Why don't you all go to the lake? There you can be as loud as you want."

"That's a perfect idea!" say Cathrin.

"How about I bring my guitar? We can have a sing along?" I add.

"Brilliant! Let's go!" says Armando with his arm around Fritzi. Everyone heads to the lake with their bottles, and I go to my room to grab my guitar and another bottle from my stash. I meet them at the pier and am greeted by cheers.

"Yes! A concert!" shouts Fritzi.

I don't think it will be much of a show, and considering how much everyone's had to drink I doubt they'll be able to tell if it's any good or not. However, on a night like tonight, none of that even matters. The evening shows us its starry diamonds and the brief backup vocals by Lake Moroscut's wildlife make it all the more special. I sing a couple of tunes from Jack Johnson, and even try to learn a few songs they request. We sing along for hours, and after each song Fritzi, who seems to have become my biggest fan, screams, *"Otra cancion!"* By the 5th or 6th time it's almost comical, and I am becoming heavily fatigued.

Armando says that he and Fritzi will go, and soon they disappear into the forest. Their departure ripples through the group's resolve and soon after we all decide it's time to call it. I think of the young Fritzi with the old Armando, Cathrin, and even the two other German girls, and am a bit relieved that despite providing the serenades and discounted booze I've made no attempts with anyone, and no one has with me. I'm happy with that. We're shuffling almost blindly through the trail and finally see the hostel in sight when I hear someone calling my name.

"Donde esta Teo!?" yells Fritzi, as she jogs from the hostel towards us.

"I'm here!" I say perplexed, as I see Armando following slowly in the distance. She jogs until she is by my side, and loops her arm under mine.

84

"What will you do?" she asks.

"I don't know," I respond. "We can keep drinking in my room. I don't have a roommate now. What about Armando?"

"Don't worry about him, he will be fine," she says. I look to see him still standing by the hostel entrance smoking a cigarette. "Let's go to your room."

The others say good night while Fritzi and I, with Armando tailing, head to my room. I feel the most awkward tension as soon as my door closes behind us and immediately suggest we move to the upstairs terrace. They agree, and the three of us walk down the hallway and out the door. Fritzi and I take the two chairs and face them towards each other, while Armando, now looking disgruntled, leans over the ledge looking out at nothingness. Fritzi rubs her hands on my knees. Any thoughts I had about going to sleep disappear. I don't care that it's 4:00am. It doesn't matter that I have work early. It seems she wants me, and I'm becoming more comfortable idea with wanting her.

I never really looked at her until that moment, mostly because she had been in Armando's gazes. She's quaint. Her dark brown hair is in a short ponytail, leaving her steel blue eyes to pierce through me. If I truly have any intention of not having sex, if there is any will power left in these bones to resist temptation, it disappears. We're locked in a gaze made almost forbidden by Armando's lingering, and increasingly creepy presence. After a few moments, he turns and says he's going to bed. He walks into the hallway and turns right. His door's slam might as well as been a gunshot sparking Fritzi and me off to the races.

She reaches in my pants stroking me into ecstasy as I grab her chair dragging her closer. We kiss electric, whispering Spanish nothings to each other. Her neck is soft, and supple, and her pleasured moans are faint as whispers. If it had been Iza the entire hallway, including some of my clients, would have heard it. But no, this is much different.

We're excelling into subtle inferno when we hear a door slam from the hallway. We stop immediately, looking wide eyed as a deer in headlights. I painstakingly and quickly tuck my manhood into my pants for the completely logical fear that I could see one of the remaining teenager's heads peeking around the corner at any moment. I think to just last week when my angel Clara sat here and consoled me with thoughts of childhood puppy love, and now I sit here possibly on the cusp of being caught in my indiscretions.

I am immediately relieved when the source of the slam finds its way into the hallway lights, and am simultaneously perplexed at the sight. It's Armando. He's standing in his boxers, brushing his teeth, looking at Fritzi and I, who are for the sake of appearances are just two people sitting across from each other in the dark. He tilts his head back as if to say, "What's up." Fritzi and I do the same to him.

"What you guys up to?"

"Smoking," she says. She takes a cigarette and lights it. She hands it to me. Not being much of a smoker, I take puff and cough while exhaling.

"Yeah. We're smoking," I say.

"Wait here," she says as she walks into the hallway and grabs him by the arm. She leads him out of sight, and I hear the door slam again. I sit on the terrace looking into night, with my cigarette and a half-chubby. I take another drag this time without coughing. After a couple of minutes, I hear the door slam again, and am relieved to see Fritzi return alone.

"What happened?" I ask.

"Oh nothing. I told him I would be there soon to see him."

"That was weird. What is he thinking?"

"I don't know, Teo!"

"Let's go to my room. I don't want anything to interrupt us again."

She smiles and takes the cigarette from my hand. After taking a long drag, she puts it out in the ash tray. We stand and tiptoe to my room as if we were teenagers sneaking out to sin. I gently open and close the door. I turn off the lights except for the reading light above my bed.

There, in the faint glimmer of light, she undresses, her eyes once again fixated on me. I oblige and begin to remove my clothes, in the silence of our anticipation. Almost nude we step towards each other. Our naked skin touching, with faint goosebumps. Her waist is at the whim of my large hands, but the subtle caresses of her slender fingers are in control of my much larger physique.

She lacks the French or English skills to communicate, and I've never been a student of German. Spanish is our only choice, as I lift her off her feet placing her gently on top of the bed sheets. Iza was an overt experience, wild and unrestrained, but Fritzi in her meek manner possesses a silent strength and sexuality. Our touches are sensual, almost loving. The sounds of kisses are faint between steady breathing. We take our time making sure that we've delicately inspected every inch of each other's bodies.

We remove the last of our clothes. Her body is beautiful in its totality. I gaze at her in wonder, as she looks back at me further captivating my moment. I lift her with one arm, and grab protection from the dresser. I slip it on as I hold her in my arm kissing her supple lips, and once again lay her on the bed.

Slowly. Surely. We connect. She moans with a wisp of air tilting her head back, closing her eyes.

"Look at me," I say. Her eyes stay opened best as possible, as we engage in the closest thing I've had to making love in ages. I close my eyes, biting my lip in a fit of sensible passion.

"No. Look at me," she whispers. I refocus every part of my body to her. My hands almost pulling her body into mine, and my eyes piercing into hers. Her delicate cries sound a sweet siren in the early morning hours. I lean back bringing her body with mine, until we're erect thriving upright. Her head rests on my shoulder as she squeezes my back. She lets out a triumphant moan climaxing in an otherwise sensual occasion. We lie down in each other's arms. The reading light illuminates her eyes right before me, but only for a few minutes.

She gets up in the dark, and begins to put her clothes on. I prop my head up on my fist, and watch her get dressed. Once she's sure she's' gathered all her things, she leans upon the bed stopping just before my face, and just enough for the light to catch her eyes once more.

"That was beautiful," she says. She kisses me and leaves the room. I turn on my back, and close my eyes.

I comfortably fall asleep for the first time in months. Tranquility found in the aftermath of sensual passions. For the first time since those old days, I am calm. The delicate roller coaster named Fritzi is fulfilling, and she is right. It is beautiful. Maybe the talk with Hermann, or even with Katia and Reda, has helped me relax a bit, but I'm far too blissful to try and figure any of it out. After spending the last year loathing and fearing the coldness of an empty bed, I find an enlightening warmth.

I bask in it.

The next morning brings an energy I haven't felt in a long time. Not optimism, not even enthusiasm I'd say; but energy. The best way to say it could be that I have an understanding, which doesn't necessarily mean peace or chaos. It just implies that I, at the very least, comprehend the moment. I'd like to think that in some way reconciles my past, and if it doesn't it is at least a step in the right direction.

Something about last night, or this morning I should say, made things clear for me. I sleep only a few hours before waking up to the idea of catching a late breakfast, but for the first time since those old days facing the sun rise alone is ok. Not good, and thankfully not bad. It's ok. I'm content. I walk into the bathroom to wash up, and look at myself in the mirror.

"Not bad, Teo," I say to myself as I think of the sensual roller coaster. I look for that boy who believed in romance, but I don't see him. Instead I see a young man and doesn't need to believe in romance, because he's lived it just as much as he's lost it. He knows it, he understands. That's the ticket. I can't say that I'm happy, or sad, but I can at least say that. I'm somewhere in between, and that's just fine. It's acceptance. I was never going to remain that boy.

When I think about Hermann's story I now see that I won't remain this way either, and that evolution depends on my involvement. I'm occupied with this concept as I walk to the kitchen where it seems almost all the food is gone, but there is at least enough to get me fed. Baguette, butter, coffee, fruits. Simple. I'm strangely refreshed for a guy who spent the majority of the night and the greater part of this morning drinking and having sex. Through the large cafeteria windows, I see Fritzi and Cathrin on the terrace. Fritzi gets up smiling. She opens the door and enters.

"Good morning, Teo," she says giving me a greeting of kisses to the cheeks. "Did you sleep well?"

"Well enough," I say with a smile. "What about you?"

"As much as possible, but I wished I could have had more time. We have to leave today for the next city."

"Well, that's how this travel life goes. The comers and goers," I say with a sense of nostalgia. "Give me your contact. Who knows? Maybe I'll find my way to Germany."

"I'm glad you ask," she says. She brushes her hair back, and takes out her phone from the back pocket of her jeans. We exchange information and kiss a goodbye. She exits the cafeteria, and I lock eyes with Cathrin through the window. She is laughing pleasantly at the whole ordeal. I return to my breakfast.

Chapter 13: Puig & Daro

It's our last work day, and despite having no program or clients , there is much to be done. Katia, Shoshana, Hermann and I must pack up the entire office. All of the decorations must be taken down. The fridge must be emptied, inventories must be taken, and the accounting must be finalized. It's all quite tedious, but we all work with the pleasant fact that the season is over. There are no clients arriving to ask us silly questions, or teenagers to give us grey hairs. However, there is a nice sum of money in each of our bank accounts. My emotional state remains in flux, but my pocketbook knows the score. I've planned a nice vacation throughout Europe for a couple of weeks before finally crossing the Atlantic. It's as exciting ,as it is uncertain.

We load the boxes into Hermann's car, which as usual is pulled up unto the grasses near our office window. He bids us adieu until tomorrow morning, when he will come to see us off as we will depart to our separate lives. That leaves the three of us who've braved a long summer to fend for ourselves. We want to hop over to San Sebastian but have no time, so we look up a place to eat some tapas in the Biarritz. We find a restaurant called Puig & Daro. I had passed it a few times during my strolls in the city center, but had never taken the time to stop in. We make sure our bags are prepped and change into some nice clothes. I dip into the staff catering budget once more.

Puig & Daro's window has rows and rows of irresistible tapas. Sardines, salmon, sausages, and peppers are just a few of the mouthwatering amenities tempting us as we take a seat on the terrace. We're in the middle of reminiscing about the season when our waitress arrives. She has long brown hair, and her bronzed skin tells tales of a fine summer at the beach. Her name is Miren.

"Ok! It is your first time here?"

"How can you tell?" asks Shoshana

"I am always here, and I've never seen you! Ok so this is how it works. Follow me," she says as she leaves to walk inside. The small establishment has high tables around the room, walls lined with wines, and meat for days. She leads us over the shelves of tapas which are even more tempting without a window separating us from them.

"Ok. Tell me which ones you want and I will place them on a platter to bring to you."

Katia and Shoshana go first, taking almost one of everything. I opt for twice as much.

"You are quite hungry!" says Miren, rubbing her stomach.

"Yes, as always. I love tapas."

"Let me guess, American?" she says switching to English.

"How'd you know? Because I'm hungry?"

"No. Maybe it's just in your eyes," she says picking up the platters to bring to our table. She tells me to go sit down and that she will bring everything. I walk outside. It takes her two trips but she finally is able to lay our full platters on the table with another round of drinks.

"Do you need anything else?"

"No!" laughs Katia. "I think we have enough for a lifetime. Thank you very much!"

Miren clasps her hands together with a smile and says she will be near the entrance if we need anything else. Before walking away, she casts a quick glance my way. I feel my face tighten into what I'm sure is jack ass smile. I shake my head coming to my senses as I see Katia looking at me.

"*Bon appetit!*" I say, while they reply with the same. Katia, however, quite habituated to my summer habits by now, doesn't let anything slide.

"Grandson! What was that look? That smile?"

"What do you mean?"

"I know you, Teo. What did you say to this nice girl?!"

"Nothing! I've done nothing at all!" I say laughing. "I'm just a man. She's a woman."

"Yeah. I really pretty woman," adding Shoshana. "Why don't you talk to her?"

"Nah. I'm leaving tomorrow."

"Pffttttt. That's never stopped you before, Teo. Maybe you'll come back next summer? You can see her then," begins Katia. She continues. "You need a nice girl, Teo. She is so sweet!"

"*Babushka,* please. I'm in no place for a sweet girl now. I fall in 'love' or lust every week."

"Maybe you will be more mature next summer!"

"You guys can keep talking. I'm gonna eat," says Shoshana picking up her first tapa.

We share a laugh and dig in. These delicious delicacies are helpless against our appetites, while further educating our palates with every bite of Basque savors. I feel a new regret. With all that has passed I feel I've hardly engaged the beauties of the Basque culture. If there is to be any second summer, which the bags under my eyes are currently opposed to, that would be something I'd focus on. Perhaps, Miren could show me a thing or two as well.

It's the next morning. Shoshana left just as the sun rose, and Katia will linger a bit to work on her studies. She wakes up to see me off. It seems she did find a place to stay in Paris, and happily without the help of that Parisian prick. She says I'm welcome to visit whenever I return to France, and I'm sad to bid farewell to my *babushka.*

Hermann picks me up from the hostel very early. It's quite nice of him to come, as he doesn't live in Biarritz. Then again, I would expect nothing less from a man who believes in rendering services. We load my bags and drive to the train station. We decide to wait on the terrace of *La Station* until my train arrives, and order two tall Leffe Blondes before sitting on the terrace, side by side.

"To a successfully passed season, Program Manager," he says. He smiles that grizzly smile of his and I raise my glass.

"We did it, Program Director!" I say as we clink them together. We take a deep sip of our beers and grow silent for a moment.

"We will see for next summer. Bernard will be in training to take my place. I could use an easy-going season. Reda will be back. I am sure of it. It would be nice to have some people who know how we function."

"We will see. You're right," I say. I take a large sip of my beer. "I have a lot to sort out, you know? I need to get back to my writing, my art, but I know that the States can't keep me. Even if I can't work here again, I know we'll meet up for a glass of rosé again."

"Or Two," he says slapping me really hard on the back. "Guys like us understand, Teo. I'm sure you'll find what you're looking for. Take your time. Live your life," he says. He gulps down the last of his beer. "*Allez op*! Finish your drink. You'll miss your train!"

We walk in front of the train station. I never got the impression that Hermann is a man who hugs often, so I skip trying altogether. We shake hands firmly, and I hide back my tears. Not because he's crushing my hand, although he is, but because it's been a damn pleasure. I carry my large bags, two full size ones, a carry on, and a guitar. I'm heading north to Paris to see an old friend, Francois. It's 6 hours direct on the TGV, so I've got the time. Luckily there aren't too many people, so there are lots of places to store my things. I sit down with my green satchel in my lap.

I let out a long sigh as the train begins to move, and soon we're zooming down the tracks through the countryside. I reach into my bag and take out the book. Her book. I run my hands over its tattered cover, pensively looking at it. I open it.

I start to read.

Winter: In between, somewhere

Four months after Summer 1

There are clouds where once Basque sunlight beat down daily on sandy beaches. There are no scantily clad women passing by, no Reda moments, and drinking rosé in the late morning is frowned upon. A leisurely life is easily lost in comprehension of the big city's rush hours and time cards. It seems that even 'the service' between men is a lost art. I watch as 'friends' argue over who will cover the tab, and even who bought the last round.

"Your drink cost twice as much as mine, so that means you owe me two," someone says.

This would never happen with Hermann. He would always say that he and I are very similar. "Guys like us understand," he'd say with his arms crossed nodding his head.

The more and more time I pass here, it becomes clear. I begin to see what he meant. People are in such a rush to get things done, that they're just going to have to do again tomorrow. Eat. Traffic. Desk. Eat. Desk. Traffic. Eat. Sleep. Repeat. I'd rather relive my heartbreak and indiscretions than settle for a routine existence. My life abroad certainly had its ups and downs, but at least it was never boring. It's been four months since Biarritz and even though I'm back in the U.S., a place that I call home, I don't always feel at *home.* I prefer a life of espressos, tapas, rosé, but can hardly afford it here. These things, and many others, were daily delicacies back in France, while here I have to almost break the bank to find a decent glass of sangria. At least I know one place where I can get good cup of coffee.

It's the late evening when I arrive at the cafe with my bag slung over my shoulder. The door creaks open as I step in from the winter's cold. It's a damned season in this city because everyone decides to sit inside, and it can be terribly difficult to find a seat anywhere in the cafe if you don't know where to look. I however, being a purveyor of comings and goings, immediately walk to my typical place tucked away in the darkest corner of the bar area. George and Anni are working tonight and bid me a good evening. Before I can even get my coat and gloves off a warm cortado is already being handed to me over the bottles of wine which line the counter.

"Thanks much," I say. "It's a bit crowded here tonight!"

"You know how it goes, Teo," says George. "Everyone gets in the mood for warm drinks during the cold months."

"Opportunists," I say.

"Don't worry. No one sat in your spot," he replies.

I'd love to chat more, but the insanely long line won't allow it. I mix in the sugar cube and look around the room. I place my bags on the barstool next to me in anticipation for Kevin's arrival. If we were not already good buddies, we certainly have become so since telling him about Biarritz two months ago. More often than not we find ourselves mixed in with the other comers and goers on any given day. I take a sip of the cafe goodness, and place it down delicately on the bar as a strong hand lands on my shoulder.

"*Menino*," he says as I rotate to meet him.

"Kevin Otto. As I live and breathe," I respond. I stand and shake his hand and move my bag from the adjacent stool so he can take a seat.

"Thanks for saving a spot."

"I had to, man. This place is a mad house."

"Opportunists," yells George from the behind the bar. I snap my finger and point at him with a nod of my head. "You want something Kev?"

"Hey there, George. A cortado please," says Kevin as he shakes his head and smiles. Despite the orders coming in from the line, George finds a quick moment to whip up it up. Kevin thanks him, and turns to me.

"So?"

"So, what?"

"What is it with you lately? There is a certain *je ne sais quoi*."

"Ha! You speaking French now?"

"I do what I can," he says as he stops stirring the drink and takes a sip. "You're different now. I don't know, you seem...Happy."

"Shhhh!" I say with a furious finger over my lips. "Watch what you say. I've got a reputation to keep."

"Whatever," he says. "What's going on?"

"It's difficult to explain. It's just a process, I suppose," I say stroking my beard pensively. "Time. Time has passed. Wounds have healed. It's not just one thing. It's just a series of happenings and decisions. I'd like to think it began with that day I told you about last summer. You remember that, yeah?"

"How could I forget? We were here until closing time talking it up."

"Well, I think it had something to do with it all. It was the first time I'd really been able to put it all into context since coming back. Talking all that out just...just...," I say with a puff of air and eyebrows arched.

"Just what?"

"It freed me up. I'm free," I begin.

"So you're all better?"

"Noooo! I'm still screwed up. I don't really know where I am. In between. Somewhere. Who knows?"

"That's a bit surprising actually. It's obvious you're 'happy' or at least doing well. I mean think about it. You're drinking less, well not that much less, but less. You're freelancing your ass off, writing every day. I even read your book!" he exclaims with his hands in the air and voice becoming louder. "In between doesn't seem that bad."

"Well, I am on the up and up."

"Exactly," he says winking at me. We both take a sip of our coffees. I pull a postcard out of my bag and hand it to him. "What's this?"

"I received this last week. It's from Iza. The Hungarian girl."

"Whoa! All the way from Cambodia?"

"She's volunteering. She's never broken contact, Kev. She's always asking if I'm coming back to Biarritz, and says it would be nice to see me again." I say.

"Do you want to see her?"

"I've thought about it. Maybe not in the sand this time, but I've thought about it. I just don't know. I've been too busy to think about these things. I haven't had sex since Biarritz, and honestly, I haven't really wanted to."

"So you've gotten over your 'indiscretions'?"

"I don't know. It's more like I've owned them as mine. That, and I'm terribly bored. Sure, all the things you said are true, but those are right now, you know? I need some inspiration. I suppose I am 'happy' because I've stopped and counted my blessings, but with women like Iza seeking me out, as well as others, how can I not be this way?"

"I understand."

"It's calling me. *Pays Basque* wants me back. Hermann e-mailed me just today reminding me that it's his last season as director. He wants me to come back so it can end with someone who knows the ropes."

"And what did you say?" he asks.

"I said maybe. If Reda comes back for the season, I just may do it," I say. I gulp the last of the coffee and twirl the empty glass in my hand. "I've thought about it since my uncle passed. Hermann reminds me so much of him. I suppose that's the attraction."

"You been dealing with it?"

"As best I can. It's all context. It's particular. Those days growing up in the countryside were some of my first memories. My uncle was a man who rendered service. We'd go into the fields and pick vegetables, and ride around giving the extras we had to neighbors. He told me never give it up."

"What up?"

"Whatever it is that I'm trying to do," I say.

"And? Teo, what are you trying to do?!"

"I don't know! I'm trying to figure that shit out, but believe me I won't give it up when I do."

"You want a brew? Yes of course you do," he says. He heads to the glass fridge and takes two Staropramens. I ask George for two chilled glasses. He hands them over the bar and adds the beers to our tab. Kevin pours mine and his. "To your uncle, to the service, to the in between, and to figuring it all out."

"I'll drink to that," I say as we touch glasses. The beer is cool and crisp. The night air sends a gust into the cafe every time someone opens the door. Even if the door didn't make so much noise, it would be easy to tell when it's open because anyone sitting near it gets a faint touch of winter's breath. The door creaks and the gust makes it all the way to our backs at the bar.

"Phew. Cold stuff, my man," says Kevin.

"Cold as my bed at night," I say laughingly when a hand gently touches on my shoulder. I turn in my chair. Derlenzistda stands before us, bundled up and beautiful. Her smile is as wide as I remember, and her brown eyes just the same. For a moment, and perhaps several moments, there are no words. I notice Kevin's eyes darting back and forth between us and can feel the heat from his brain when it arrives at the conclusion that this is the woman he's heard so much about. I want to tell him, but he already knows.

"Hi, T," she says as she opens her arms. I stand up and give her a massive hug, and a kiss to both cheeks.

"Derlenzistda," I say slowly. "Fancy seeing you in these parts."

"I could say the same for you too, vagabond boy."

Kevin says he needs to step outside for a smoke, which is funny. I didn't know he smoked. Derlenzistda takes his seat, as I call out to George. He looks at us with wide eyes, barely able to hide his amazement that we're sitting side by side. He remembers us from days before Biarritz, and tries to play it off. She orders a glass of red wine, Spanish rioja, just like I remember. He passes it over the counter and I tell him to put it on my tab. She looks at me out of the side of her eyes and smiles.

"That's really kind. Thank you."

"Well it's the least I could do. It's been so long. What brings you here? I mean, I know I haven't been back too long, but I'm here all the time and I haven't seen you."

"Honestly, I'm not sure. It's the first time in over a year or so. I guess I just needed a familiar place."

"Maybe a familiar face or two as well?"

"Perhaps," she says nodding her head. She takes a sip of her red. "What's new with you, Teo?"

"You don't know?" I ask.

"A little bit, yes. I've known you were back for a few months now. I got your letter too, I'm sorry I didn't respond to it. I've just been terribly busy these days."

"We all have our moments. No worries," I say. I take a sip of my beer, and glance quickly outside to see Kevin peeking through the glass giving me a thumb up. "Anyways. What's new with me? A lot. I'm putting a lot of time into that and other projects. Also, trying to capitalize on my book. It didn't do half bad. Otherwise, I'm just adjusting to being back."

"I read it, you know? I really enjoyed it. Haha. It's funny when I think how crazy you were about writing it, and now I see that you can relax and enjoy it a bit," she says with a smile. "Can you sign it?"

"The book?" I ask. She pulls a copy out of her bag. "Wow. Sure. I'm not really used to doing it, but why not, yeah?!"

"Well you should get used to it. I think you've got something here."

"Thanks," I say. I sign the book. "So is that all that's new? You've just been reading my book?"

"Haha. No. I'm in law school now. It's death and a half, but I love the workload," she says. Her smile fades. She twirls the wine glass around in her glass, looking at it with an intensity I know all too well, with a melancholy that one shouldn't look at alcohol with. "Professionally I'm perfect. It's what I've wanted. I suppose it has a cost though. Ryan. He left me. Last month."

"Wow...I thought you two were practically married," I say. Her countenance falls to a low I know quite well. "I'm sorry to hear this."

"Yeah. We were engaged...My career is my dream. It's my life. He wanted me to be some housewife and raise his kids, but I wasn't ready. I couldn't just abandon all that I'd worked for. I had to go for it, and he left me because of it," she says voice almost trembling in sadness. She finally looks up from her glass to me. "I guess, I understand you a bit more now."

"Don't do that. Don't go to that place. I've been there...I lived there. I made my decision to leave and I lived with it in ways you can't imagine. I don't know what you think of me, or if my advice is worth anything anymore, but don't do that. You made a decision. It has its pleasures, just as much as its pains."

"Shit."

"What?"

"If you'd been that direct when we were dating then we may have had a shot."

"Maybe, maybe," I say toying very briefly with the concept in my mind. "That was a long time ago."

She smiles and leans back in stool. She glances around the cafe for a few moments whipping that long dark hair as if the send a gust of the past into my face in the form of her scent. It's the same perfume from those old days. I look outside to see that Kevin has indeed found a cigarette and is looking in at me as he takes a drag. He gives a thumb up again, and I am shaking my head 'no' when Derlenzistda turns back to me.

"So," she begins.

"So," I respond immediately refocusing on her.

"Did you find someone over there? Is there some French woman waiting for you to cross the pond?"

"Not exactly," I say. She almost seems to be relieved at these words until I continue speaking. "There are probably a few."

"Oh...What do you mean?"

"You read my letter, so you know how I felt. There were some days I couldn't even enjoy my adventures, because I couldn't stop thinking about you. I tried to replicate you. It didn't work so replacing you was my only option, but even that just left me empty. I tried everything I knew to move on."

"And have you?"

"What?"

"Moved on."

"Yes."

I respond without flinching. She seems almost shocked, and I am equally rattled without showing it.

"I was gone for almost two years. I've seen a few places. Some would say it's too many, while I say it's not enough. Ran across some faces, and made some friends. I'd like to see them again. Don't take it personally. I don't even know if I have a place to say that, but you should know it's not personal. I've moved on from everything, because that's what I do. I keep moving. Sometimes fast, so fast that the past is just a blur of context. Sometimes so slow that I wonder if I'm stuck in between a rock, a hard place, and my ego."

"Hard as rock," she says coming back to life. She nods her head and smiles.

"This is an adventure. I believe that even more now than before I left," I say. I finish the last of my beer. She takes a big sip of her wine.

"I understand. Completely. Good. Good for you, Teo," she says. The look in her eyes has a depth that I recognize quite well. She is somewhere in between, in whatever sense that means for her.

"Hey do you have my number? We should maybe have a coffee again," she says.

"I don't have a phone," I respond. "But sure. What's your email? That's the best way you can reach me. In any case, you know where to find me."

"Of course. Either here at the cafe, or on the other side of the globe," she says as I wink at her at her in response. She finds a small piece of paper in her bag and writes her email on it before handing it to me.

"Exactly. It *is* nice to see you again, Derlenzistda. If you need some help with anything just let me know. Yeah?"

"Sure," she says. We both stand to our feet and hug tight. She starts to walk away, but I stop her.

"Hey. By the way...I read your book too, you know? The one you gave me," I look in my bag to pull it out, but realize for the first time in two years that it's not there.

"That's funny."

"What is?" she asks.

"Nothing. I just thought I had it on me. Hemingway. Remember? It was a great book. A perfect read for a guy like me."

"I told ya," she says with a large smile. She walks out the front door.

Kevin, who is still staring through the window turns away as she passes by. He puts out his cigarette and comes rushing inside. He takes a seat, and I go to grab two more Staropramens. I return and fill both our glasses. He takes a sip and looks at me in silence waiting on me to say something, but I won't let him win this game.

"Ok ok! What happened, man? That was Dee, Der."

"Yes. It was Derlenzistda. Nothing happened that didn't exist already.

"Meaning?"

"I didn't have the book, Kev. *As the Sun Also Rises.* I carried that thing everywhere with me. I had no idea it wasn't there anymore."

"You no longer carry the book. You no longer carry the feelings for her."

"Yes, perhaps. Simply put. I recognized flashes of long ago, because that's my history, but I don't really know that woman anymore. She could hardly understand me."

"And here you were thinking there was something left between you two."

"It crossed my mind, but I didn't feel it."

"Ok. So, that's water under the bridge. That's done, or just beginning of something new. What now?"

"*Pays Basque* is calling me. It wants me back. Maybe it's this cold weather getting to me, but I want to be there again. I always wondered how all of this affected me. I spent half the time looking at my adventures through Derlenzistda's memory. No matter how far I went, it followed me. It even controlled me. What if I couldn't fully appreciate those journeys in that state of mind?"

"That's a question worth finding an answer for," he says. "That's on you, Teo. Wisdom is the ability to look retrospectively at the present. I think you've done that. I think you've got to think about the next time."

"What next time?"

"The next time you tell a long ass story. Two months from now. A year from now. Doesn't matter. The next time you are able to take your life into context will you be 'in between', or will you finally be somewhere? No matter what you find by going back, I'd imagine that you will want a second summer, for the sake of Hermann or whoever, to be a part of your memory."

I go silent. He nailed it. Everything in and around me is pointing back to the Basque Country. Its life force and rhythm fit my palate, like the foods and wines I crave. Unfinished business, in unwritten stories. The chance to use my somewhat reconciled past as inspiration for the future, is incredibly enticing. Shit. That's most compelling idea I've had in months.

Summer 2

Chapter 1: A Familiar Air

Sleeping while traveling has never worked for me. I used to think that it was because of the excitement of going to a new place, but now, having slummed it around Europe alone on several occasions, I think it's a survival habit. I don't like to sleep because I am always on the lookout for the next step, the next encounter, because if I can see it coming, it's much easier to handle.

I'm on my way down from the north where I passed a couple of weeks in La Roche and Paris. It was nice to see some of those old faces again, including the legend himself, Reda Tj. We drank like the old days, but had to part ways as he needed to be in England for some advanced training. It sounds like a cut and dry operation, and especially with me having already crossed the Atlantic. Everything is in place. However, it wouldn't be Reda without a Reda Moment. I am somewhere in between Bordeaux and Biarritz when he calls.

"Fuck."

"What?" I say. "Fuck what?"

"Me, Teo! Fuck me! I think I screwed up."

"What did you do?"

"Nothing, I swear. I mean I've just been really outgoing in the training. I had an issue where I was mugged the night before too...I spent the night roaming the streets and drinking with bums. Needless to say, I smell and looked pretty shitty when I arrived for training."

"You gave them the Full Reda, didn't you?"

"No. Well. Yes," he begins. "I know, I know. I just felt I was the new guy and had be impressive. I didn't have any training last summer, so I wanted them to know I could get shit done. Still, I don't think they like me very much. I think they're going to fire me before I even get started."

"I should have warned you, Reda. Trainings are not like Biarritz. They have a system and structure, but they don't know how it functions for us in *Pays Basque*. You have to play by their game on their turf."

"A bit too late for that. Anyways, Bernard was here doing some training as well. He told me he put in a good word for me before leaving yesterday."

We talk for a few more minutes before finally deciding that this decision is completely out of our hands. I've never been able to sleep while traveling, and but now there seems to be a good reason. I am in no way prepared for this.

My contract in Biarritz is signed and ready to go, but I'll have to wait until arriving to know Reda's fate. Part of the reason why I agreed to return was the fact that he would be on my staff, which in my mind meant an easy going and fun summer. The season is long and hard, and who would they send to replace my wingman to survive it all? The idea is almost diverting enough to keep me from noticing the change of the landscapes and the sun's brilliance. The fields have a certain *Basqueness* to them, and I like to think that the sun is shining just a little bit brighter with every passing kilometer.

The train stops. I grab my large roller bag and guitar moving swiftly through the aisle and down the exit. It's funny to think how much luggage I had last time. I can enjoy the familiar air a bit more now that I'm not carrying my entire life with me. I pass through the station and exit left to see Bernard leaning on his car. His hair is much shorter, but he still has a cigarette dangling from his mouth, as I expected.

"Ciao, Teo!" he says as we meet halfway and exchange kisses to each cheek.

"It's great to see you, B! It's great to be back."

"Even better to have you. Let us go!"

"Wait. It's been a long journey. Let's take a drink first," I say with a smirk on my face.

"Opp!" he says smiling with his cigarette still dangling from his mouth and clapping his hands. "Not a bad instinct."

"Let's just say I know a thing or two about how things are done here," I respond. He takes a seat outside on the terrace, while I go in to grab two Carlsbergs. I take a seat as he hands me a cigarette. I take it despite it not being one my bad habits, and he lights it for me. We clang our glass together. Despite the evidently casual nature of the scene there is the lingering question of what has become of Reda, and I can only resist for so long.

"Do you have any news? Will he be coming?"

"Teo, it doesn't look good."

"What happened? I mean, you were there. It can't be that bad."

"I was in the private meetings, yes. Doing a different type of training so I could prepare to take Hermann's place...Let us just say there were many things that went wrong. I was shocked by how different things were there, and they don't understand how things go here. We have the same product, but the destination is different. Biarritz is different," he says shaking his head almost disappointedly.

"What did he do? I know Reda. He's brilliant and the best person for this job, so how could it go so wrong?"

"He showed up smelling like booze three hours before training. He couldn't check into his room because we hadn't begun officially, so he napped where everyone could see on a bench. He walked into a private meeting and introduced himself and was asked to leave. It was not a very good first impression even with his story of being mugged."

"Well..."

"I'm not finished."

"There's more?"

"Yes. They thought he was a bit flirtatious with some of the women, which is a bit bizarre. I mean he was leading all of the workshops and the first one to step up to the tasks. There was a woman who was the only other French person there, so obviously, they got close. She's supposed to be coming here too, so I guess they thought there was some conflict of interest. I don't know if either of them will come now."

"That's bullshit. He performed well at the training, so why is there a question?"

"I don't know. I fought for him in those meetings, and told them about the great work he did last summer. They just don't think he's mature enough. We will see. Let's finish up here. Hermann will meet us to tell what they've decided."

The five-minute drive to the hostel seemed like hours with the weight of the impending decision on my mind. Bernard tries to lighten things up a bit asking what I've been doing, and I respond as best I can. I can't even seem to enjoy the fact that I'm arriving at the hostel again. I'm here because so many things are supposed to be the same, and now it seems that things are going to change quite fast.

We park, and I chuckle a bit upon seeing Hermann's car parked in his parking spot on the grass by the office window. Bernard and I grab my things and walk to the office where he sits with the window open working on his computer. As soon as he sees me he smiles wide and shouts,

"Hello, Program Manager!"

"Hello, Program Director!" I yell back as a place my things at the office door. We enter and shake hands all around. His handshake is as crushing as I remember. "It's a pleasure to see you."

"You as well, Teo," he says as he grabs three glasses from the cabinet and a cube of rosé from the fridge. He begins to pour it before asking if we'd like some. "I need to drink. I'm thirsty. Would you like some?"

"No," I say. He turns his head quickly in my direction with a shocked look on his face. "I'm just kidding. Can you pour faster please?"

"Op la!" he says. He finishes and hands them out. "Team. To a great season."

We clang the glasses in tribute to uncertainty as far as I am concerned. I'm not sure how thirsty Hermann really is, or if he is just trying to get some wine in us before breaking bad news. We stand looking at each other for a moment before he asks us to take a seat. We turn three chairs facing each other in center of the room.

"Reda will not be here. Wait, Teo," he says before I get a chance to go on a rant. He knows me well. "I don't agree with their decision, as I don't agree with many things happening. They're trying to change the structure of everything here, but I put them in their place."

"What do you mean?" I ask, still restraining myself.

"I started this center. It may be my last year, but I'm still here. As long as I am here we will function as we always have. Reda made a mistake, and he is difficult. But I am difficult and so are you, Teo. I like difficult people. They get the job done with a bit of help. They don't understand that at the home office, and they have a completely new administration team who has no idea how things function here."

"I tried to tell them, Hermann. I fought for him, but they hated him from the start."

"This can't be right. We decided that the three of us would come back for this. You all came from your homes for this meeting, but I've come from across an ocean to be here and now everything's changed? Do they know that? What's their solution? Who are they sending me?"

"They don't know yet. There is no one prepared."

"So they solve a problem, with a problem? *C'est quoi ce bordel de merde!? Ça casse les couilles, quoi!*"

"Teo! Calm yourself," says Hermann calmly in a way that only someone who has seen twenty-five seasons can say. "You have a right to be upset, I won't take that from you. However, the anger will solve nothing. Don't worry. We will arrive."

"Ok," I say decompressing with a puff of air. "We will arrive."

"Teo, wow! You're speaking some good French!" says Bernard.

"Yes I am the epitome of class. Sorry for losing it," I say. I gulp the down my wine, and they do the same. "Is anyone coming?"

"Not for now. You will work the first week and a half alone, but don't worry. There are only a handful of people. Business isn't so good for the first couple of weeks to be honest with you," says Hermann as he refills our glasses. "Have you news of Katia?"

"I saw her last week in Paris. She's actually looking for some work...I'll send her a message."

"Thank you. We could use some experienced hands," says Hermann. We continue drinking and are a bit more relieved, or at least accepting of the situation for now. A moment later a woman knocks on the door. She is tall, slender, with long hair and glasses, and obviously sun bronzed skin.

"Oh. Look at this office. Drinking during work?"

"Just a little aperitif," says Hermann. "Teo, this is the new hostel director. Greg is on sabbatical."

"Oh! Hello. Pleasure to meet you," I say thinking about the wonderful first impression I'm making, already halfway through my third drink in the last hour.

"Pleasure as well, Teo. I am Augustine"

"Is there anyone here from last year? Working for the hostel?" I ask looking around at everyone.

"Yes of course. Aude is still here, and so are Hamza and Gil. There are new interns as well," says Hermann. I smile at the great news. At least I have some familiar faces to make things smoother, and most obviously to keep me company during my week and a half of program solitude.

"I hear this is your second summer here?" says Augustine.

"Yes, it is for sure."

"Well that's great. I'm glad to have you all here so that I can understand a bit of how the season works. Do you do this type of work normally, Teo?"

"No, not at all. I'm a writer. I wrote a book a couple of years ago."

"Whoa! That's incredible. What in the world are you doing here then?!" she asks jokingly, as we all laugh.

"Hey. It's Biarritz and it's summer. What do you think I'm doing here?" I respond inciting a bit more laughter, but behind my smile, and glass of wine, the answer is not so sure. I know 'we will arrive'. I trust Hermann in that respect. How we'll actually do it? Not even he knows. What am I doing here? *Merde.* I should ask myself the same question.

Chapter 2: Julien

Hermann, Bernard, and I set about to fix the office up with relative ease. They take care of the tasks that my 'team' would normally do, while I set about organizing documents and administration. For the first time, I think it could be a good thing that Reda isn't here, because there are only a handful of people for the entire first week. Technically, I'll be doing the job of 3 people, which doesn't include much with such a small group. Four adults coming for surfing courses means that I have to do a welcome meeting, city tour, direct them to the surf school in Anglet, and give them a tour to San Sebastian.

Not bad for a week's work.

With Reda on hiatus and no other team in sight, I've got plenty of time to sort my thoughts out. What am I doing here? It was one thing for Augustine to ask, and I can understand how it doesn't make sense professionally. However, my reasons for being here have almost nothing to do with my profession.

Derlenzistda is now just another experience in my life. It was what it was, and, as like with everything else that's happened, I've at least been able to keep our relationship within its context. As nice as it sounds, it's only freed me from a melancholy bondage in exchange for a certain uncertainty of circumstances.

I told Kevin just before leaving that I would make Biarritz my grand experiment where I am the test subject, and the variables are the wilds and wonders of another summer. I'm not sure if I believe that people change. Perhaps, it's just that they mature and learn how to better appropriate their personalities, character, and desires. Have I matured? Did Derlenzistda, Justine, Fritzi, and Iza, who may or may not be around this summer, teach me anything? Hermann says 'we will arrive', and I believe him, but it's my own personal venture that remains uncertain.

Hermann and Bernard have their own lives. Once the office is settled they return to them, leaving me to my own devices, and not much work to do at the hostel. It's nowhere near high season, and the first night at the hostel's bar is rather calm. I meet the new intern, who is a bit shocked when I walk behind the bar grabbing at bottles of wine. Julie, a tall French redhead, calms down a bit after I explain who I am.

"Ohhhh! Ok. They said there would be some sort of program here. Are there others?" asks Julie.

"Well yes, but I'm not sure when they'll arrive."

"Ok, cool. You want something to drink?"

"Of course. I'll take a bottle of red," I say while handing her four euros.

"It's eight euros."

"I forgot to mention that the team and I have staff pricing."

"No one told you?" she asks.

"Told me what?" I respond.

"There's no more staff pricing...The new director changed it," she says with an apologetic face.

"Wha...What?" I begin taking a twenty euro bill out of my wallet. "Give me two of them. Didn't know I'd be drinking to the death of sanity *and* staff pricing tonight. I'll just have to go into the city to do some light shopping tomorrow."

She laughs. I don't think it's funny. First my right-hand man, and now my staff pricing? I may be over my past romantic woes, but I am still a thirsty man. The only difference is that I don't drink to escape, and I have a hard time remembering the last time I drank myself to sleep. I drink because it's tasty. That's gotta be some type of progress.

The next afternoon I head into the city. It's beautiful even from my view on the bus. It's like I've never left and I remember almost every sign, building, and bus stop along the way. I exit at *Bois de Boulogne* and stroll through the streets admiring everything from the city center's beauty, to the variety of people I see. Overtones of French, Swedish, German, Spanish, English, and several other languages are strung along with the sounds of the bay's breeze as I arrive on *Rue Gambetta*. I smile for a moment at the sight of Puig & Daro, and halfway hope to see Miren working today as I enter the *Petit Casino* market across the street.

Despite food being the most immediate necessity, I head straight for the beers. I am not much of a cook, so I save the difficult decisions for last. I grab two six packs of San Miguel without thinking, and begin to roam the aisles. I'm able to gather a few things and am feeling pretty confident when I see an old man looking at me while passing on the same aisle. I nod at him and say 'bonjour'. He replies the same. As I pass I can see his head turn to watch me, but think nothing of it as I go to another aisle to look for cue tips. I'm looking at the prices when he approaches me.

"Excuse me. Hi!" he says. He's short with a kind of round in frame. He has slicked back gray hair, large glasses, and obviously sun bronzed skin. He's got to be at least fifty years old. "What's your name?"

"Teo. What about you, sir?"

"Julien, *enchanté,*" he says. "Are you from around here?"

"No. Not at all. I'm just here working for the summer," I say quite nonchalantly as I continue to search for the perfect cue tips. For the sake of conversation, I continue. "What about you?"

"Oh, much of the same. I work here and in Nice. I pass two weeks here and there. Actually, I don't know a whole lot of people here. You want to hang out? Take a drink sometime?" he asks with a smile. I'm not one to just befriend old men, but it seems like a good idea considering my relationship with Hermann. Perhaps this Julien has some sagely wisdom he could give me for my quest. "Could I take your number?"

I am suspicious, but not that suspicious. I give him my work number, knowing that I could just block him if he gets weird.

"Thank you," he says. "Do you work out?"

"What? Why do you ask?" I respond.

"Well, you seem quite big and muscular."

"Oh. Well, not really. I'm not as active with heavy weights because of some issues with my knees."

"Oh. That's really too bad. You know I am a nurse. Maybe I can take a look at them?"

"*Non.* Don't worry about it, man," I say a bit confused, but still respectfully. "I'm cool."

"No problem. OK, so, when would you like to hang out? Do you have a car? I could come and get you? Where do you stay?"

"I'm living at the hostel near *Lac Mouriscot,* but don't worry. I have unlimited bus passes, so just let me know when you're in town and I'll see my schedule."

"Oh, ok."

"I need to get back actually. Nice to meet you, Julien," I say a bit rushed. Something about this guy doesn't sit right with me, and I am terribly hungry. We shake hands goodbye and I walk quickly for the checkout line. I leave the store with my bags and glance to Puig & Daro, but still no Miren in sight. I head directly back to hostel and walk to the kitchen. A start to cook up some pasta with bolognese sauce and several chorizos. It's simple and doesn't take me too long, and as I look at the plate I can't help but being pleased with myself.

"Not bad, Teo. Not bad at all," I say sitting down with the plate a San Miguel in the bar area. I'm poised to take a bite, when I hear my phone go off. It's a text from Julien.

So, when do you think you'd want to meet up? Maybe tonight?

I look strangely at the phone in my hand, and respond that I can't.

I'm eating. Been a long day. Another time.

He says 'ok', and I start eating. It isn't half bad. A few minutes later my phone goes off. It's him.

So, you did want to meet eventually? Right?

My general social courtesy is no more. I place the phone down without response and continue eating. It's not proper to be on the phone while eating, so it's a bit rude that he would keep messaging. Not to mention creepy. I hope that my silence speaks volumes, but it doesn't. He messages me again.

Is something wrong? Am I bothering you? I don't mean to.

Look, Julien. You've got to understand that it is a bit weird to meet someone in a supermarket and then be asked to hang out. You need to relax.

Oh. I'm sorry. Talk to you later.

I think he's finally got the picture. I continue to eat in relative peace. There is a World Cup match on the bar's projection screen, so the situation is perfect. Food. *Futbol.* Beer. I eat the last morsel of my masterpiece when my phone goes off again. It's Julien.

Would you like to sleep in my bed?

I set the phone down. I stare at my empty plate. It's gotta be my fault. This meeting was strange from the beginning, so why did I think anything savory could come of it? It seemed a bit obtuse to ask if he was gay at the beginning. After all, he's an old ass man, and what would he want with a young fella like me? I think a bit further, and I can imagine what plans he had in mind. He perhaps imagined I could be his Nubian stallion, his cabana boy, strutting around *la Grande Plage* in my banana sling thong. I shudder at the thought snapping back to the moment as someone in the bar cheers for the game. I take my phone. I respond.

No. Not at all. I have my own proper bed.

I pass the rest of the night like it never happened. I watch the remaining games and drink a bit with the rest of the futbol enthusiasts who are glued to the projection screen. He doesn't respond, so I pay it no mind.

I don't even think of it again until I have my first meeting with Gil the next morning. It's good to see some things haven't changed as I can hear the music and beatboxing coming from his office from down the hall. We spend a few minutes looking at videos, just like last summer. It's nice until he starts asking about *les meufs.*

"So you had a pretty good summer last year," he says with his customary wink.

"I was wondering when you'd say it. It was fine."

"Did you take some of your Biarritz training back to the US?"

"No! I've actually been out of the game since I left here last year."

"*Quoiiiiii?*" he says in shock. "Wait. You must have just been taking a break so you could have stamina for this summer, yeah? You dog!"

"I don't know. We will see. It's actually starting off a bit different," I say. I tell him about Julien, and his mouth drops as far as physically possible. His eyes widen almost out of the sockets.

"Wait!" he says. He gets on the office phone. "Hamza. Hey come to the office. I have a, uhhh, question about a reservation."

"What are you doing?!" I ask, but Hamza's large figure is already passing by the window before Gil can respond.

"Ciao, Teo. How are you?"

"He's doing quite well," responds Gil chuckling. He tells the story, which I hadn't even finished, and adds his own twist. Hamza darts his eyes between the two of us shaking his head in disbelief.

"Teo, I mean. I thought you love the ladies," says Hamza in awe. "Well, there is a gay community here, if it is what you're into."

"I do! Gil didn't even hear the whole story!"

"What? There's more?!"

"I responded 'no' when he asked me to sleep in his bed!"

"Ohhhhhh," says Gil shrugging his shoulders.

114

"Haha," laughs Hamza. "Teo, in any case you have to admit it's pretty funny. I mean you've only been here a couple of days."

I'm about to speak when my phone goes off. It's Julien.

Hey, Teo. Look I am quite sorry about last night. Perhaps I was too aggressive. Perhaps we could see each other in a more polite way.

I read it out to them and about to send a response when Gil leaps across the office reaching for the phone.

"Let me respond for you!"

"No!" I yell laughing. "I don't trust you!"

Hamza blocks him from me as I turn away with the phone. We've passed the point of politeness at this point, but still I've got to know for sure.

Look, man. Are you gay?

Yes, but it's not a big deal.

Yes, it is. I am not gay. I sleep with women.

There is no response from him at this point, but it doesn't keep Gil from giving me a hard time. Even Aude even chimes in from the office next door.

"Wow, Teo. You know gay marriage is legal here in France? You never know where you will find love!" she yells. We all laugh; some a bit louder than others. I admit the entire situation is funny and it's my fault for trying to confide in Gil. We're having a pretty good time at my expense when Augustine comes walking by.

"Hello everyone, what's going on?"

"Oh, um. We are just finishing up some work," says Gil as he closes out a music video on his computer screen. Hamza, as tall as he is, somehow slips past her unnoticed.

"Ok, great. You and Teo had your meeting? All the documents are ready?"

"Yes, Augustine. We've just finished."

"Ok Great. Gil, send them my way when you have a chance," she says as she leaves the office swiftly pass the windows.

"*Putain,*" begins Gil. "She's a lot stricter than Greg."

"Seems like it. No worries, *mec.* I'll let you know if I get another message," I say with a wink. He winks back at me and I leave the office.

It's one of the last days before clients arrive and even then, it seems like I will have plenty of time to think to myself. I may not know what my intentions are this summer, but I know Julien's. I'm not at all intrigued. I didn't imagine that my summer of 'love' and self-discovery would begin like this. It's about time I start figuring out what I'm doing here, before Biarritz makes up my mind for me.

Chapter 3: A Brand-New Dress

The next days are some of the most silent I can remember. There is simply nothing to do. The arrival of the first clients is a blip in an otherwise uneventful day. I give a small welcome speech at the bar, all information regarding the surf school, and a tour of the city center. I don't see any of them again until a couple of days later when some stoner type passes by my office asking if I know where he can score some weed. I look at him and shake my head 'no', and go back to my busy work, which isn't really work at all. Music videos, backgammon, siesta, repeat. Things are moving so slowly that Hermann, who would normally critique my work ethic, tells me I need to take it easy.

"Teo, listen. You know the season is long, and we will be understaffed even with the replacement that arrives on Sunday."

"Who are they? Have they been trained?"

"She is a half German and French girl named Camille, but don't worry about this. I want you to take it easy now. Get out the office while you can."

He's right, and why didn't I think of it sooner? Sunday our numbers will jump from four to thirty clients, and I'll be getting this rookie replacement. I've got to enjoy these last days of peace while I can, so I set about doing that. I work a couple more hours, taking care of the tasks I would normally have to do on the weekend so I can have the next couple of days completely free.

I decide to pass most of my time watching World Cup games, which keeps me pretty busy and give me an excuse to drink beer at all hours. One day I take the bus into the city, and hoof it pass the *Les Galeries Lafayette*. I continue past the tourists, boutiques, and bars, until I arrive at Puig & Daro. No sooner than I sit down on the terrace does Miren emerge from the inside. She sees me, smiles, and walks over to my table.

"Hello, would you like something to drink?"

"Sure, a Heineken, please," I say smiling with happiness to see her pretty face once more. "Do you remember me?"

117

"Hmmm," she says folding her arms with an inquisitive look. I see the memory rush into her eyes as she switches to English. "Yes! You are the American guy! You're back for the summer?"

"Yes. I am here again."

"You couldn't resist the Basque lifestyle, could you?"

"Something like that," I respond with a smile. She asks me to follow her inside so I can choose which tapas I'd like, but food is the last thing on my mind. Over the next few minutes I learn that she's a business student and is just working the summer again until she starts an internship for non-profit organization in the fall.

"That's very impressive," I say.

"I love it," she responds with a smile. It seems like we could have gone on forever but the terrace begins to fill up with customers. She says she will stop by in a few minutes and leaves me to my tapas, beers, and imagination. I'd like to dwell on her, but the first bite completely steals my heart. I've waited over eight months to taste this savor, and even if she wasn't here, I'd be still be face deep in Basque delicacies. Not even the threat of a Julien sighting at the Petit Casino across the street could keep me from this.

Even while devouring tapa after tapa I can't help to think of the whole market debacle. Perhaps it was fate? The summer has already been completely unexpected so why not expect something outlandish? The idea that Julien could be a catalyst pushing me into monogamy and a sense of romantic sanity isn't a farfetched idea at this point. I like it. Miren glances at me as she brings some food to another table. I smile. She finishes with them and returns to me.

"So, American boy. It seems you were quite hungry?"

"Perhaps. I normally eat a lot, and it's not every day I get to come here. I have to devour as much as I can."

"In any case, you are here for the summer. Just come back often so you don't have to eat so much in one sitting!"

"Ok, ok. Maybe I will. Are you working again this week?"

"No, but I will be back next Thursday and then for the whole weekend."

"Ok, Basque girl. I will be here next Thursday," I say.

She reaches her hand out and we shake to seal the deal. I pay the tab, and even leave a tip despite it not being customary. I say goodbye to her and all the other workers who seem to remember me from last year's drunken night. I decide to brave a visit to the Petit Casino so I can stock up on more food and drinks, which I've already devoured since the whole Julien adventure. I peek around every corner cautiously, and am able to get in and out without making any new friends. I carry my bags to the bus stop, along with a faint sense of sanity. Even after I've placed my items in the fridge and settle in for a long siesta, I still feel that sense of calm. Everything works together with everything else. Maybe I'm on the right track after all.

I wake up to a breeze from my open window. It cools the small amounts of sweat dampening my skin. I've missed this life. This sun. Even my room, which is exactly the same as last summer's, is perfect. It seems my planned two-hour nap turned into five hours meaning it's time for dinner. I roll out of bed refreshed and ready to eat again. I take some rice and sausages from the fridge and begin to cook them in the small kitchen. There is a game being shown on the bar's projector so I grab a beer from my fridge to go along with my meal. As I pass by the reception I see a woman chatting with Hamza. She's got to be a client because she's toting a large bag, but her clothes show she's not exactly from around these parts. She's wearing a white skirt with flowers and a white button up blouse to match. I'm sure she wouldn't have so much trouble carrying that suitcase if she took those high heels off.

She whips her red hair in my direction and we lock eyes for a moment. I'm standing there with my food and drink in hand, and casually, if it's possible at all to be casual, turn and continue to the bar. I sit down to watch the game. The Netherlands are playing and they have every bit of my attention. Julie is behind the bar cheering along with myself and the few clients scattered along the couches and chairs. I'm just finishing my meal when I hear a voice asking Julie for a bottle opener. A few moments later, I hear the same voice grunting and cursing.

"Shite. This bloody bottle," she says. I turn to see it's the redhead from the reception. She has the bottle in her hand and is trying to yank the cork out.

"Give me the bottle," I say.

"Huh?"

119

"The bottle. Give it to me. You're going to break the cork," I say finally standing up and walking to her. She hands it to me and I pull it out with ease.

"Whoa! Thank you."

"You're welcome," I say as I return to my seat. She sits at a small table next to mine placing the bottle and a glass down.

"Fancy a drink?" she says looking in my direction with her green eyes. "It's the least I can do for you helping me out."

"Sure."

She takes another glass from the bar and pours the red wine for both of us.

"Cheers," she says as we clink glasses. "To Biarritz and bottles!"

"Sure. What's your name?

"Lily. Lily McConnell. You?"

"Teo."

"Just Teo?"

"Yes."

"Pleasure to meet ya."

We hit it off extremely well. It turns out she's Scottish, and not Irish as I first guess. She makes sure I understand the difference and then a five-minute discourse about how they're completely different accents. We finish the first bottle of wine.

"Shall we take another?" she asks.

"Of course, but this one is on me," I say.

This bottle service dynamic continues for a couple of hours as she goes on and on about the stories of her life. I'm buying the 6th bottle when she finally explains that she's on vacation after leaving her 'prick of a boyfriend'.

"I don't even know what I was doing with him. I'm older than him and he's a liar."

"What did he lie about?"

"It's stupid. It's my fault anyway. I was with him for years before I figured it out."

"C'mon. Lilyyyyyy. Tell me."

"Ok, fuck's sake, Teo. When we met, he said he was an electrician and that he was a year younger than me. We dated for a couple of years and things seemed fine. I never asked about his work. Then one day the truth came out."

120

"Which was?"

"He's fuckin eight years younger than me! I'm bloody thirty-two for fuck's sake!"

What? How'd you not know that?" I ask. I can see she becomes a bit bothered by the question. "Nevermind...Was he at least an electrician?"

"Kinda."

"How can you 'kinda' be an electrician?"

"Sigh...He's an apprentice. He's an electrician's apprentice."

"Oh...Oh my...," I say taking a hefty sip. "Drink your wine."

The last drop drops from our last bottle. The sun has gone down, Julie has closed the bar, and we're all that's left of what was a pretty busy night. We swap a few more stories, although none could top the apprentice one. Eventually it's time to call it a night. At least, I think it's bedtime.

"Let's go out!" she says excitedly.

"No."

"Yes. You have to come with me. I don't want to go alone. I have a brand-new dress I bought in San Sebastian and I want to show it off."

"No. There's not even a night bus this time of the summer and taxis can get to be expensive."

"Don't be a pansy, Teo! I'll pay for a taxi. Get dressed and call it in, because I can't speak a lick of French."

Her mind is made up, and it seems mine is as well. I call the taxi, and switch out of my Biarritz slacker gear, which are flip flops, shorts and a short sleeved button up shirt opened just enough to expose my chest hair, into some slacks and a nice long sleeved shirt. I'm waiting in the lobby as she walks through those doors wearing a short black dress. She looks great, and her red hair contrasts brilliantly with the dark colors.

"Shall we go, Sir?"

"Sure thing, m'Lady. Our chariot awaits," I say as the black Mercedes pulls in front of the hostel. We walk outside and I open her door. She slides smoothly along the black leather, as I tell the driver to get us as close to the city center as possible. I place my arm around her. As soon as the car starts moving our lips collide in a fury. We're inseparable. I can hear the driver turn on the radio to drown out our lustful sounds, and he speeds up. I suppose I can't blame him for that.

We arrive at the city center. Lily pays and we stumble drunkenly out of the car. We walk just minutes before arriving at *Le Cafe Biarritz*, and can hear the thump of the music from outside. You'd think we were a long-time couple they way we're hand in hand, instead of two strangers sharing a random summer evening.

The multicolored lights dance in tandem with the bodies as smoke machines blaze brilliantly. For a small place, there are big things happening. A Dj rocks back and forth to Modjo's *Lady*, as some guy wearing sunglasses and a wig plays saxophone. I grab Lily by the hand and take her to the bar where we kiss until our turn to order. I ask for two Desperados, and pay. We polish them off surprisingly fast before stepping onto the dance floor. We navigate the mass of people, never separating. I've always adored the certain closeness that comes when dancing with someone. It's just as potent and profound as a kiss. We explore that closeness and each other's persons. I run my hands along her legs caressingly and she grasps at my shoulder blades. We kiss periodically, only stopping to smile. It's been awhile since I've been out like this, and admittedly I'm having the most beautiful time.

We only break from each other's bodies to buy more rounds of the 'French-Mexican' beers, before immediately reuniting. It's kinetic. Passionate. I feel that we could walk out of here and go anywhere, that tonight we could be anybody. However, the sensation is momentary.

"I'm hungry," she says. "Really fucking hungry, Teo."

"No problem. I know this burger joint a couple of minutes away. It should still be open."

We exit just as slovenly as we had entered, still inseparable. It's a good thing the *resto* isn't far because neither of us is in the best of form, and she's even carrying her high heels to give her feet a rest. The spot is still open and I am impressed as she orders two super large fries, two hamburgers, and a small bottle of white wine. I take a large fry, burger, and another Desperados.

We sit on a nearby bench with our faces completely engulfing the food. If only one of us was doing it, it would be the biggest turnoff in the world. However, we're not special. There are several others; would-be 'couples', dudes on the prowl, and teenagers eating, each one of them just as inebriated and hungry as we are. The scene is pretty familiar to me for a Biarritz early morning, until I look over to Lily. She has half of her second burger sitting on her lap and tears in her eyes as she stares at the ground.

"Lily? What's wrong?"

"I'm fat. I'm just gross."

"What?"

"Look at me? I'm just eating my life away. Ahhhh!" she cries.

"Keep it down," I say as I notice that people watching us. "You're not fat or gross."

"Whatever. Only enough to bag a bloody apprentice. If I was any good I would have a real electrician," she says. She sticks her finger in her mouth. I tell her to stop, but she snaps. "I need to throw up, Teo."

"What?! Why?"

"I am bulimic. Can't you see. I need to lose weight. She coughs pushing her finger further into her mouth."

I watch as she tries to make herself vomit with wide eyes; I'm half scared out of my mind. I reach out to her but she stands up with her burger falling to the floor and knocking over the bottle of wine. She stands to pick it up bending over exposing her underwear. I wanted to see them at some point but not like this, and not with everyone who had a hint of drunken hunger looking on.

"We're leaving," I say. I throw the food away, and of course get rid of the booze. I take her shoes, her hand, and walk her to the taxi stand a couple of minutes away. Her makeup has left black tear stained rivers. I have to explain to the driver that she's just having a bad night before he lets us in his car. She leans her head on my shoulder wiping her eyes, still pretty shaken up when we arrive at the hostel.

"I don't want to be alone tonight," she says. Usually there is some sort of sensual ring to those words, but this is different.

I tell her she can stay in my room, and she goes to change out of her new dress. I hardly have time to change clothes, and certainly not enough to process the situation, before she arrives at my door in a sweat shirt and shorts. We sit on the bed and she leans in to kiss me. It is just a brief peck with no semblance of the passionate taxi escapade or the dance floor.

"Thank you," she says.

"For what?"

"For taking care of me. It's been a long year. It's all made me a bit crazy, I think."

"Don't worry about that. Maybe we're all a little crazy at some point."

She lays down and immediately falls asleep. I turn off the lights, leaving only the reading light on. I lay next to her. She feels me near and puts her arms around me. I return the favor.

Chapter 4: The Replacement

My bed is cold. Lily left sometime during the night. I'm pretty sure I'm lying here, but it's difficult to say where I *really* am. It's probably my fault. Yes. I imagined things would be so simple.

Teo the artist, the traveler, finally gets over his past, and takes full advantage of his life and liberty.

Perhaps I'm doing just that. I'm not drinking myself to sleep every night or staring at unread books in bags. I can look at myself in the mirror, and I almost never think of Derlenzistda. However, these last few days have thrown me for a loop. I can't tell which has gone off the rails: Biarritz, with its geriatric sexually aggressive community and crying tourists, or the guy who thinks simply thinking things are figured out, means they're in fact figured out.

Shit.

I take a long hard look at myself in the mirror. I can see the young boy from my past once more, but even he looks at me with shrugged shoulders. I shrug mine back at him, shower, and brush my teeth before heading to breakfast. I'm strolling in the lobby where Gil and Hamza beckon for me.

"Teo, mec. Hamza says you were close with that redhead last night," says Gil. "Did you *nik* her?"

"Who?"

"What? C'mon, T. You know which one. The Scottish one."

"Oh. Yeah. No. Lord, no. She...I don't know."

"Oh, Teo is a gentleman," begins Hamza with a wink. "He wouldn't kiss and tell."

"Good morning!" yells a frighteningly familiar voice. Lily comes over to the reception startling me. She's all smiles, with new makeup, and a bright yellow dress. I can feel my eyes widen and may or may not have yelped upon seeing her. "What's going on mates?!"

"Hallo. Did you have a good night?" asks Gil, with his customarily sly smile.

"It was perfect! Teo took me dancing!"

125

"Yeah. It was perfect," I say laughing nervously. "I have a lot of work to do though...So I think I'm just going to see you guys later? Yeah? Ok, ciao."

"Wait," she begins. "Do you have a moment? I'm leaving in a couple of hours."

"Sure, but just a moment," I say hoping to avoid discussing last night. We get some coffee from the machine and go to the bar area, where it all began.

"How are you feeling?" I say.

"Like shitte. I hope didn't act too much like an ass last night," she says.

"Hey now, this is summer. This is Biarritz. If you can't lose yourself a little bit, then why do they call it a holiday?"

"You're just being nice."

"I'm trying," I say laughing. "Listen. Everyone has their moments. I had a bit of a relationship issue too...Lady wasn't exactly an apprentice, but I guarantee I didn't know how to handle it."

"Did you make an ass of yourself too?"

"For sure. Then again, I don't think I needed heartbreak to do that," I say. She smiles again.

"Thanks, Teo. I haven't had much luck with guys."

"I never heard of 'Luck of the Scottish'. Irish maybe, but not Scottish," I say jokingly.

"Really?" she asks. It's obvious from her unimpressed expression that she doesn't find it humorous.

"Hey, I told you I'm trying here."

"Ok, ok. Thank you in any case. You have bad jokes, but you're an ok bloke," she says.

"Thanks."

I tell her I need to get back to my work, even though I have absolutely no work to do until tomorrow when Reda's replacement arrives. Perhaps, it's the thought of actually being an 'ok bloke' that frightens me, or even that having some semblance of human decency would require responsibility, but it's all a bit much for a summer morning. She gives me a kiss goodbye on the cheek, and I shuffle to the office.

It's time to take all things into consideration. I sit for a couple of hours going over my personal budget and doing a collateral damage assessment while looking up plane tickets. I begin to think:

If I leave now, I can travel around Europe for at least two months. I'd lose a few thousand euros for not completing the season. I'd certainly lose Hermann's respect and doubt that I'd be getting a recommendation letter from Summers by the Sea headquarters, but maybe, just maybe, I'd have a shot at sanity.

"I could go to Bulgaria," I say to myself nodding my head. At that moment Hermann's blue Volkswagen pulls onto the grass in his customary spot by office windows. He honks the horn and sticks his hand out of the window. It's almost a relief to see him because out of all of the changes happening this summer I know that at least he's the same. I know what to expect.

"Hello, Program Manager," he says extending his arm for a handshake to crush my hand.

"Hello, Program Director. How's it going?"

"It's fine. Hot, hot. I'm thirsty. *Il faut que je bois quelque chose,*" he says as he walks to the fridge for his cube of rosé. He offers me a glass, which I gladly accept, and we sit in silence for a few moments at our computers. His next move will certainly be for food, and if I play my cards right we will end up lounging in the Maria Cristina today. After about an hour he lives up to my expectations.

"Hmmm. I'm so hungry. I need to eat something. Teo, you a bit hungry?"

"I could eat."

"Ha. Of course. I think our friends chez Bar Gorriti could use a visit, don't you?"

"I thought you'd never ask."

Before I know it, we're zooming down the expressway, just as I've always remembered and even how I've dreamt of doing again. Last summer I would fall asleep trying to dream of Derlenzistda, but after returning stateside I only dreamt of these hills. They haven't changed, and give me a much-needed calm today. With no work to do, Hermann and I are free to soak up San Sebastian in a way that we never have.

We stop in Bar Gorriti first, and despite it being customarily packed the barman looks at us and nods. How could he forget the dynamic duo of a tall sixty-year-old German man and his brown, afroed, almost as tall, stocky sidekick.

"*Moreno!*" He yells at me. "You gained some weight?"

"Yes, a little."

"Hey, look now! Don't eat all my food you hear?! The other customers need to eat too," he says with a smile.

We order our usual. Chorizo and egg. Spicy sausages. Sardines. Grilled chicken with peppers. These are merely starters and fine complements to our pints of beer and glasses of white wine. I watch marveling fondly as if it were my first visit as he pours drinks with the bottle extended in the air; but crumple the tapa paper tossing it to the floor like I've done this dance every day of my life. Several tapas and drinks later Hermann suggests we walk to help digest a bit. We stroll through the streets, past the shops, past the children and families, until we arrive at *La Concha* beach with its marvelous sea wall amenities.

We turn back towards the city center walking until we arrive at the *Plaza de la Constitución* with all of its restaurants and filled terraces. Our walk has made us fatigued, so instead of taking a siesta we take a seat on the terrace under an umbrella with a couple of beers to keep us company. This moment is exactly what I hoped for. Two men of 'the service' passing an afternoon in *Donostia.* It's perfect.

"I'm a bit hungry again. Are you too, Teo?"

"I could eat," I respond with a smile.

We settle the bill and stroll a few minutes more back to Bar Gorriti which has just happened to reopen for its evening crowd. We eat about half as much as we did at lunch, but are just as full and satisfied with the portions. This calls for another siesta. Only this time, with the sun calming down and the streets bustling with the evening rush, we opt for our typical bourgeois reservations at the Hotel Maria Cristina. We walk past the doormen and concierges en route to the bar area. We each order a Guinness as we sink into the plush chairs admiring the decor. Even with all of the *hard work* we've done today there remains some things that must be discussed.

"I have some news." he begins.

"Is there any chance of this being that the corporate office has regained their sanity and decided to send Reda?"

"No. Unfortunately no, but there is still good news. It seems Katia took your advice. She put her application in and has been accepted for another summer. However, she will not arrive until next week."

"I thought it would be that way. She couldn't get free from her other job until then, but you're right. It's great news," I say as I take a sip. "What of this replacement?"

"She arrives tonight. A bit earlier than I thought. You will need to meet her at the train station at 10:00pm. Use the transfer budget to take a taxi to the hostel."

"Agreed," I say nodding my head. "And then what? I mean...What am I supposed to do with her? She's no Reda, and she has no experience. She doesn't know how things function here."

"You're right, but I doubt anyone is like Reda."

"He'd say that was a compliment."

"I'm sure he would. Ha! In any case, and I will just be honest, you will need to guide her a bit. There isn't much administrative work to do, which is good because you will need to walk her through everything for the first couple of days. I know, I know," he begins putting his hand up to stop me as he sees my mouth open ready to respond. "It's not what you thought it would be, but it is what it is. She will do fine. She's good. With Katia, next week, we should have a good head on our shoulders, but you will need to stay in form."

"I can do it."

"*Allez.*"

We rest a bit more, and take a tour of the bathroom facilities to make sure they're still in tip top condition before getting back on the road. I pass out after a few moments as Hermann drives humming some song that's stuck in head. He drops me off at the hostel and I go to prepare some welcome information for this Camille. I can't help but to pass the next couple of hours wondering about her. I only know that she speaks perfect French and German, which is a bit inspiring as we will need both.

I watch half of a World Cup match at the bar before walking up the hill towards the bus stop. The train station is a good fifteen minutes by foot, so the journey is great to help me walk off all the tapas and beers of the day. I wait in the lobby and am happy to see that her train is arriving on time. Tired from my leisurely day, I am in no mood to be social, but as the train arrives I find a way to stand to my feet and force

129

a smile. I'm holding a sign with her name on it and am terribly surprised when through the cluster of people a gorgeous woman smiles at me. Shit. She has bright hazel eyes and dark brown hair. From the tone of her skin you would think she had been already passing weeks on the beaches of Biarritz. She's just my cup of tea.

"*Bonsoir*. You are Teo?"

"Um, Yeah. Camille?"

"Of course. Pleasure to meet you!"

"You as well. Welcome to Biarritz," I say. I grab her large bag and take out my phone to call a taxi.

It's been awhile since I read company policy on relations with coworkers. I vaguely remember that it is not allowed, and especially since I am the manager. I'm still thinking of it as we stand in front of the station waiting for the taxi.

"Have you been here long? In Biarritz, I mean," she begins.

"About a week and half," I promptly say, hoping to keep the conversation as short as possible while trying not to look at her again. Thank God the sun has gone down. The taxi arrives saving me from having to say much more, and we're at the hostel in a few minutes. I give her a room key and ask Julie to heat up her pre-made dinner. Camille arrives about thirty minutes later showered and relaxed.

"So! What shall we do?"

"Nothing. I mean, nothing tonight. It's quite late, so we can start early tomorrow before our clients start showing up. For now, it's as you want. I've heated up your meal. Would you like a beer or some wine?"

"Oh, no. No, thank you. I don't drink much. How about some tea?"

"Oh, I see," I respond looking inside the fridge filled with rosé and Leffe Blondes. "We will see what they have in the kitchen. Follow me."

We walk in silence down the hallway, which makes it even more monotonous as we hear our steps echo. Julie places her meal on the bar. She's able to find an Arizona tea, which just happens to be her favorite.

"Oh, it's just perfect!" she says. "You two are so kind."

"Thank you," says Julie.

"Yes, ok. Well I am going to bed," I say.

"Really, Teo?" begins Julie "It's just 10:30."

"Umm. Yes. I need to, uh, rest. Big day tomorrow, yeah? *Bonne nuit*," I say.

I nod and walk through the hallway, past the reception, through the double doors, up the stairs, through more double doors, and then to my room where I let out a sigh of relief. Suddenly whether or not she is a newbie is the last thing on my mind.

"No, Teo. No. It doesn't matter. You have a job to do, and she works on your team. Get it together," I say to myself.

I reach for the bottle of red wine that I keep in my armoire, and uncork the top. I pause with it ready to pour into my glass. *Not tonight*, I think. I put the cork back in and place the items away for another day.

Chapter 5: Run to the Hills

Trees, green foliage, and bushes whip fast and furiously against the bikes pedals and frame pinging, ringing. Relentless hills are no match for the bike, which shockingly careens through the ups and downs of the forests surrounding Lake Mouriscot. I wish I could give all the credit to the bike's manufacturer, but these wheels are turning to the tune of my body and mind which are taking the frustration of having no solutions to how strange this summer has started out on the backroads and trails.

I was able to get back in pretty good shape after last summer and decided to bike every now and then to keep up some form. It has turned into an everyday obsession since my first day, and the arrival of Camille has only added fuel to these legs. If she had been a hostel client, if she had even been a passerby in the city center, I would have already gotten her number and invited her out. But this is not the case. I'm tempted and there's not a damn thing I can do to change it.

Almost effortlessly through the hills, I speed. The sun is as cool as it's going to be for the day, and the breezy moments are heightened by my expeditious movements. In any other the context, it'd be the perfect morning ride, but now it seems to be a method of facing the tasks ahead.

I exit the trails heading towards the hostel. There is a bike rack just in front if it so I lock the bike there before entering the front doors. I am preparing say hello to Gil at the reception when Camille comes through the double doors, smiling like the morning's sunshine.

"*Bonjour*, Teo! Wow, did you just come from a run?"

"*Bonjour*. No, I was riding my bike around the lake."

"Oh great. I was hoping there was place where I could make some sport. I am a runner," she says. "You will have to show me where it is. Perhaps we can train together to stay in shape during the season?"

"Uhh, sure. We can go tomorrow morning if you want," I say. I can see Gil's eyes darting back and forth between us. "Excuse my manners. This is Gil. He is the Logistics Manager for the hostel."

"*Bonjour!*" he says. He stands up and comes all the way around the reception and out of the office to give her kisses on each cheek. "If you are in need of anything, anything at all, I am at your service."

"Oh wow, that's so sweet. Thank you, Gil," she says naively.

"Camille have you had breakfast yet?" I interject. "I'll go to wash up in a moment, but we should be in the office by 9:00am to start."

"Oh! Ok. No problem, Teo. I'm ready to get to work!"

"Yeah, cool. See you then," I respond.

What the hell is wrong with me? I sound like a robot. Even Gil looks at me strangely probably wondering why I interrupted his romantic introduction and also how I have suddenly become serious about my work. Before anyone can figure it out I dart through the double doors, only slowing down as a whiff of what must be her fragrance grabs my nose.

Shit.

I take my shower, and completely ignore looking into my own eyes for the fear of what they may tell me. A bit of post biking hunger has struck me so I swing by the kitchen as it's closing to grab a croissant and coffee. Camille is waiting for me enthusiastically at the office door. I nod while unlocking the office door and let her enter first. I am happy to feel the pressures of the tasks at hand overshadow my attraction. We really do have some tough work ahead of us, and I need to make sure she is capable. I place a chair in the middle of the room while turning my chair to face her.

"Welcome to the office. It's my second home. Sorry. It, uh, is where you, I and the rest of the team will keep ourselves organized for this season, which if no one has already told you is long."

"I understand. They've told me of a situation where someone was supposed to be here. I understand that I am a replacement, and maybe it's not what everyone had in mind," she says in a reassuring tone. "In any case, I'm happy to be in Biarritz and to be a part of this program. Just tell me what we need to do and we'll get it done."

If I didn't know this job so well I would be at a loss for words. This visage of a woman came ready to get her hands dirty. I don't even think I was as ready for the task when I arrived last year.

I show her around the office, and give her copies of the handbooks which we review almost page by page sitting side by side. She laughs as

I tell her which rules are bullshit, and which things we absolutely won't be doing.

"But on the skype call they said this was very important."

"Maybe they did, but that's how things go for different centers. We have a system here in Biarritz based on our climate and needs. It's impossible to function exactly like a center in London or Barcelona, because they're not the same cities. We do things a bit differently here in *Pays Basque*," I say with a smile. We go silent. If it weren't for Hermann's honking horn I may have fallen into her eyes and off the face of the earth.

"Opp la. Hello Team!" he says with his bellowing voice as he enters the office. He shakes her hand, crushing it as always to be expected. "Pleasure to meet you, Camille. Has Teo gone over everything?"

"Yes. He was very thorough. I have a few questions, but I believe I'm ready."

"Well, look at this. All-Star Program Manager," he says with a smile on his face. He looks at me hand on his hip while shaking his head. "It seems like we're off to a good start."

Hermann takes her to the airport to greet our first clients, while I stay behind to double check their arrival documents and room reservations. It provides me with a rather fortunate break as they make transfers to and from the airport and train station. Throughout the day they bring in clients, while others arrive by car and taxi. By the early evening we have everyone, and just as last year Hermann leads the welcome meeting. I hand out the itineraries, and Camille stands there, drifting through her first welcome meeting, before we shepherd everyone to the center city.

I opt to do the city tour, but she asks to take over just minutes into it saying that she can handle it. I'm not sure how, but she's already gotten all of information memorized. My fears of some lackluster replacement are quickly disappearing, and being replaced with a very conflicting hope. Partially that we can actually pull this off, and the other half wondering if I can keep myself from falling for her until Katia arrives in a few days.

It's 7:00 am. She's dressed in her running gear with her hair pulled back in a ponytail. I unlock my bike, and we head off down the trails. We stick to the main paths, and I maintain a steady pace as not to lose her. The sun is brilliant yet calm, and while our goal is to get a proper workout we have a moment to get to know one another better. I learn that she's a traveler, and that her mother is Moroccan, but from Paris. She still has some time left in university in Muenster, Germany. I've returned to Biarritz to find whatever it is that I'm looking for to continue my life, while she is just a student looking to make a little money in a summer job.

What a pair.

We finish our morning run with enough time to shower and eat a quick breakfast. Today is the busiest day, because I will need to show all the clients and Camille the routes to their language schools, recreation centers, and surf schools. It's actually a nice change of pace after passing a week alone in the office. Fortunately, the youth program hasn't begun, so Camille has some time to get used to things before chaos ensues. By the late afternoon I've shown her the drop off points and introduced her to the instructors. I leave her in the city center knowing that she can handle herself and head back to the Hostel where Hermann and I have a few administrative tasks to handle.

"How goes it, Program Director," I say as I arrive at the office.

"Perfect. I think it's the hour," he says as he opens the fridge to pour some wine. He doesn't even ask if I want one, because by now he knows I'm just as thirsty as he is. "How's Camille working out?"

"She's...amazing. She learns fast and takes the initiative. I think she will do just fine," I say with a smile on my face.

"Good, good. Make sure you look out for it though. The season is long and we don't want her to burn out this week before Katia arrives to help and high season begins. Also, there will be another team mate arriving the week after Katia. It seems like things will shape up just in time for high season."

"Understood. She's in great shape too, so I think she can handle being out for the sports activities."

"Oh, is she?"

"Well, yeah...We uh, went for a tour of the lake this morning. She ran and I rode the bike."

"Oh la la, Teo!" he says smiling and shaking his head.

"What?! I didn't do anything!"

"Don't feed me that salad."

"She's gorgeous, Hermann. How am I supposed to spend a week alone with her?"

"Normally, I would have some advice to give you, but this time...I guess you'll just have to deal with it! She's very pretty. Quite obviously, a German girl," he says jokingly with a sense of pride.

"Hey now. She's only half."

"Of course, but seriously, Teo. The work comes first. Just keep yourself distracted until Katia comes."

It's easier said than done, but I think it may be the only advice I'll be getting for a while.

The days pass calmly. We take a tour of the lake every morning and even do a bit of yoga together. I slowly feel myself slipping further away from Hermann's advice and my better judgment. Even the fact that she's taken to the work like a pro doesn't help, because it only makes her more impressive in my eyes. We take meals together. We have daily meetings. We send text messages back and forth joking about some of our client's silly requests. Each occasion moves me closer and closer to making a decision. Gil keeps saying that I need to make a move. We can hardly get through our weekly meeting without him asking questions about her, and Aude doesn't help by coming next door to say how perfect Camille is. It's a strange revelation. This thought that I haven't wanted to invite anyone, anywhere, since last summer. I'd take her for drinks, but she's no reveler. The idea of a nice lunch in San Sebastian seems perfect, but we have no time. I think a bit of inviting her to my room, but that's clearly a terrible idea. Somehow, I resist.

It's the day of Katia's arrival. I've made it to finish line, and am relieved that there will finally be someone here to break up any tension we may have. I know it can't work, but that doesn't stop us from going for a midafternoon tour of the lake. The sun is not as bold, and there is a perfect breeze. I'm riding right by her side heading up a gravel road. She looks at me and smiles as her hair whips around to the rhythm of her feet. I smile back.

Pop!

My knee gives out in an extreme fit of pain and I jump off the bike rolling onto the gravel road. It's immediately stinging, and I grasp at my leg with both hands wincing in agony.

"Teo!" she yells. She runs back to where I am lying and places her hands on my shoulder and leg. "Are you ok?!"

"It's my knee. I don't know what happened," I say through the pain.

"Can you move it?"

"Yeah. Ouch! It hurts quite a bit, but nothing seems broken or torn."

"We need to get you back to the hostel for some ice."

"No, it's fine."

"Teo, no. We are going," she says firmly while reaching out her hands to help me off the ground. With a bit of effort, and bit more pain, I stand to my feet. She braces me under my right arm which wraps around her shoulder, while she rolls the bike on her right side. "How does it feel? Does it hurt to walk?"

"Not much. We're not too far from the hostel, so let's keep going," I say. I look down to her breathing heavily. She looks up into my eyes with concern. "I'm fine. Thank you."

We arrive at the hostel at the worse time since the reception is closed for the siesta. There's no one to alert, so she walks me to the office leaving my bike in the hallway. The pain is extreme as I sit down. She takes my leg and places it on a chair, while I give her keys to the kitchen. A few moments later she returns with a bag of ice and places it on my knee.

"Ahh! Shit!"

"What?! What?! I'm sorry!"

"No, haha. It's fine. It's just damn cold."

"Haha. Oh, ok," she says brushing back a piece of her hair that had come untied. She looks to me with those eyes.

"Thank you, Camille. You don't have to do this. I can take care of myself."

"You're welcome, but I insist. We've got to keep you in form, and I feel it's my fault. I was pushing it too much trying to go every day."

"No, it's not at all. I normally don't ride that much. I've been pushing myself every day because you...," I pause. I want to say because I enjoy spending time with her. In another life, I'd mention it's not her fault that I fancy her. That I'm willing to get up a couple of hours earlier just to have more time with her. I'd say how great of job she's doing, and how impressive she is. I say none of these things. I don't even finish the sentence.

"I am what?" she asks. Her breathing has calmed down a bit. I can tell my lack of words told her everything, but it's not something she can mention. It's for me to do.

"You're incredible."

Honk, honk! Hermann's car pulls into grass and I can see Katia's head sticking up in the passenger seat. Just in time. Camille looks at me for a few more seconds before jumping to her feet. Katia waves from outside and Hermann grabs her bags. They walk through the hallway doors.

"Teo! What happened?" asks Katia

"I hurt my knee while biking. Camille was just helping me ice it."

"Opp la!" begins Hermann. "If I didn't know any better I'd we've interrupted a day date!" We all laugh, although mine is nervous from imagining what could have happened if they didn't show up. Camille switches to German to explain the whole story, while Katia comes to hug me.

"So, Teo. How is the season going?"

"It's pretty solid," I say as I down some pain pills. "Camille is a genie."

"Good, good," she says. She leans in a bit and lowers her voice. "And are you behaving yourself?"

"Trying to. I'm trying, *babushka*."

Chapter 6: *Vnuk* and *Babushka*

Katia knows me all too well. It's almost hilarious that she could already see that my mind has been wandering to promiscuous pastures, and she's only been here for five minutes. Her presence is my saving grace. No more couple's breakfasts or staff meeting 'dates', and I doubt I will be going on a bike ride anytime soon. Whatever fancies I've for Camille will have to wait, as the summer must now pass through the ever-truthful eyes of my *babushka*.

Camille and Hermann stay in the office to discuss things for the new arrivals, while I, slowly but surely, hobble with Katia to the reception to take her room keys and linens. Ideally, she will be staying with Camille in a double room. It's the only thing that makes sense economically, and has been planned for weeks. However, when I ask Gil for the keys there's an issue.

"*Putain, c'est chaud.*"

"What do you mean?" I ask as I watch him clamor about his logistics spreadsheets.

"We messed up?"

"We did?"

"*Bah, ouais*. I don't know how it happened, but...There is no space for Katia in the hostel."

"Wait, she should be staying with Camille correct?"

"I thought so too. We're completely booked here, Teo. Augustine must have gone back and changed something. Even Camille is staying in double room with some traveler from Spain for the next few days. I can get Katia in after that, but otherwise she will have to stay in a room of four or with you."

"*Merde.* Well she can't stay with me, it's against the rules. Katia is this ok? It will just be for a few days. You can leave anything valuable in my room."

"Oh. Umm. Ok," she says very skeptically.

"I don't know how this could have happened Gil. I mean I've sent you all the arrivals a week in advance. Maybe this whole staff mix up confused us?"

"I'll double check. My mistake, T."

"Teo, do you mind if I take a shower in your room? I just want to relax a bit before having to mix in with others. It's been a long trip."

"Sure thing, Katia."

We head to my room. It's not exactly the tidiest of living spaces, but it's mine. I leave a key with her and head down to meet with Hermann before he leaves for the night. There really isn't much to discuss. Camille is a pro by now, and Katia is a veteran. Tomorrow should be an easy-going day, and we should be just about ready for high season. I go to the bar and take a beer or two to decompress for the day.

What would I have said if Hermann didn't honk his horn? If Katia was arriving tomorrow, where would this night have gone with a Camille tending to a battered bastard? It's stupid to imagine, and I think I've become sick of it all. These thoughts are exactly how I get myself in these situations. I've been up to my oldest of tricks, falling for beautiful women, building some romantic fallacy around fleeting moments. No. No more. I am here to do a job, not to fall in love. The summer lasts only so long and after that she will be out of my life. That's how things function here.

I take a deep breath and reflect on the last weeks. I *think* I've figured it out. I have evolved. I am about my business and my work, and have no interest for fleeting fancies, woeful electrician's apprentice stories, or old men looking to get their rocks off.

I gulp down the last of my beer triumphantly. I am a man set about his mind and on his way. I walk back to my room, completely forgetting about Katia. In fact, I haven't seen her since I left my room. It's well into the evening. I open the door cautiously and am met with a blast of flower power. No, no that's not it. It's like spring time blooming. Wait. That can't be it. It smells like a girl.

I can feel it even before seeing her. She's still here. I turn on the bathroom light to see that her toiletries are neatly placed on the right side of the sink. Mine, which are normally placed wherever I've left them, are now organized on the left side. I leave the light on so I can see into the rest of the room, and to no surprise, she's sleeping in the second bed. She's forgone the hostel's sheets and placed her own on the bed. Her clothes and personal belongings have been neatly placed in the cubby holes. *She's moved in!* I think to myself.

It's too late to wake her up, so I decide to just go to sleep, but when I look for my pajamas everything has changed. My clothes are folded up and placed neatly into my dresser, even the desk has been arranged with my items now in neat order.

I turn to her, sleeping there peacefully in her bed. I almost say something, but she looks too serene. Little Russian doll. Suddenly, I could use something to drink. I chuckle a little as I quietly exit the room and walk down the hallway. At least now I know I won't be inviting Camille to my room.

The next morning, we wake up at almost the same time. Or at least, I am waiting for her to open her eyes so that the first thing she hears is my voice.

"Sleep well?" I ask.

"Oh. Good morning, Teo. Yes. Quite well. And you?"

"About as good as always," I say pausing. "I see you, um, moved in."

"Yes, yes of course. I mean think about it, Teo. I don't want to stay in a room with 3 other people whom I don't know, when I can stay here with you for a few days. Yes?"

"It makes sense. Also, Hermann will be happy that we're not paying for a bed in another room. You cleaned up a bit?"

"Yes of course! *Vnuk*, how can you live like this. It was not possible for me to stay here with a room in this condition. So, I brought it up to code. It is better, yes?"

"No! It smells like a girl is in here!"

"Because I am a girl! I am surprised that you've had any girls in here at all with this condition. I have made it better. It is like real home now."

"Yeah, but where are my things? I don't know where anything is now, and what is a *vnuk*?"

"It means 'grandson'," she says coming from under her sheets and standing to her feet. "I put your pants and shorts in the bottom shelf.

Above are your shirts with short sleeves, with your nicer shirts hanging up in the closet. Finally, your undergarments and socks will be on the top shelf. Yes?"

"Ok, and where are my shoes?"

"Look under your bed."

I lift up my sheet to see that all my shoes, flip flops and slippers have been lined up in a row.

"It is good, yeah? If you are going to find a nice woman you need to take care of yourself, *vnuk*."

"Yes, *babushka*."

"Now, I am going to take shower first. I will see you at breakfast," she says as she grabs her towels and clothes and walks into the bathroom. I chuckle at the thought of it. In the office, I am the Program Manager and it's my job to make sure she has what she needs to do her job correctly and that she does so. However, behind closed doors, at *home*, she is my *babushka*. It seems I have a couple of things to learn about being a Russian grandson.

Chapter 7: The Phoenix

It's been awhile since I've spoken with Reda. Admittedly, there hasn't been too much to say. In the beginning we spoke every other day, venting about the how this summer began. He would complain that he was unemployed and had not heard back from the corporate office about any of his appeals. The last thing they had offered him was a week-long position somewhere in the U.K which would pay him only half of the salary he would have made with me. He of course declined. My situation was much different, but just as complaint worthy. Complaining is something we do quite well in France

However, it all faded with time. As my grievances lessened, our conversations became less and less common. It did no good complaining to each other, because neither of us could change our situation. We got to a point where we simply accepted it, and moved on anxiously awaiting summer to tell us our fate.

For this reason, I am surprised when I receive a call from the corporate office apologizing for the rough start to the season. It is terribly diplomatic, and I am more or less apathetic seeing as how things have been going smoothly with Camille's arrival and of course Katia's return. I give my thanks for the call and hang up with a sneaking suspicion that Reda would be reaching out to me shortly. If they'd apologize to me, then they surely would have reached out to him as well.

"What's up bosssssss!" he yells when I answer the phone 5 minutes later.

"Tj Reda, it's been awhile since I was your boss. Haha. How are you, my friend?"

"Fuckin' great, mate. Haha. Have you heard?"

"Heard what?"

"I got a job! Man, they asked me back!"

"Wait, what?! That's phenomenal. I actually just got off the phone. They just said they were sorry, but not much else."

"Ha. They're being modest. The shit has hit the fan, T!" he says so loudly that I have to pull the phone away from my ear.

He goes on to tell me that the people who decided that he wasn't fit to work in Biarritz, the same ones who wouldn't listen to Hermann or Bernard, had quit the company. The pressures of high season were simply too much for them. This led to a chain reaction causing the company to backtrack through all the events of the last month to clean up the mess and hire a new staff, which completely explains the call I had received.

"Man. That's heavy," I begin. "Wait, so does it mean you're coming Biarritz after all?!"

"No... That is the downside."

"That's bullshit. Cute of them to apologize, but we're still understaffed going into high season."

"Teo, everyone is understaffed. Imagine this same situation in programs all across Europe. Biarritz is one of the smallest programs; imagine it in London, Nice, or Rome. Someone fucked up. They fucked up big time."

"Wow. Well at least we're fine here. We will arrive as we always do. Anyways, what did you end up with? Supervisor?"

"Man. I am the doing the same job I was supposed to do in Biarritz, but in London."

"You're kidding, right? That's the biggest center in the entire company! That sounds amazing!"

"Not at all, T. It's a shit-storm up there and they need someone crazy enough to take on the task of organizing for a few hundred clients."

"They've got the right guy."

"There's more. This is a youth heavy program, so there are a lot of language courses going on. I'm pulling double duty. I've got to work and organize the programs during the week and leave every weekend on the Eurostar to go to Paris to bring a group of kids back on Saturdays, and return with another group on Sundays."

"Wait. So, you are spending every Saturday for the next month and half in Paris?"

"Yes man! I have a stipend, I'm put up in a hostel, and I get paid extra for making the trips."

"*Meccccc*. Wow. This is incredible. I thought we had the sweet life in Basque Country."

"It sounds nice. It will be a lot of work of course. We're at least 5 times bigger than you guys in high season."

"If anyone can do it, it's you my friend. I'm glad this is worked out for you," I say. At that moment Hermann walks in to do a bit of work. "Hey, chef. Guess what?"

I proceed to tell him about Reda's new position and Parisian perks, to which he can only shake his head in pleasurable disbelief.

"This guy. What did I tell you both last year and at the beginning of this cinema?"

"We know, we know. You said we would arrive," responds Reda on speakerphone.

"Exactly! Opp la! Guys like us, we always arrive," says Hermann nodding his head in satisfaction. "And of course only Reda could do it such class and style."

"Aww, Hermann. That almost sounds like a compliment."

"Congrats," he says as he turns to his computer. I take Reda off speaker phone.

"Well he is right. You've done it like only you could. Perhaps, a Reda moment isn't such a bad thing?"

"I'm at my leisure, boss."

"You're like a phoenix."

"What?"

"A phoenix. I mean, look at this situation. Just a month ago you thought your life was done. No job for the summer, trouble in school. You've come up from the ashes my friend. You have a second chance."

"Thanks, Teo.... Thanks for being there, man. Maybe some of that second chance stuff you talked about rubbed off on me. Who knows? How's your second summer going?"

"Complicated," I say looking to see that Hermann is still in the office. I stand up and walk outside just beyond the hostel so I can have some privacy. "It's ok."

"You see Iza yet? She said she was coming back, right?"

"I have no idea what her status is. I haven't heard from her in weeks. It's probably for the best to be honest. "

"Why do you think Julien would get jealous?"

"Piss off. NO, it's not that. I still kinda have a thing for her. Camille."

"My replacement? How do you *kinda* have a thing for someone, Teo? You don't know what you feel, or what?"

"It's more so that I don't know *if* I should feel. Right?"

"I understand, but listen. I know you, man. You overthink things, especially when it comes to ladies."

"Sage advice from The Phoenix."

"If that will help you get over this shit, then sure. Sage advice from the Phoenix," he says laughing out loud. "Look. You don't have to be like last summer, and let's face it. Nothing has gone the way we planned. But, you're still there. It's still summer and you've got the entire world passing through the city center, but you're stuck on one chick who you probably shouldn't deal with anyway. You're still in Basque Country man. Take advantage of that in whatever way you need."

"That was pretty profound."

"Let's just say I've had some time to think about shit."

Reda's wisdom, which sounds like the strangest combination between Hermann's and my own advice, strikes a chord. How much have I missed of this Basque life? What good does it do to be blinded by indiscretion when there's enough sunlight to keep my eyes full for the entire summer? Nothing it seems. Meanwhile, *le Pays Basque* buzzes all around me, a brilliant world and region waiting for me to take advantage.

The only way I can think to achieve this is by starting something new, or at least picking up where I left off with a pleasant beginning. I find myself on *Rue Gambetta*, as I do quite often. Most of the time it's for groceries at the Petit Casino, but the adjacent Puig & Daro is becoming more and more a place of fascination, especially considering that I don't always have time to cross the border to San Sebastian for my tapas.

I think of Miren. Beautiful, charming, and seemingly smart. She's Basque, and even if there is nothing to be had with her romantically there could be some experience worth having. I almost feel silly that I didn't stop in to visit her last week as promised, but will make up for it today.

146

The terrace is empty, and I don't see her anywhere in sight. It's strange. She told me that she works on Thursdays. A nice bald waiter approaches me. His name is Felipe. We exchange our greetings, which are always entertaining. Something about being a foreigner, and a foreigner that speaks French, just tends to open people up. They always have so many questions, which admittedly makes me feel nice. He takes me inside, as is custom, and I choose at least one of each tapa they have. I take my seat on the terrace and moments later he arrives with my platter and beer.

"Is that all?"

"Yes," I begin. "Wait, um. Is Miren working today? I expected to see her around."

"Ahh, no. Not today. In fact, she won't be for a while. She had to have some emergency surgery on her leg."

"What?! I mean how? She seemed fine to me."

"Well my friend, it is just one of those things. She went for a normal checkup and they found something off in her blood. She is fine, so do not worry. It could have been worse. They found it early on and can give her treatment. It is only that she cannot be on her feet for too long as she recovers," he says almost sadly.

"Wow. That's no good."

"Yes, for sure. She is a great girl, yeah?"

"Well, yes. Part of the reason I come here so much is because of her. I mean, she remembered me from last summer. It's nice to see a familiar face, I suppose."

"Miren is the best," he says. We both look down and nod our heads. I think quickly of what I could say to reach out to her, but everything that comes to my mind sounds strange. 'Would you like to be my Basque guide?' or 'Hey, get well soon. Want me to bring you some tapas?'

Shit.

"Hey, Felipe. Could you tell her something for me?"

"Sure, my friend."

"Just tell her that the American says he hopes she gets well soon."

"Will do, American. I know she will appreciate it."

Chapter 8: *Les Amis*

The dawn before the storm that is high season is upon us. However, not before a brilliant fluke in the corporate office's planning leaves us with two days of free time. Well, there is a bit a logistical planning on my part, but as far as clients are concerned we have nothing to do. Hermann told us about this 'break' a couple of weeks back, and we took it lightly. Katia and I, having already lived through an entire season, thought it wouldn't be as he said, and that there would surely be work. However, we planned accordingly for a brief holiday before an abrupt high season, which would include double the clientele, a new team member, and as expected a group of youth campers.

Enter Francois and Jean-Henri. Old friends from my old days, arriving just in time. Francois studied in my home city, and I at his university in Strasbourg. Jean-Henri is Francois' buddy who I've ran into on more than one occasion during adventures around Europe. Between the U.S. and Europe, we've made quite a good deal of memories, and it seems they'll arrive just when I need them. I've been in need of some guy time to make up for a lack of Reda running as my wingman every step of the way. Katia and I get on well, but there's only so much I can tell her. I imagine that works both ways. She's huddled up to Camille as they pass the days working around Biarritz, which has left me to my own thoughts. Unfortunately, in the quiet of my office I find my mind wandering to Camille.

I tell myself I don't fancy her, but I seem to have done everything to appear 'fancy'. Some people would call that cleaning up my act, but I'm not too sure how true that is. I've turned down more glasses of rosé than I care to admit, and a blind eye to more than a couple of cute travelers passing through these walls. It's fatiguing without any reward, but the arrival of my buddies should be a good change of pace.

It seems even Katia is taking advantage of our holiday. One of her best friends, Irina, is coming down from Paris to visit, as well as her boyfriend Ilya who's coming over from Lisboa. I've already imagined a spectacular evening for us. Katia, Camille, Francois, Jean-Henri, Irina, Ilya and myself; a group of young adults looking to make the most of a moment in a Biarritz Summer.

It's the late afternoon. Everything's coming together as brilliantly as I imagined. Francois and Jean-Henri's are staying at Jean's parent's summer home, while Irina has bunked up in Katia, and Camille in a triple room where Ilya may or may not be spending the next two nights, depending on who you ask. I don't ask. I don't tell.

Hermann stressed to me that I still have some work to be done. Camille organizes taxis for our leaving clients, I handle all of the administrative duties. Katia and Irina go shopping at *les Galeries Lafayette,* while Francois, Jean-Henri, and Ilya stock up for our evening soiree. Instead going out to eat and having to deal with the hassle of drunkenly taking the night bus back from the city center, we opt for a few pizzas from *La Boîte à Pizza* on the back terrace of the hostel.

We have two tables combined with chairs all around them. The pizzas are placed in the middle with plates, plastic ware, napkins, and cups for each chair at the table; with bottles of wine strategically flanking. It's about as classy as one can be with a pizza dinner, but I expect nothing less with Katia at the helm.

"*Babushka*! This is pretty fancy don't you think?"

"*Vnuk*, if we are going to have old friends over then we must give them a proper welcome. Haven't you learned anything??"

"Sorry. I should have known better," I say giving her a hug. "Irina, Katia has told me a lot about you! Is it true that you two are besties?"

"Yes. I suppose so. We know each other from back in St. Petersburg, but it is just a pleasure to see each other in a different place."

"I thought you both lived in Paris?"

"Yes. It is true. But that is like home. This is a vacation from the busy life in the north!"

"That sounds about right," I respond. I look into the terrace doors to see Francois, Jean-Henri, and Ilya return from the city center carrying bags of beers and wine. My eyes widen at the site of it.

"Whoa! You guys brought all that for me, eh?"

"Well, Teo! If I know you, you probably can take at least half of this down!" says Francois. "The rest will be for us."

"Oh really?" says Camille who had been quietly placing small candles on the table and lighting them. "I didn't think you much of a drinker."

"You must not know him that well," says Francois.

149

"Yes," begins Jean-Henri. "You know we remember the mess you made in Roma."

"Well I don't!" I respond laughingly. Camille seems a bit perplexed by the whole exchange, so I quickly change the subject. "*Cough*. Um, so Ilya. How are you liking Biarritz so far?"

"I enjoy it very much! It's a very interesting region, and of course I admire the Russian history," he says as he reaches into his backpack. "I even brought a piece of Russia with me to share with you all."

He pulls out a bottle of Beluga vodka, still chilled in his cooler. He hands it to me with reverence, which I mimic as I slowly take the bottle in my hands.

"It is good enough?"

"It's incredible," I say smiling widely.

"And I brought shot glasses!" says Francois.

"Really? You walk around with 7 shot glasses?" I ask

"Oh, um no. Ten actually. It was a pack of ten...I just bought them," he says. We laugh at him and return to the preparations. I hand the bottle back to Ilya who gladly fills up 7 glasses. Camille says she doesn't want one, so Ilya suggests that he and I split hers since it's already poured. It'd be a shame to waste such good vodka. I gladly accept.

"To a great evening," he says holding his glass in the air. "*Na zdravie.*"

"And to *mes amis*. Old and new," I add. "*Santé.*"

We shoot the vodka. It is smooth. I normally chase shots, but there is no need for with this fine liqueur.

"Whoa," I say looking at Ilya.

"*Da.* It is the best."

It's as if Francois and the boys had a premonition when buying that much to drink. I'm not anywhere near drinking half of it, but it isn't long before our small soiree expands. Gil happens to be on call and is staying the night at the hostel. After closing the reception, and hearing our commotion, he decides to join us with his girlfriend, or whatever he considers her.

"Teo, I cannot believe this! I haven't had a drink with you since last summer! You have been much calmer this year!" he says. "Anyways, this is Marina. She's Romanian."

"Hello all. I hope you don't mind that we join you! I have brought a bottle of wine to add to the party!"

"Wha? More wine," says Francois who has been sitting progressively more sideways in his chair throughout the night. "Perfect. It is exactly what we need. Hah!"

We pull up two more chairs and continue reveling in the cool night air. Gil regales us with stories past seasons, while we listen in amazement. At least most of us do. Katia has to keep translating for Ilya who is the only one who doesn't speak French, causing a delayed laughter on his part.

"I have seen some crazy shit in the summer seasons. You cannot imagine it. Biarritz is Biarritz. There are reasons why tourists come here every summer, and that is not even considering *la Fête de Bayonne.*"

"Gil, so tell me. What about these two? Katia and Teo. How do they compare?" Says Ilya nudging Katia. "Translate please, dear."

"Shit, c'mon. I can at least understand English. *Putain.* They're alright," he says making a sour face and shaking his hand. Everyone laughs as he takes a sip of his drink. "Actually they are quite cool. Most people come here and are so strict and worried about their work, but they seem to at least try to enjoy the summer. Especially, Teo! Haha."

"No, no. It's not true," I say with a wink.

"Oh it isn't? Hmmm. What was that redhead's name again? She was Hungarian, right? Or was she German? I lost track!"

"Haha. Ok, ok. I give up. I think I've had my share of fun."

"And then there was the teenager who slept with the same woman as you?"

"Whoa!" exclaims Jean-Henri laughingly. "This is becoming much more interesting than Roma."

"Not true! Well, I didn't sleep with her...at least," I say chuckling, slightly. "Besides that was last summer. This one has been a bit different."

"Do you mean Julien?" he says laughing loudly. I completely forgot how my summer had begun. "Katia, please tell me he told you about Julien?"

Everyone's eyes look to me as I try to hide behind my wine glass, which doesn't work so well because it's completely empty. I laugh and tell them the story of the legendary Julien, much to their enjoyment. I thought I would be embarrassed to tell these stories, but for some reason I'm having a good time. I probably should have stopped at that one, but I continue. I talk about Lily and even how Iza may stop by this summer.

"Dammit, shit," says Francois. "I am in the wrong city it seems."

"Maybe so. I doubt it would make a difference even if you were here," jokes Jean-Henri.

"*Ta guele, connard*, At least I didn't have sex on the toilet at a stranger's house!" responds Francois.

"Opp la! Yes, Jean! You want to keep bringing up Roma, but you forget I know what you did in Zagreb!" I say.

"Zagreb? Go on," says Gil. I look around the table. Almost everyone seems interested. I am about to start talking when Irina interjects.

"Is that all you gents have gained in your travels and time in Basque Country?" she asks immediately provoking silence. "I mean there have to be more stories. Ilya, is it like this in *Lisboa* as well?"

"Umm. Of course not. I mean there are parties all the time, but I do not have time for any of this," he says shooting a quick apologetic glance at me. "Maybe we should change the subject? More vodka."

"I'll take one," I say.

"Make it two and three," adds Jean-Henri. Ilya pours the shots as we all sit in a bout of silence. Katia and Irina share some words in Russian, which only Ilya can understand. It seems only the men are in the mood for more drinking as Katia and Irina keep talking. Camille has been nursing one, and maybe even two, glasses of wine for the whole night. I can't say I've ever seen that look on her face, and at that moment I realize how much I'd said in the good spirit of the soiree.

"What should we cheers to?" asks Gil.

"To *Euskadi*," I say firmly.

"*C'est parti*," he says. The five of us touch glasses. Ilya says another *na zdravie*, as Francois and Jean-Henri add a *santé*. We shoot the vodka and sit back in our chairs. It's still just as smooth, but definitely is a bit much after all we've had. Finally, the girls stop speaking Russian and Katia switches to English.

"Teo and I have had some very great experiences, and there are perhaps more to come with this summer. Last year was chaotic. Remember *Les Quatre Fantastiques*? Ooooo Teo! Haha! We were so stressed out! This summer I think is better, and look, *Vnuk*. We even have a nice break to be with our friends."

"Well that's true. A lot of crazy things happened last summer, but that's just life. You and I were different people in those days, and I like to think that the experience made us better."

"I can agree to that," she says with a smile.

"So now? What's different for you this summer? Have you found something, or had some experience to change things?" asks Irina inquisitively. I look at the empty bottles and the table nodding my head, and run rapidly through the stories I've told tonight. Then, I steal a quick glance at Camille, who like most of the table is waiting on my response. Is this the time to conjure some kind of feelings? Is this the soiree that tells all? No. Not at all. My face; void of emotion. I'm good at that. Just as Katia had neatly placed my shoes under the bed out of sight, I very keenly hide any semblance of sympathy. I drink down the entire glass of wine, which is a bit over half full.

"No," I say reaching for the bottle to refill my glass. "Not yet."

The hangover is unrelenting. I awake the next morning. No wait, afternoon. Actually, I'm not sure when it is. The sun has already heated my room, so I know it can't be a respectable hour. I respond to this by closing blinds, and try to get back to sleep. However, it's to no success. It's like every shot and glass I remember drinking adds another level of pressure to my head. Funny. I can remember the drinks, but not the details.

My phone goes off shooting sound waves of pain through my head. I forgot that I left it right by my pillow. To my horror, I look to see that it's Augustine's number. Despite having the day off, this is certainly I call I can't skip. This hangover will have to wait.

"*Oui? Bonjour.*"

"*Salut,* Teo. Are you available now? I need to speak with you."

"Sure, I'll be right there," I say. I hang up the phone and roll out of bed onto the floor. After struggling to my feet, I slip on some shorts, flops, and a button up shirt, and shuffle on down to the reception where Augustine and an equally hangover ridden looking Gil wait for me.

"Hello, Teo. Have a fun night?" she asks.

"Well it was last night. Right now, is not so fun."

"Yes, it seems Gil did too. So much that he left a huge mess on the back terrace. I know you have some friends staying here. Yes?" she asks. I come to my senses, and speak up.

"It's my fault, Augustine. Gil showed up to have a drink or two after the reception closed. I told him I would lock up and clean things up, but we just got a bit out of hand. We haven't seen these friends in a while, so I think we went a bit too far last night. My mistake. I will clean it up now."

"Is this true, Gil?" she says looking at him.

"*Bah, Oui*. I thought it was taken care of," he says with a puff of air.

"Ok. Ok. I really need your help here. It is high season for us, and well it is my first summer. This can't happen again. I don't mind what you do so much at night, just make sure that everything with your position is taken care of."

"*Bien sur*, Augustine," says Gil.

"And Teo. There aren't really supposed to be outside drinks in the bar area."

"Oh wait, I understand why," chimes in Gil. "There used to be staff pricing for us, including Teo and his team. I meant to tell him to stop, but he says it was too expensive with the normal prices. Maybe we can change that back? That was something we had before."

"Hmmm," she says looking at the two of us. "Well it worked like that before. Let's keep it that way. Have a good day you two?"

She walks up the spiral staircase into her office. I wink at Gil and he winks back. He reaches into his pocket and pulls out a small bottle of painkillers and hands them my way. I smile and shuffle towards the office to look for my sunglasses, where Ilya is working on his computer. We glance at each other with the same parched look.

"Did you find some water in the fridge?"

"Yes, but I could use some more," he says. I take out two cold bottles. Water is about the only thing we have left in there after last night. I toss one over to him. "Thanks"

"Don't mention it. You hungry?" I ask.

"I could, and probably should eat something."

"Where are the girls?"

"Where do you think? They're from St. Petersburg, Teo."

"Shopping then. I'm sure they dragged Camille along too. I invited Francois and Jean-Henri for tapas in the city center. Come with us."

"Ok, what time are we supposed to go?"

"I think around 1:00pm or so."

"Teo, umm. It's half past 4:00pm..."

We opt for an early dinner. Francois and Jean-Henri are still sleeping, so it takes a bit more time for us to get going. Eventually, they swing by in their car at about 6:00pm. We all seem to be over the hangovers, but don't take any chances; dawning our sunglasses as we ride into town. We park and I guide them to *Rue Gambetta*, for some Puig & Daro, which is perfect. Jean Henri says he vomited so he can't eat too much, and Ilya is supposed to have a romantic dinner with Katia for his last night. However, the beauty of tapas is that you can eat just a little, or a whole lot, and still be satisfied. Felipe sees us walking in the distance and nervously looks around at the almost full terrace. He smiles when he sees a space big enough for the four of us.

"Teo! Great to see you! I see you have brought friends!"

"Of course! I had to show them what my life is like here!"

He takes us in groups of two to choose our tapas. I go on the second round, and look around briefly for signs of Miren. There are none. I help Ilya choose his tapas, and we all adjourn to our table. The tasty bites don't stand a chance. I finish in no time, and even Jean-Henri seems to have forgotten that he spent this morning with his head in the toilet. Even Ilya stuffs his face and has no shame in going for seconds. We have another round of beers and sangria. Finally, someone is brave enough to bring up last night.

"It got a bit out of hand," says Jean Henri.

"Or a bit out of your stomach," says Francois with one of his terrible jokes.

"Ughhh. Stop telling jokes. They're not funny," I say.

"Yeah," says Jean-Henri burping.

"I thought it was quite funny," adds Ilya as he chuckles. "I am not even sure we're touching on the most humorous parts of the night."

"Which were?" asks Francois.

"Well for one we gave a detailed story of Teo's sex life for the last two years."

"Shit, that did happen, didn't it?" I respond.

"Oh yeah. Katia tried to clean it up a bit, but I am not sure it helped."

"What do you mean?" I ask.

155

"Oh, well it was all of the Russian talk with her and Irina...Irina thought it was silly to be discussing, but Katia was trying to say that it is just a party and that she should relax a bit."

"I knew it was something sneaky!" says Francois.

"What did they say?" asks Jean-Henri. "Wait! You were in the room with them, right? Is there any gossip."

"Yes...It is actually a bit funny."

"You will tell all!" I say with part of me laughing, and the other half a bit worried.

"Well the girls thought Francois and Jean were in a couple. Like, a gay couple."

"*Putain de merde!*" says Francois. "That is just bullshit."

"Yes!" adds Jean Henri. "I mean we even have my story about the bathroom sex."

"I'm sure you have better examples than that, Jean. If you two want, you can go to the market across the street. Perhaps my good friend Julien can help you!"

"Very funny, Teo! Ok what did they say about him? There's gotta be something, right?" asks Jean-Henri.

"Yes," begins Ilya. "Irina says she thinks you're immature. She asked Camille how she survived a week alone with you as a manager."

"Ouch!" says Francois looking to me. He knows more about me than anyone here, including my little crush on Camille.

"Damn...Well what did Camille say?" I ask.

"She said she did not know what Irina meant, that you were always kind, and even sweet," he begins. He pauses. "Look I am not even supposed to know this stuff. I told them I was sleeping but they talked the whole night. How could I ignore it?!"

"Ok, ok," I say. "Did she say something else?"

"Ummm. I was quite drunk. It is a bit fuzzy. There was some talk of whether or not she fancies you, but it stopped when Camille talked about some guy back in Germany."

"Shit. She has a guy?" asks Jean-Henri. "I was hoping to make a run at her tonight."

"Pfttt. You would not stand a chance with her," responds Francois.

"I do not think either of you would!" jokes Ilya. "She does not seem like the type of girl to pass the night in a bathroom!"

"I will never live that down, will I?" says Jean-Henri shaking his head and taking a sip of his beer.

"Perhaps," says Francois.

I sit in silence. The girls thinking Francois and Jean-Henri are in a relationship is funny, but I'm not so sure if I'm immature. I don't get it. Here I thought I had come so far since last summer. I thought I had changed, and was simply looking for definition. According to Irina, that definition is 'immature', and she may just be right. The news of Camille's guy back in Germany affects me in a way it shouldn't; at least not if I truly see her as a friend. I order another beer. The guys keep talking, but I just sit there waiting for my drink.

"Here you go, Teo. Anything else?" says Felipe.

"No, thank you. Hey, is Miren doing ok? Any chance of her coming back soon?"

"Sorry, but no. She's doing much better, but I doubt she will be back this summer. She does say thank you asking though!" he says. Before I can respond a family arrives and he has to go attend to them. My silence must be having an effect because Ilya has to snap his fingers to get my attention

"Teo! Haha. There you are. Hey man, don't think anything of it. We were all drunk anyways."

"Don't worry. I wasn't thinking about that," I say. It's a lie. "Who wants to go dancing tonight?"

Everyone except Ilya agrees, but then again he's the only one in a committed relationship. He heads off down the street to catch a bus back to the hostel, while Jean-Henri heads inside with our money to pay the bill. I stand, and walk slowly off the terrace looking at the day's remaining sun.

"Teo," says Francois as he walks and stands next to me. "I would ask what's on your mind, but I know you too well."

"What?"

"Camille and this guy back in Germany. Don't think of it. Maybe he is wrong about it."

"Maybe."

"In any case, I see that look in your eyes. Last time I saw it was that one night was back in Paris. Remember?"

"We drank and danced all night. It was so long that we missed the metro back to *Rueil Malmaison* and had to wait until 6:00am for it open again."

"Yeah, and then you missed your flight," he says. He pauses. "I guess what I'm saying is to take it easy. Don't worry about what was said, especially the whole immature thing. Let's go have a good time, but keep this girl out of your mind. It is just going to bother you."

"Don't worry, my friend. She's already a memory."

Chapter 9: Immaturity

Nothing can truly end, when we don't know where to begin. I didn't know where to start this summer. I had no definition, no end game. The idea was simply to come and see things work themselves out. I didn't decide where and how to begin, so Biarritz did it for me. Irina did it for me, and maybe she's right. Why would I revel in those stories, no matter how entertaining they are? Furthermore, how could they end without me deciding where to begin? Perhaps, it's a touch logic in an illogical world, just as this summer's sexual and romantic exploits have been a dash of madness beyond all reason. If I don't have an idea of where to begin, did last summer ever end? I accepted who I am, content but not satisfied, considering all factors past, present, and plausibly futuristic. That's cute. That's a plateau made monumental, and suddenly I'm not feeling very stable. I have a sneaking concern that I haven't changed at all.

The friends come and go bidding us their most earnest adieus. If it wasn't for the fact that I in some ways agree with her, I might have shunned Irina during her last moments in Biarritz. Instead, I opt for a cordial goodbye under the auspices of Ilya's sworn secrecy and whatever possible dignity can exist between brethren. Ilya heads back to Portugal, while Francois and Jean-Henri head to Nice for more vacation before passing back through *Pays Basque* by summer's end. It was fun while it lasted.

It's time for work, and I almost feel that this break in the season did more harm than good. In any case, I view high season as a way to distract myself, from myself. Today we have fifty-five new arrivals, twenty of which are teenagers. The spike in clientele warrants the arrival our new teammate, Adriana, from Spain, who I remember from trainings over a year ago. She has experience from working in different programs last summer, so she's a vet like Katia and I. With a little crash course in the Basque comings and goings, I expect her to do swimmingly.

Katia does what she does best; giving a tour of the hostel to a large group of Dutch travelers. Camille, Adriana, and I sit in the office going over some on-site training. Katia will take more of an administrative roll when possible, so it will be up to Camille and Adriana to look after

159

anything in the field, especially with our youth group. If my lists are correct, we should be seeing a few familiar faces from last year.

"Ok, ladies. This will be a very particular two weeks. Not only will it be the busiest time of our season, it is the most occupied for the hostel and all of Biarritz. We have the *La Fête de Bayonne* taking place next week, which you should try to check out if you can. I know I will...Anyway, we also have a large group of teenagers, which is a completely different ball game than our adult clients."

"Is it like in other cities?" asks Adriana, "I know you said there are some differences here."

"The amount of attention we have to pay to them is just the same. In fact, it's even more important here. We're staying in a hostel mixed with our adult clientele and separate hostel clients. I can hardly explain to you how insane it can be when you have teenagers sneaking out at all hours of the night. It will be stressful, but you two and Katia can alternate days on who is mainly responsible for them."

"Ok. Awesome. I'm excited!" says Adriana.

"Good!" I say.

"It's a lot of work," begins Camille, with that strong smile of hers. "But we're in Biarritz. If you ever get stressed just go to the beach or for a jog around the lake. It's all quite beautiful."

"She's right," I say looking in her direction. A look turns into a gaze. Said gaze evolves into daydreaming away to the week we spent alone. The meals, the lake. Even the knee incident doesn't seem so bad. I reach down massaging it. It's still slightly sore. Adriana speaks up.

"What lake?" she asks. I don't respond.

"Teo," says Camille.

"Huh? Wha? Oh. Yeah is anyone hungry? I may order a pizza or something."

"The lake," begins Camille. She smiles wide and brushes her hair back behind her ears. "She asked about the lake."

"Oh yes. Lake Mouriscot. It's beautiful and preserved by the E.U. Camille and I used to make a turn or two every morning, but I banged up my knee. Strained tendon. Still I do some yoga from time to time. Camille, why don't you take her to see so she knows where it is?"

"Sure thing," she says still smiling at me.

Shit.

It is in that moment, those seconds it takes them to leave the office leaving me to balance the budgets, that I have a profound thought.

What am I pretending for?

I sit here, and have sat day after day behaving myself like a good little Teo, and for what? For her? She'll be gone in two weeks and I will be here until the end. Beyond that, I will still be living my life after the season. Will I pretend to be ok then? To be sober? To be mature? Let's face it. If Reda had been here I probably would have been making notches on my belt down by the beach, and if Iza shows up I'm sure I will have wild sex with her. If Katia hadn't stayed in my room for those days I would have invited someone already, and it would probably have been Camille if she'd even shown the slightest of desire. That's probably all true. This is it.

Reda is settled in his job and I no longer am worried about his replacement, or whether or not the team can do the job. I have no *babushka* to keep me from inviting someone to my room, and Camille, despite smiles and knee massages, may have some beau back home. This is it. This is the first time this summer where I have no buffers. There is nothing to keep me from seeing just how *immature* I can be, and maybe it's not even that. But if moments indeed need defining, then now is the hour of definition.

A familiar horn sounds. It's of course Hermann pulling into his usual parking spot in the grass right by the window. I think perhaps it could be a good time to ask for some of his advice with the girls at the lake and giving a tour, but that quickly changes.

"Hello, Program Manager."

"Program Director, what can I do for you?!" I say trying to exchange a firm handshake, but failing under the grip of his German mitts.

"I have a surprise. Just arrived at the airport."

I look for the first time at the person getting out of his car. As she approaches the door under a sunlit silhouette, I immediately remember who it is.

"My angel!"

"Hi, Teo!" says Clara, as she reaches her arms out for a huge hug. I embrace her like seeing an old friend.

"Look at you!" I say delightedly.

"Do I look older?"

"Darling, yes. You're a young woman now! I'm happy to see you. Where are the others?"

"Their parents will bring them soon," she says smiling.

With so much having changed since the last summer, it's a sign of relief with slight salvation to see my angel again. Camille and Adriana arrive from the lake just about the same time as Katia finishes her tour. Katia embraces Clara just as I did, happy to see how much a year can make a difference just by appearances, and it makes all the difference. Even the way she speaks has changed. Maintaining all the innocence a seventeen-year-old could have, it's obvious that life, for whatever that's worth, has passed since we last met. Camille takes her to her room with Adriana following, while Herman, Katia, and I hang back in the office.

"Do you see that?" begins Hermann. "I love that. Look at her. Back again for another year. She's grown up, hasn't she?"

"It's incredible," says Katia.

"You can see it in her eyes; that maturity. That's what we do, you know? We do a good job, then people will come back. That's the service," he says. He folds his arms looking out of the windows with his lips tightened and head nodding. I begin to ponder. I try to wonder. What maybe she saw in me, or even what Katia and Hermann see. If a year is indeed that important, then it had to have counted for something. That could mean that I am immature. Sure. Maybe immaturity is actually an improvement for me? Perhaps, that's ok.

There isn't too much time to dwell on it all. We have to pack nearly sixty people in the bar area for our welcome meeting. Hermann's voice bellows and even he seems to be in good spirits. I take over with a new spring in my step. This morning I wasn't impressed by anything, but in front of these people I'm in my element.

"We're here to make your holidays more special, and if you have any questions feel free to contact myself and the team for your needs," I say looking to *Les Quatre Fantastiques* who have returned for another summer. Even after all the insanity of last summer I'm happy to see their young faces and delighted they're so happy to see me too. The meeting adjourns and Katia takes Camille and Adriana for the massive group tour of the city. Hermann pulls me aside.

"After a season and a half you finally got the hang of these meetings!"

"Opppp laaaa!" I say. "I could say the same for you, chef."

"Ha! Good, good. Look. There is some good news about our little Spanish friends here," he says. He takes out 4 documents. "After the age of sixteen their parents can opt for a less strict program. Here are their forms."

"Meaning?"

"They're only required to go to classes; otherwise, they're free to do as they want. That is, considering they don't involve the other youth, or mingle with adult clientele."

"Brilliant. I've got that settled. I've organized it so all of the adults are in a separate building. Those four are in my hallway along with some hostel clients. I can keep a good eye on them that way."

"Well, look at that. A Program Manager, who manages," he says with a slap to my back. He leaves the bar area, as *Les Quatre Fantastiques* approach me with their Spanish whispers.

"Hello Teo!" begins Ester.

"We're so happy to see you again!" says Miri.

"Hello ladies. What can I do for you?"

"Well, we were just trying to check if you had gotten some very important forms," says Ester.

"You mean these," I say as I hold them up in my hand. "Yes. I've got them. Here's the deal. You're my girls, but we did have a couple of issues last year."

"No, no, Teo," begins Clara. "We are a year older and much more mature! You will have no trouble from us!"

"Yeah, T. We are much more mature now!" adds Sandra.

"Ok, ok. Don't miss class. Don't cause trouble!"

They nod ok and run off down the hallway leaving me satisfied. I feel like I am doing what I said I would over a year ago. My job. With a good meeting under my belt and some returning customers, I'm riding on a high. I enter the back-storage room leading into the bar and take a tall beer. Julie is working tonight. With high season being upon us there are a lot of clients. Anyone looking on would think that I actually was a barman. By the looks of it, I am. I help Julie sell beers and wine indulging in a few sips of wine myself thanks to the recently restored staff pricing.

There is a felicitous spirit as clients come in and out of the area. Most of them are using this as a platform to their nights, downing a few drinks before heading into the expensive Biarritz nightlife. However, there are several stragglers who are content with our selection and my latest music playlist which is patched in through the speakers. Julie and I are tapping our feet when a man with well weathered skin and thick beard approaches the bar.

"*Bonsoir*. Do you have beer for sell?"

"Sure," I say handing him a menu.

"*Merci*," he says. A few moments later he looks me directly in the eyes. "*Kronenbourg*, please."

I began to pour it from the tap, delicately minding the foam. It seems I've almost become an expert after all these nights. He speaks up again before I finish pouring.

"You're not from around here, are you?"

"Not quite," I say. I place the beer down before him. "How did you know?"

"In your eyes. I could tell," he says with a smile. I look directly at him.

"I can say the same for you, friend," returning the smile.

"American?"

"Something like that?" I say taking a sip of my beer. "Bulgarian?"

"*Quelque chose comme ça. Na zdravie*," he says as we touch glasses, never breaking eye contact. Normally, the story goes that to break eye contact means seven years of bad sex, but I don't think either of us is worried about such a thing. We both take large gulps.

"You've seen a few things. Been a few places, huh? I can see it in your eyes," he says as he takes out a bag of tobacco and starts to roll a cigarette.

"I like to think I have. Ha. Life has a way of showing me otherwise. Funny. I didn't know it showed."

"It's the depth, my friend. If you blink you'll miss it," he says fluttering his eyes. We both let out a hearty laugh along with Julie who is listening in. 'I'll drink to that,' she says extending her glass. We all exchange glances for another round of cheers before taking sips of our beers. As I set my glass down I see a woman approaching the bar out of the corner of my left eye. I turn to her as she looks directly at me, into me.

Neither of us blink.

Chapter 10: Almost Perfect

"What can I do for you?" I ask.

"Ha! Where do I begin? Do you know anyone in Italy?" the woman responds.

"I have a few names I could toss around...I meant if you wanted something to drink."

"I suppose that's the question of the night. I've already had one or two, and I know where this goes if a take a third."

I start to pour a pint of *Kronenbourg* for her.

"What are you doing?"

"Pouring you a beer." I respond.

"I didn't say wanted a beer," she says with a cocky smirk.

"You didn't have too. You took too long, so I did it for you. Sometimes we all need help in making decisions," I respond as I place the pint on the counter. "In any case, if you really know where this third one takes you it shouldn't be intimidating. Besides, it's on the house."

"Never bet against the house!" she says laughingly as she takes the beer. "And where's yours? I've been drinking alone tonight, and refuse to do so anymore."

I gulp down the last of my pint and pour myself a new one. By this point Julie and the Bearded Stranger have receded into their own conversation, allowing us to continue in this increasingly interesting exchange. My pour is perfect. I extend my glass out for a toast and without words she raises hers. Our eyes locked the entire time.

"*Santé.*"

"Cheers," she says. "And to not having seven years of bad sex."

"What's your name?"

"Mara. Yours?"

"Teo."

"American?"

"Something like that. You?"

"Lithuania."

"Oh my. You're the first I've met."

"Don't say that."

"Why?"

"It puts a lot of pressure on me to be interesting."

"Absolutely true...So. Wow me."

"Do you know how I got this scar?" she asks while pointing to her face.

"What scar? I can't see anything."

"Come closer," she says. I lean over the bar until I am just inches away. "See?"

"Oh my," I say as I notice the actually impressively hidden mark between her eyes. It's amazing I didn't see it before considering its size. "How'd you get it?"

"I was quite young and was trying to feed my uncle's dog. All of the kids were taking turns and it seemed like a really sweet animal. I was the last to go, but when I stuck my hand out with the meat the dog jumped up and bit me in the face."

"What?!"

"Yah. I know. Ridiculous, right?"

"Among other things. Seems like you turned out ok."

"Yeah. I'm a quick healer," she says still inches away. "What's that scar from? The one on your eyebrow."

"I was hit in the head with a metal baseball bat when I was a boy. I was knocked almost unconscious and had to be rushed to the hospital where I received twelve stitches in my head."

"Shit! Who did it?"

"Some other kids."

"Did you deserve it?"

"Yes," I say smiling fully, and finally leaning back from the bar.

She is interesting. Very interesting. In fact, she seems interested. So much so that I leave my barman duties to sit next to her on the opposite side of the bar, only returning behind the bar to retrieve more drinks or to help when Julie is called to the reception.

Everything is easy. Normally tension exists between two people because of pretense, because before even a word can be uttered, a hand can be held, or a kiss can be exchanged, they already have a motive in mind. It's this energy which feeds fears and fuels suspicions despite the fact that these preconceptions can be completely inaccurate.

166

This tension is nothing like that. In fact, we are arbiters of tension, wielding it as a tool. Where most are victims, we are possessors of social chaos, purposefully creating those moments unabashedly for the sake of it. Because we don't know. We have no idea. We use tension to help us move past ideas in search for facts. I knew her before she opened her mouth, and I am almost certain she knew me before I offered a beer.

She's brilliant. She's absolutely insane. The UK is her home, only because she can speak the language. She doesn't speak French, but at least she appreciates it, and after all of this has decided that Italian is the language for her; hence why she asked about it.

"I know a couple of people. I'll send you a name or two."

"Perfect! I just love that language. It's like music to me."

"Do you like music?"

"You have a peculiar talent for asking the right questions, mister."

"What kind of music do you do?"

"Jazz. Soul. I sing and play a little guitar. If I had one here, I'd show you a thing or two."

I look around the bar. Julie has been gone for at least an hour, and the only patron is some old man smoking a cig and nursing a beer on the terrace. I stand up and without a word and walk behind the bar. I turn off the music still playing on the speakers and lock up. I bring my laptop to the office, and return with my guitar. I hand it to her, and sit back in my chair.

She brushes back her short dark hair as she sits with it in her lap before strumming the first chords. E minor. Deep and profound. She belts out a sultry melody whipping her head back. If she had much hair at all it would have been like a black wave whipping, but she doesn't. Her fingers are long and slender, sliding down the neck. I wish she would open her eyes, but she doesn't until the releases the last note.

She hands me the guitar after. Without a word. I strum through some chords. Jazz chords. A minor 7, B diminished, to C major 7. It's as if I don't know what I'm doing. I began to sing, which is like liberty. I don't sing much anymore, and I can't believe I am doing a private concert for this woman I've just met. But I am. I don't close my eyes, but I'm not turned in her direction. I look into the distance as if to look into my past, as if to dictate my future. My voice rings out until there are no more lyrics.

"Who was she? The girl you wrote that song about?"

"An old girlfriend. But that was a long time ago."

"I see. Good."

"Let's go to my room. I need to kick that guy out and shut the bar down."

"How about not."

"Ok. Let's go to my office. I need to shut the bar down."

"And kick that guy out?"

"Precisely."

The man leaves without much gruff. After all, it's 3:00am. I turn off the lights and we walk down the hallway to my office. I turn the office lights on, and place my guitar in the corner. I grab two beers from the fridge and a bag of chips. We sit side by side talking, eating, and drinking. Suddenly she says;

"I'm not having sex with you."

"If I wanted to have sex with you, I would have told you by now."

"Oh...Well. Good," she says with a smile.

"Let's go to my room."

"Ok. But only for a moment."

"You keep this place clean!"

"It's a new habit. Want some wine?"

"No, I'm good. I just want to lie down. Is that cool?"

"That's cold as ice," I say.

We take off our shoes and lay in my bed. I turn the lights off using the switch by my night light. I turn the night light on as she wraps her arms around me. I return the affection and that is all. We hold each other. We talk more shit than should be talked for two people in our situation. It's brilliant.

"I'm older than you, so I know these things," she says.

"You're just a year older than me."

"I lot can happen in a year, Teo."

"Maybe. Maybe. But most of the time we just get a year older," I say as she laughs. I'm looking down on her face which is the only thing illuminated in the night's hour. "You're cute when you do that."

"What?"

"When you laugh. When you laugh you slightly stick your tongue out and bite down. I like that."

Our tensions shift.

"You are the second person to ever notice that."

Unleashed is a kiss worthy of the hours and hours of innuendo, signs, and fancies. She's strong, fit. She pulls at my shirt until it comes off, and feels on my chest as I am still above her. She moves me forcefully unto my back. I oblige. She takes her seat on top of me removing her shirt to expose toned abs before making my lips her own.

She climbs off of me standing just before my bed, and unbuttons her black jeans. My shorts are simple. I unsnap the buttons and toss them in time to see her standing before me. Her black undergarments contrast starkly with her pale skin. I taste her with my eyes, fully appreciating how her form uses the light. Her long legs intertwine with mine. She slips into the bed. Warm skin; Her body wraps around me like a towel fresh from the dryer, distinctly with no substitute or comparison. I reach for a condom on one of the side shelves of my armoire.

"No," she says. "I told you I can't have sex with you."

"You said you were *not going* to have sex with me."

"Oh yeah. Well I'm not because I can't. Well, I could but I don't want to. I'm on my period, dude," she says. I pull back from her for a moment and rest my head on my hand looking down at her once again.

"Well that complicates things doesn't?"

"I really want to." she says.

"You speak for us both."

"Dammit."

"Among other things."

"Well, we can do other things. That could be fun."

"Sure."

Being between her legs leaves everything to the imagination, which crawls, walks, and runs wild. The caressing pulses are all we have, and they increase with every motion. Swinging back and forth like the sway of a clock's pendulum until there is no more time. We hastily remove the last of our clothing and pause just moments from carnal enlightenment, but shadows linger just as the condom which is still on the shelf.

"Other things?" I whisper.

"Other things," she says as she reaches for what could not be more profoundly in her position. I despite knowing what awaits me place my hand where I could be inside otherwise, and to both our delights this suffices. For now, for never. It does nothing to have reality in flesh and fluid before you and still be left with everything to the imagination. But that can't happen. That won't happen despite how much we want it to.

"Dammit. I want you to fuck me."

"I know," I respond in between wild kisses. She's aggressive. It's overwhelming. So much that when I tell her to slow down she doesn't, so much that I'm done long before my time. It feels just fine, although untimely. I kiss gently on her neck as she grabs at my hair. Kiss by kiss, we become calmer, until we lay silently, blissfully.

I am almost asleep with my arms around her, when I feel her shoulder gyrating vehemently. I think it could be a muscle spasm, and open my eyes to see. I look to find that her hand has found herself. She begins to moan viciously as the motions repeat wildly what perhaps I failed to do for her myself. She becomes louder giving heat off of her body as I uselessly watch her please herself. Eventually, she lets out a triumphant moan. A second later she begins crying.

"Wha?" I whisper at first. She curls into the fetal position with her hands covering her face. Her sobs are almost as loud as her once satisfied state. "What's wrong? Are you ok?"

"No! Dammit! No!" she exclaims. I reach out to touch her causing her to move to the foot of the bed, which is impressive considering how small it is. "Don't touch me!"

"Shit, ok ok! I'm sorry. Did I do something?!"

"No! It's not about you dammit. It's me! It's my fault. I said I wouldn't do this again! I've done it again."

"What? Finish yourself off?"

"No, Teo! I'm a nympho! Ok? I always meet a new guy and this is how it ends up. I have to get myself off just to be happy."

"Whoa. Don't say that. We didn't even do anything"

"You just don't know! This is how my life is. I'm so fucked up."

"Hey now. Maybe it makes me fucked up too. Right? I mean we're both in this bed," I say trying to calm things down. She responds by getting out of the bed.

"Now we're not," she says.

She walks, still nude, to the bathroom. I am concerned that her mind has gone somewhere far away from this room to its darkest destination. This is more than I signed up for, especially after already having dealt with Lily's meltdown. However, something won't let me move past the pain in her voice. I've had crazy nights, and normally wouldn't care to pry into whatever my partner was dealing with. However, this is different. Something in me is different.

I hear the water running in the bathroom sink and moments later she returns, nervously looking for her underwear, which she begins to put on.

"I'm going to my room."

"No, you're not. You're staying here with me. You don't need to be alone right now," I say putting on some shorts. I stand to my feet and take her into my arms as she places her head on my shoulder. I take her by the hands and lead her to the empty bed on the other side of the room and we lie down.

"Are you sure you want me to stay?"

"Yes. Why?"

"That's crazy to me..."

"There seems to be a lot of crazy things going on this summer."

She begins to tell me about her lovers, her flings. They're numerous. Where I once sought to neglect sex for the sake of sanity, it drives her insane pleasure and pain. She's embraced nymphomania and harnessed it for everything its worth, but this trip isn't supposed to be about that. She tells it's meant to be an adventure away from her normal way of doing things, which more often than not includes multiple partners in a week according to her. Despite her best efforts, she still found her way into my arms.

"You know. You can't get away from it. You can't escape it," I say.

"What do you mean?"

"Those feelings, who and how you are. You carry it with you, no matter how far you go. Those impulses pass through customs. They don't weigh your past at the airport, so it doesn't matter how much baggage you have."

"So...What do we do? How do people in general deal with themselves? Can we just continue to carry our burdens? It's too heavy, Teo."

"Sometimes, yes. I've had a lot of things to get through. Emotionally. Personally. I tried to drink through it. Screw through it. And then I learned that that's simply where I was. It was for that time, for that place. Just like whatever's happening now in this bed. It's for this time. We just have to deal with it," I say. I pause for a moment looking to my right where she lays waiting for my response. "You can keep trying, you know? Your trip isn't over. Changing yourself ain't easy. It's damn difficult. I know it, and even now I'm not sure of where I'm going. But I know I'm living. At the very least, I'm trying. I suppose we just have to keep trying to change until we've actually done it."

"Not bad...I think I understand...You're pretty smart for a young fella."

"I don't think so. I just hurt a lot, and lived to tell the tale. Had some good advice along the way. It's all easier said than done," I say feeling pretty happy about her compliment, and pretty relieved that I'm not the only one trying to figure things out this summer. "You don't find me immature?"

"Hey now. You may be a bit screwy, and if you're lying in bed with me you're probably bit off anyway. I'm not sure if that's immaturity. Promiscuous. But not immature," she says. She looks at me smiling for the first time since crying. "Thanks, dude."

"You're welcome...Thank you, too."

Chapter 11: *La Fête de Bernard* and Promiscuity

It's been three days since she left my room at 6:00am. I remember watching as she jumped hastily from the bed to prepare for the day. Neither of us had slept. She slipped into her jeans. Cracked a few jokes. She said she was off to prepare her bags and wash up before catching an early breakfast, and a carpool into Spain. She knelt down to the bed where I still lay with my head draped over its edge in admiration.

"Keep in touch," she said.

She kissed me on the forehead before leaving the room. I went back to sleep. In retrospect, it wasn't the best idea. Staying up to until 6:00am, two damaged, yet experienced, individuals scraping up what bits of wisdom they have to try to make sense of it all. Even if she is right, and it turns out that I am not immature, it didn't help me get to work on time.

I've become habitually latter to work in the mornings since the visit with *mes amis.* I'm always tired, and if I'm not still slightly drunk in the morning, I'm certainly hung over. I can't help what problems people have, but I at least thought I could control myself. If it wasn't for my three superwomen, Katia, Adriana, and, Camille, the only women I haven't thought of promiscuously about recently, this operation would already be sinking against an iceberg of my indiscretions.

I'm here, but not here. The encounter with Mara, despite being organic and explosive, has led me to an interesting space in my mind, and I've yet to decide if it's going be productive. I thought I was dealing with my problems, but it seems there are others with more complicated issues than me. I don't try to make myself throw up in front of a crowd wearing a fancy new dress, and I don't cry after fooling around. Instead of pondering on budget shortages, logistics, and whatnots, I only am thinking of ways to explore promiscuity, as it has become my new definition. I think I can be ok with that, if it's true. However, I've had almost no way of putting it to the test.

The team and I have an extended lunch break to have a meeting about how things are functioning. Normally, I'm the one who comes to them with questions for which they must find answers. Typically, I critique them and give feedback like the Program Manager I am supposed to be. However, today is far from the case.

"Ok, Adriana. Do you have your schedule made for beach soccer tournament?"

"Ummm...I sent it to you three days ago..."

"Op la! Yes, I remember getting that. My mistake," I say as I shake my head looking down at my notes.

"Actually, I was still waiting on a response," she begins. "I asked if we had room in the activities budget for two more balls, because one washed out to sea and I think another was stolen."

"Sure, sure. Just see me after the meeting. I'll free up some funds."

"Teo," interjects Katia. "I need to start planning the activities for the next week, but you haven't sent any of the budgets and client sheets. How can I plan a week of recreational activities if I don't know who has booked what and how much I have to spend?"

The three of them look at me unimpressed. I'm still looking down at my notepad where I've been doodling my social itinerary for the weekend. I think about Miren. She still hasn't returned to work. Maybe she would have been a positive force to keep me focused. I'll never know that now.

"Teo. Are you ok?" asks Camille. The sound of her soft voice breaks me from my train of thought. The others seem notably aggravated, but she seems to care enough to inquire. "Are you tired?"

"I'm good. Excuse me, ladies. I was just going over some numbers in my head to see about your requests. I'll have that info to you by day's end."

"Thank you, Teo," begins Katia. "And what about this complication with the surf school? Are we going to be able to refund the monies?"

"That I don't have an answer for. It's complicated because polluted waters are why the lessons were cancelled, which is a proper reason for a refund. However, we haven't received a deposit to cover the amount," I begin. "In any case don't worry about that. I'll talk to Hermann again about it."

We end the meeting. I turn to my desk to comb through the budgets. This actually requires updating the documents, which I was supposed to do days ago. The truth is that there is no money. Not for refunds for departing clients or for next week's activities. The ladies set about planning the best they can. They've done such a great job in spite of my lack of focus, and perhaps even apathy. I'm typing an email about the budget to Hermann when I receive a phone call. It's Bernard.

"Ciao, Teo! What's going on?"

"Just got out of a staff meeting. What about you, B?"

"Oh, just here at the school dealing with this *bordel*. These 4 Spanish girls are driving me crazy. They're the same ones from last year, remember?"

"Oh... Yes, I do."

"Well you should talk to them about participating in class. But look that's not why I called. What will you do Friday?"

"Friday...No plans."

"Yeah right, Teo. You know it's *la Fête de Bayonne* this week."

"Oh. Is that what all that red and white is about? I had no idea."

"*Putain. Tu fait ma gueule, où quoi*? If you don't already have plans, let me give you one. I will be having a party at my house in Bayonne. It is in the city center. You can come and meet a lot of nice people, have some drinks, and just enjoy *les ferias*."

"That sounds amazing...I've needed a change of pace."

"Perfect. Tell the girls too. Just be at my house around eight. I will give you the address by text. Bring something to drink! Ciao!"

La Fête de Bayonne. We meet again. Why didn't I think of this before? It's the perfect playground for would-be promiscuous persons, and it seems as of recent I am during my leisure.

"Hey, Ladies! It was Bernard."

"Oh really? Did he mention something about the school?" asks Katia.

"Well yeah, something about *Les Quatre Fantastiques,* but we'll get to that. He's having a party at his house we're all invited."

"That's nice Teo. What about the girls? They've been giving us a hard time," says Katia.

"Yes! The Spanish ones? *Mierda.* I am Spanish and even they make me angry," says Adriana. "They listen to no one but you, Teo."

"I know, I know. I will talk to them,"

"And don't play favorites, *vnuk*. "
"Yes, *babushka*."

Bernard was right. I knew it was the week for *les ferias*, and in fact had been planning for it since I arrived. Laying aside all of the depressions from last summer, and all the bizarreness of this summer, *la Fête de Bayonne* is something I know I have to do, and not even for the sake of all the beautiful women filling the streets. It's something special. Something worth experiencing at least once in life and the fact that I had a chance to do it again doesn't escape me.

I remove last summer's red scarf and belt from my green bag. They had replaced Derlenzistda's book in the months prior to returning, as I counted the days until I could wear them once again. My last shirt was ruined with splashes of sangria and mud, as most clothes are when you get thousands of people in the streets drinking and dancing. I bought a new one, which has a huge Basque flag on the back. I get dressed in my room, adding the final touch with some red shorts before heading down to the office.

"Oh la la! Teo, you look ready for a great night!" says Adriana as I enter with more energy than I've had all week.

"I've got to be for *la Fête*. Are you ladies coming?"

"We will see. We've got to close out some things here, but perhaps we will stop by," says Katia.

"Okay, okay," I say as I grab two massive bottle of sangria and a six pack of San Miguel from the fridge. "Well, if you are, call me on my personal number. Hopefully, we can find each other!"

I start the long walk up the hill when I see *Les Quatre Fantastiques* coming down. It's impossible to avoid them, and they begin to yell upon seeing my party gear.

"*Roder*, Teo! It's great!" says Ester looking at me with a smile.

"So you're going to party?" begins Miri. "And you gave us such a hard time about partying last year! Haha. Look at our role model."

"I'm not going to party. I am going to blend in to catch any youth who are sneaking out to *la fête*!"

"So you need sangria for this too?" adds Miri jokingly. They begin to giggle in unison.

"I have to be convincing to blend in... Anyway! I better not see you there, it's dangerous and I don't care if you have signed documents. You've been missing class again."

"Oh..." says Clara.

"We will talk tomorrow. I have to go now," I say as I continue to walk up the hill realizing that I've somehow done my job and been a hypocrite at the same time.

I take the special *ferias* bus directly to Bayonne, which with all its stops in Biarritz and Anglet turns an eight-minute trip into forty. Luckily the bus stop is just a few minutes away from Bernard's apartment. I walk through the gate and buzz his apartment number. It is a large house that has been altered into a complex of 4 large apartments. There is a pebbled terrace with chairs and tables, whose earth toned rocks match the much larger stones that make up the building. A buzzer sounds and I push through the large red door to see Bernard waiting for me at the first door on the right.

"Teo! Come on in," he says greeting me with kisses to each cheek. "Make yourself at home."

His place is just as I expected. Completely feng-shui and easy going, with plush couches, hardwood floors, and some musical instruments around the room. There are bookcases and a record player at the end of the large salon style setting with stacks of records piled around them.

"I need to shower quite fast. Put some music on if you want and relax. If anyone comes just let them in."

I do just that. I place my drinks in the fridge and pour myself a large glass of sangria. Sergio Mendes' *Timeless* album is my choice for tunes as I relax looking out of his windows at the street. People are trickling by with their red and white outfits. Most of them are families and the elderly. They're clearing out before the real revelers show up. *Buzz!* I open the door to meet a group of women all dressed in their *feria* attire.

"*Tu n'es pas, B,*" says one jokingly.

"No. I'm T. Teo. B is in the shower," I say with a smile.

They all enter as we make our introductions. They complement my French. I ask if they're Basque. It turns out they all are, much to my liking as the idea of getting to know a Basque woman has been lingering in my mind since meeting Miren. I take all of their bottles of wine and place them in their proper place in the kitchen before preparing drinks for them. By the time Bernard gets out of the shower, passing briefly through the living area in just his underwear, we've already got a small soiree going.

"Oh la la, Teo! You've got things moving I see?" he says quickly wrapping his towel around his waist at the sight of Audrey, Florence, Jade, and Lea, who burst into laughter.

"Yes I've got it taken care of. Now please put some clothes on and come and join us!"

This is my speed. This is my pace. I would like to say that Bernard and I hosted only the four Basque beauties. However, being a man of considerable sociability, Bernard lives up this reputation. In just an hour the apartment is full, with most of the party goers adorned in the proper attire. It almost feels like we don't need Bayonne. Who could need it when we have *la Fête de Bernard* in full swing? There is a group sitting on the terrace smoking cigarettes and ganja, while having political debates. The true drunkards hover around the kitchen door waiting to refill their cups. I occupy myself with the third and more party focused group of dancers and hob nobbers who all have it in mind to head to into the streets once the evening reaches its peak. A few of us are dancing to the Bee Gees when the record stops.

"B!" I yell out of the window. He's sitting on the terrace with a cigarette in his hand and a slew of people surrounding him. "The music!"

"*Merde!*" he says. He jumps up from the group and somehow is able to hoist his long figure up into the window, which is several feet from the ground. "What has happened?"

"We need some good music," I say feeling a bit of slur in my words.

"I have got the remedy!" he says as he runs to his collection. In a few moments, the entire house delights as Marvin Gaye's *Got to Give It Up* begins to play with Bernard taking the lead vocals. "*I used to go out and partayyy!*"

He begins to shuffle around his apartment with a cigarette dangling from his mouth and I join him lighting an uncustomary cigarette of my own. We snap a few photos to mark the moment before he returns to the terrace, and I to the original group of ladies, one of which in particular. Audrey dances so controllably. Her movements graceful and calculated as her red belt sways with the turns of her hips, and her hair sways in front leaving her beautiful face only to be imagined. She tosses her hair back looking my way with a smile. I, still hoisting a cigarette in my mouth feel silly as my mouth drops, allowing the cigarette to fall to the floor.

"Shit," I say as I quickly grab it from the ground and put it out in an ashtray. "So, Audrey. Ladies. Shall we go into the city?"

"Yeah! Let's go!" shouts Lea who is already halfway out the door with the half full jug of sangria. The rest of us grab what drinks are available and follow her into the streets, which have changed a lot since I arrived. It's like last year all over again with buses filled with red and white pulling up to release their drunken passengers into the streets.

The five of us hold hands making a chain as we navigate the bodies. We stop occasionally to pour sangria into each other's mouths laughing as some spills onto our shirts and the ground. A street DJ has attracted a large vibrant crowd in front of a bar, so we stop to pick up where we left off at Bernard's. I grab Audrey spinning her to her delight. Her rhythm and beauty are tandem parallels, as her body tells my hands and feet where and how to move next. I feel like I could kiss her at any moment until Lea grabs her.

"C'mon! Let's go to the square!" Lea yells taking her hand leading her away as Audrey grabs my hand. We navigate the crowd, our quintet now made a trio. It is just like I remember from last year. Only the strong survive and once you're lost; *les ferias* have you. They won't give you back.

As we arrive on the outskirts of the mass it becomes apparent that Lea actually has brought us to meet some friends of hers. I soon get to know pretty well both of their boyfriends, and I shake their hands with a smile all the while thinking how good it is that I thought twice about kissing her. We all stand chatting for a moment until it dawns on me that I've become the fifth wheel.

If it wasn't for the music blaring from the stage, and the sea of bodies and probable promiscuities, I would have called it a night. However, the sangria won't let me and neither will Audrey who still seems intent on having me around. We enter the crowds. A group of red and white clad dancers take the stage with the DJ moving in unison to the beat, while a huge lighted projection of "*La Fête de Bayonne*" is blazoned on a brick wall in the background.

179

It doesn't take long before I find a willing dancer. With thousands of bodies colliding side by side we're forced to be as close as possible, and it takes only a couple of minutes to connect with the brunette's lips. Without names, we kiss as thousands of people are sure to do and have done. We disconnect and in that moment, someone grabs my arm. I turn to see Audrey. She attacks my face kissing me wildly, and I kiss back with my eyes still open in shock, looking out for her boyfriend who seems to be nowhere in sight.

The brunette grabs me back into her arms, kissing me gently, potently, as if to say I am hers for the night. I draw back dazed at the amazing kiss and turn to see Lea in the mass of people yelling at Audrey's boyfriend and pointing at me.

"Let's go!" I say to the nameless woman, taking her by the hand and quickly leading her out of the sea and into the alleys. The hour runs late. Just as expected. Every now and then there is some private corner, in some dim passage. That's where we find ourselves when I finally ask for her name.

"Aida."

"You are Basque?"

"Non, *belge*."

"I like Belgium...Close enough," I say. I pull her close to me doing my earnest justice to return the kiss which she so prudently placed on my lips earlier. We are a match made in revelry. She unbuttons my shorts and reaches in. I lift up her skirt while pondering the condom in my pocket. It seems as if we're made to consummate our *feria* in this alleyway, until I see, or at least I think I see, a glimmer of my angelic Clara passing by.

"*Putain!*" I say backing up nervously trying to zip up my pants.

"*Quoi*?! What is it?"

"Nothing! Nothing," I say with my eyes squinting in the distance. No one is there. However, the thought of my angel or any of the *Fantastiques* catching me in my immature promiscuity is too much. Maybe I'm both of these things, or perhaps even neither. I'd rather find out within the privacy of my room. "Where are you staying?"

"I'm at the youth hostel in Biarritz, in one the female dormitories."

"Not tonight," I say taking her hand. "I have a private room. Let's go."

180

It feels the essence of success to walk arm and arm in the chaos. Aida and I stroll near the Nive River, where there are still crowds of people. There is even a race taking place as two men see who can climb a light pole the fastest. The crowds cheer while throwing plastic bottles at them. We laugh a bit and kiss en route to the bus stop. It's just 3:30am, which is quite perfect because to wait until the last buses around 5:00am means being herded through metal barriers like cattle and possibly missing a ride home.

We enter giving the driver our tickets and head to the back of the relatively empty bus. We can hardly contain our kissing. I lean my head back against the headrest as she leans her head on my shoulder. At that moment, the most terribly timed of occasions, enters Katia and Camille.

"Ohhhh Teo!" laughs Katia. They come and sit on the seats facing us.

"Ladies, ladies!" I say quickly covering up my shock, which isn't hard to do considering the sangria to blood content ratio of my body. "How was your *feria*?"

"It was really fun Teo!" begins Katia. "We see what the fuss was about. We had to leave though because it was getting a bit crazy."

"Yes I agree. Who's your friend?" asks Camille.

"Oh, umm. This is…," I say before stopping. My mind draws a noticeable blank realizing the compromising situation I've put myself in.

"I'm Aida," she says with a bit of sass, as she reaches her hand out to greet them.

"Yes, yes! Belgium. Aida. Yes. This is Aida. Aida, these are my co-workers."

"Oh great! Did you have a great time at the *fête*? Is it your first time?" asks Aida moving past the fact that I'd forgotten her name.

"Oh yes! I had to see it for myself. What about you two? How do you know each other?" asks Camille inquisitively. I still sit silently with quiet horrors exploding in my brain.

"We just met tonight. We were dancing and he kissed me. No wait. I kissed him. Pftt. I don't know anymore."

"Oh. I see," says Camille slowly nodding her head. I cast a glance to Katia with a smile, but she knows me too well to look into my eyes. She knows I'm embarrassed.

"It was really something. We actually went a bit earlier and saw some of carnivals and played some games before getting to the parties," says Camille.

"Those things are nice, but I just love dancing in the streets. Don't you? Did you meet someone tonight?" asks Aida.

"Oh not me! I have a boyfriend. He's hardly comfortable with me even being here," says Katia.

"Oh! You're a good girlfriend! What about you, Camille? Some boyfriend looking out for you too?"

"Oh, not at all. I don't have a boyfriend, but I don't think some guys would have cared. I would try to dance, but they kept trying to kiss me. It was funny at first and then it got pretty desperate," she says simply glancing at me in a flash. "There's a lot more to *la Fête* then dancing and kissing strangers, but I think I got to see a bit of it all."

By now I am looking out the window. By now I am far, far, from here. Take me back to sanity. Render me unconscious to my consciousness. Aida's hand rests on my leg, while Camille reemerges in my mind. Aida places her head on my shoulder for the last twenty minutes of our ride. I sit in silence. Camille and Katia exchange a few memories laughing about the entire night. I can feel her looking at me on occasion, but I just ignore her glances. Even as the four of us walk down the hill to the hostel there is nothing for me to say. Only now does violating company policy to confess my crush to Camille seem like a good option. She's single and after everything that's happened I simply don't care anymore. We arrive at the hostel and enter using our keys for the back door by our office.

"Hey, Camille. You have a second?" I say.

"I'm quite tired, Teo. I've got to bring the youth to class tomorrow, so I should get some rest. Lunch tomorrow?"

"Ok...*Bonne Nuit, les filles*," I say as they disappear down the hallway leaving Aida and me.

We stand just at the office door. She moves closer to me and we begin to kiss. She wraps her arms around my waist, but I don't return the sentiment.

"So, Teo. Shall we go to this 'private room' of yours?"

"No, Aida. Maybe another time. I have a lot of work to do tomorrow," I say half-reluctantly. She swiftly removes her hands from around me and backs up.

"I see. *Connard*," she says as she walks down the opposite way of the hallway into her dormitory room. She's right. I am an asshole.

I open the office door. There's a bottle of sangria in the fridge with my name on it. With the office door safely locked, I shuffle to my room. There's a music playlist on my computer made for nights like these. I turn on the lights and look at the mess of clothes around the room. Katia would cringe if she saw this. Amos Lee's *Black River* plays. He sings about the sweet whisky that's "gonna take his cares away." Perhaps this sangria can take mine away. I engage in a battle with the bottle to see which one of us will become empty first. Half-way through, it wins. I slump over. Confused and full of *feria*.

Chapter 12: The Joker and The Angel

The phone rings. It rings again. It rings once more until it rings no more. Instead, there is a knock at my door. I finally open my eyes, shielding them from the sunlight which shines unrelenting through the window I left open last night. I look down at my filthy ferias outfit. The morning after, sullied in sangria spots. It looks pretty damn ridiculous.

"*Attendez*," I yell as I hoist myself out of bed. I shuffle to the door not thinking twice about my appearance, and feel probably just as ridiculous when I see Hermann standing there.

"Rise and shine, Teo. Did you forget there is a program to manage?" he says looking a bit unimpressed with my dirty *feria* attire. "Nice clothes."

I ask him for a minute so I can make a wardrobe change, but it doesn't matter. Taking shower and brushing my teeth does nothing to change how filthy I feel inside. Partially from the alcohol still within my veins, and the rest from the bits and pieces of the evening's events which are slowly coming back to me. I emerge a minute later as promised. We walk down the hall and to the right through the double doors, before taking the stairs. I'm assuming we're heading straight for the office, but instead he hangs a right out the front doors of the hostel and heads in the direction of the lake. Shit. He doesn't want anyone to hear how loud his already booming voice can become.

We arrive at a bench looking out unto the lake. Its waters are deep blue and serene, as he asks me to take a seat. He takes a place right next to me on the bench and sits in silence before finally speaking up in a calm tone.

"Teo, is everything alright?" he asks looking in my direction. I purse my lips and shake my head.

"Not exactly. I guess I have a few more problems going on than just a hangover."

"Business life is business. We will get to that, but it's your personal comings and goings. Normally, I wouldn't ask, but I feel we have that understanding to speak freely. It seems...Well it seems to be affecting

184

your work. Everyone has noticed it. The team, the main office, even Augustine. You're doing just enough to survive it seems. I know this is not your field. *Merde!* This has even been made extra difficult with the Reda situation. But what's the story?"

"*Je suis perdu.* I'm in a space I don't know. I can't define it. I, I don't recognize it. I tried to let it tell me how to be, and that just got out of hand. I tried to let others define it for me, but they were all wrong. I was in a different situation last summer and thought I could figure some things out by coming again."

"You know, Teo. You and I have some things in common. We roll the dice. We take risks. That's why I approved you to come for the first summer, and is one of the many reasons why I invited you back for this one."

"I appreciate that...I mean part of the reason I am here is so I work with you again. I figured I still had a few things to learn about rendering services."

"We can always learn something about the service, Teo. But the service comes from an understanding of what we owe ourselves. Self-respect. Sometimes you've just got to be able to take a decision for yourself, and that is the best service you can render to others. It makes you a better person. You can do better for others if you're in form, which is why you not being in form troubles me. You were stronger in your resolve at the beginning of this summer. I could tell you'd grown. Now it seems some new troubles have found you."

"You remind me of my uncle. You know? He would sit down and talk to me about these things. He...He was a man who rendered services. I grew up around him. He'd ask me to go on a ride with him to the fields to pick vegetables, and then we'd bring them to folks in the community. Those trips to San Sebastian remind me of that. I suppose I'm just looking for my field to pick from. I thought I once knew what and where that was. I hoped to find it here."

"You're so dramatic!" he says with a deep laugh.

"I'm bearing my heart here, man!"

"I know, I know. But listen. You have decisions. You are the only one who can make those. Sometimes they work, and sometimes they don't. But you still have to live with them, you understand?"

"*Ouais.*"

185

"I made a lot of choices in my life. God, I was a wild card, hopping on trains. I worked here and there. Some of it was brilliant and other times it was just a *bordel de merde*. I took it in stride. I don't know if it was half and half, but it was what it was. You have woman troubles. That's nothing new. Getting one doesn't make those go away. You will have a whole new set of concerns then! Ha! But the least you can do is decide for yourself."

"You're right," I say nodding my head. "I've got to be willing to make a decision, and stick with it."

"Exactly," he says clapping his hands loudly. "Now. *Allez op!* We have an issue. The budget has gone to hell."

We walk back to the office and pull up the spreadsheet. He came here personally to respond to yesterday's e-mail. It seems the mix up in personnel at the corporate office has caused a vacuum. Sure, Reda got his job, and we were able to *physically* do our jobs, but it's been a damn task and half to get an answer about our funding. He explains that it's because a large booking company has yet to pay their fees.

"Hermann, look. I've emailed them and even called almost every day asking when we'll get a deposit. They keep saying it's coming. I've used the recreational budget to pay for transportation and even used deposits to pay off our vendors. We've got over half the clients leaving this weekend and an empty cash box."

"Don't worry, Teo. I remember you told me about this, but I just thought all of this cinema would be resolved by now...I mean, where are we? What is this?" he says as he tosses his hands up looking out of the window shaking his head. He takes out his phone and makes a call, which I can only imagine is to sort things out because it's in German. At the end, he aggravatedly presses the screen to hang up. "*Merde*."

"What?"

"It's the same salad they've been feeding you," he says as he stands to his feet. He slowly paces around the room.

"What will we do? I need at least a couple of thousand euros by tomorrow to settle everything."

"Don't worry. That's it. I'm making a decision. Can you get me the exact amount needed?" he asks. I go through my spreadsheets and a few minutes later arrive at the number. "Perfect. Let's go to the bank."

We hop in his car and head into the city center. He has a crazed look on his face of almost self-satisfaction.

"What is it?"

"I am going to front the money to the program budget. I'll need you to write up a receipt and invoice to send to the main office."

"Are you sure? It's not your fault?"

"Yes, but it is my responsibility in the long run. No worries. Despite, how shall I say, my personality, I've done well for myself in all these years."

"Well there it is," shaking my head in pleasant awe.

"I told you we would arrive. We always arrive. It's a game and I always have the joker up my sleeve," he says looking at me with a grin and taking his hands off the wheel as he points to where his sleeve would be, if he were even wearing a long sleeve shirt. It seems like he lives for moments like this.

There is a lingering hangover. At least all of the business affairs are taken care of. Even the site of beers in the fridge causes my head to pound harder, so I don't open it for the entire day. Hermann jokes with me after getting back from the bank offering me a glass of his rosé. I almost vomit, and nervously sip my water without turning to acknowledge his jokes.

It's time for dinner and today's barbeque seems to be just in time. Katia and Adriana, being the champions they are, have already taken the adult clients into the city for one of their prepaid nights on the town, leaving Camille to check in on the youth students who eat at the hostel. Slowly the night is coming back to me.

I don't know how Ilya could have gotten it wrong, but I don't think it matters. I pass through the line seeing that the youth are already eating and chatting. Some yell out to me asking how the night was, but I ignore them taking a seat by myself still wearing my sunglasses. At least the food looks and smells delicious, and I am anticipating the first bite when someone yells out my name.

"Teo, Teo, Teo!" yells Clara as she and the other *Fantastiques* come and sit at my table. "You said you wanted to talk to us, so now we have come to talk to you!"

"Oh. I am so happy," I say as I place my fork down with a bit of uneaten sausage still skewered. "You ladies have been making trouble at the school."

"No, no, Teo," begins Ester. "We've been going to school."

"Yes, true. But when you arrive you play on your phones and don't participate."

"Oh. Well maybe," she responds.

"Look, you don't have that much time left here. Just do me a favor and go to class and be good students. It will help me out a lot, ok?"

"Of course, Teo. Anything for you!" says Miri.

"And now it is your turn, Mr. Program Manager," says Sandra. "You were out partying all night. We passed by your office to ask something this morning and you were not there. Can you explain yourself?"

"I, uh. Wow. I already got in trouble today, and now you guys are gonna get on me to?"

"Yes, of course, Teo. You look out for us, and we look at for you. That is what friends are for," says Clara with her angelic smile.

"Well, thank you. It was a long night."

"Oh we know," says Ester.

"Shhh!" says Miri.

"Wait! You were there? You went to Bayonne?" I ask scared out of mind. It *was* them who passed that alley. If they saw me with Aida, I'll never forgive myself.

"Well it's too late now, Miri. He knows. Yeah, we were there," says Ester putting her head down.

"We thought we saw you," begins Clara timidly. "You were running almost holding some woman's hand, but you disappeared. Then we ran into these assholes."

"What assholes?!"

"We don't know who they were. Just some guys trying to dance with us," adds Sandra.

"Yeah and one tried to kiss Clara," adds Miri.

"What?!" I respond.

"It's fine, nothing happened. They were just being stupid."

"No, I don't think it's fine. Are you all ok?"

"Yes of course, Teo. I mean it is not the first time we've gone out. We do it often in Spain."

"I know, I know. It's just...This nightlife can get the best of you. People can be...promiscuous. People can do some pretty silly things, trust me I know," I say. If they could see my eyes they would have watched them looked across the terrace to Camille who is dining with some German students. "You're young ladies, so just be careful. Just do your studies, finish school. If you have a dream, go for it. Don't try to meet guys in this craziness. Try at nice places. Take your time. Ok?"

"Yeah, that sounds better. Maybe at school," says Miri.

"Or at a cafe. Yeah a cafe would be nice, calm, and mature," says Clara. I begin to chuckle a little and think about Derlenzistda for the first time in a while. I should know a thing or two about romantic relationships in cafes. They all nod and look to see how I'll respond. "That's a good place, yeah?"

"Sure. That's a fine place," I say with a smile. "Just do your best to make good decisions. You know? Be good to others, and yourself. I think that's a good place to begin."

"That's great advice, Teo! Hey can we make a photo with you?" asks Clara.

"Yes, yes!" adds Miri.

"No," I say finally taking a bite of the delicious food. They ignore this response, much like they've been ignoring their teachers, and gather around me just as Camille is passing by.

"Hey, Camille! Can you take a photo of us?" asks Clara.

"Sure!" she says as she places her tray down. I remove my glasses and smile as best I can with a lingering hangover and the sun in my eyes.

"Thanks, Teo!" says Clara as they run off. I can only hope that they're ok. That after this summer they can make good decisions for their lives. I don't know if anything I said helps or matters to them, but I said it. Even if I'm not sure I can live up to it, maybe they can. I'm still pondering on my Fantastic Four when, Camille speaks up.

"Hey, you said you wanted to talk to me about something?"

"Oh," I begin, trying to remember exactly what that was. "Yes, but nothing pressing. I, uh. Just wanted to say thank you."

"Really? What for?"

"You're amazing. When they said you were coming, I was completely against it. I didn't want a replacement, which I think you knew."

"Yes, I could tell at first," she responds with a smile.

189

"Sorry. Well, in any case. I am glad you came. You've done a knock up job, and I don't think the season could have gone any better without you."

"Awww. That's sweet, Teo. Thank you. I've enjoyed my time here. I am almost sad that I have to leave so soon" she says. She looks at me the way she did that day when I hurt my knee. "Do you have travel plans for after the season?"

"No. Not yet. Why?"

"Well if you find yourself in Germany, let me know. Yah? I'll be in Berlin for the rest of the summer."

"If I find myself anywhere near Berlin, you will be the first to know," I say with a smirk.

I remember now. Last night I wanted to confess some type of drunken love to her. Saying anything would have been an incoherent disaster. But this. This is something else. It happened so fast. This job will end in two weeks and by then everyone will be back to their respective places, just as I will be most likely held up at the cafe. I'm not sure if I'll pass by Berlin, but if I do it will be just that. It will be for what it's worth, just like Camille's time here. Step-by-step. Moment by moment. If anything at all.

That's my decision.

Chapter 13: *El Camino De Santiago*

With high season over, there simply aren't enough clients to keep the kitchen open all the time, which means a return to my culinary arts. It's nice to make some trips to the market again. The Julien debacle has come and gone, but I still peek around corners as if he could show up any moment. Fortunately, he never does, and I can keep about my domesticated ways. I pick up a six pack of Leffe Blonde, which is obviously the first ingredient in making a proper meal. I add some eggs, spices, chorizos, fish. I'm not sure what I plan do with all of it, but I think Katia could figure something out. I stop by a cheese shop for some *ossau iraty*. It's a Basque cheese which I first tasted during my days in La Roche Sur-Yon, before I had any idea that I'd end up here. It tastes the same even after all this time. The end of high season causes for an insanely abrupt drop in clientele, for our program and the hostel. Without revelers for *les ferias* and *Les Quatre Fantastiques* around, things are almost quiet. I can use quiet.

I open a beer and bring my eggs, chorizo, and spices into the kitchen. I put on some Charles Aznavour while sipping the cool delight. It's nice to think that anyone passing by the kitchen window, en-route to the bar, would look in and think, 'that guy is cookin' up a storm,' and perhaps I even feel that way as a dice up chorizo to mix in with eggs. Truth is, I have no idea what I'm doing. It's pretty hard to fuck up breakfast foods, so as long as I don't burn them it's probably ok.

A woman enters the kitchen and is startled by me belting out lyrics to *La Bohème* with a beer in my hand. She laughs a bit and quickly grabs something from the fridge, placing it on the stove just behind me. I stop singing and settle for a humming instead. In a fit of curious courtesy, I ask;

"Does the music bother you? I can turn it off."

"Oh, um. I don't speak French," she responds. She's not American, or even British by the sounds of it.

"Is the music ok?" I ask in English.

"Oh. Yes. No worries," she says with a soft voice. I continue to cook, humming from time to time. I finish, wash the dishes, and leave without a word towards the bar area. I sit in silence. Eating breakfast food for dinner. It's damn good. Edible at least. I should have made more.

With a clean plate and empty bottle, I stand to my feet. I toss the bottle in the recycling bin, and am walking back towards the reception when I see Hamza talking to the woman from the kitchen. She's wearing all black, leggings, a tank top, and shawl around her shoulders. Her black hair is long. She laughs at him blinking her eyes behind the thick black squared lenses. I try to pass covertly.

I'm fine with quiet. I'm doing ok. I'm so ok that I skip the kitchen altogether and take the plate into the office. It can be put back later. I sit at my desk for a few minutes twiddling my thumbs. There's nothing to do, so I grab another Leffe from the fridge and put it in one of my plastic cups. As I lock up the office, I decide to let my feet take me where they want. Honestly, I could go outside and sit on one the picnic tables or I could make some more eggs. I could take a stroll by the lake or even just stay in the office. There are many options, but I take the most interesting one.

Hamza sits at the reception desk as I *un-casually* come strolling by. I pretend to look at some pamphlets about destinations and surf classes, until finally he can't take it anymore.

"Ok, Teo. What is it?"

"Oh. Hamza. Hi. Sup dude? Um, who was that?"

"Woman in black?"

"Her? Oh, I was going to ask about something else, but since you mention it...."

"Teo. If you didn't already know you were crazy, I'd tell you you are myself," he pauses for a second as we both look around to see if anyone is near. "She's magnificent, yeah?"

"I tried, man. I tried to just pass her by, but I can't help it."

"She's sweet, Teo. You know we have a lot of people passing through here, and sometimes they can be rude. Not this one. She's a darling."

"I think I could feel it. She's not here like the others. I can see a surfer from a mile away, and I already know who is here for *les ferias* before they even put on the red and white. I couldn't read her."

"It's the Camino."

"*El Camino de Santiago*? She's doing that?"

"That's what she says. You should talk to her. She's really nice, Teo."

"Maybe."

She sits on the back terrace. Alone, with hardly even the sun to keep her company. Her legs are folded into the chair as she sits writing in a notepad, with her face just inches from the page. Only the most pensive of words can be found there. Inches away. The closer one is to the page the more earnestly they've considered their thoughts and inspirations. That, or they need glasses. She's not wearing hers.

"Excuse me," I begin, almost timidly. "Would you like some company?"

She looks up from her notepad, startled at my voice breaking through the evening's silence. I can see the thoughts and fancies turning and toiling behind her eyes.

"Sure! Please," she responds. I take a seat at the opposite end of the table and stick my hand out, as she introduces herself. "I'm Sara. Your name is?"

"Teo. *Mucho Gusto.*"

"*Igualmente*," she says pausing for a moment. "So, you enjoy singing?"

"Yes. What do you enjoy?"

"I play some music. Nice weather is always great. I love children! Um, I hope to work with them someday," she says looking down at her notebook.

"Will you? I mean...Is that what you want to do in life?"

"I have a lot of questions at this point. It's rather complicated."

"Is that why you're doing the Camino?"

"Does it really show? How could you know this?" she asks laughingly.

"Well I can't take all the credit. Folks doing the Camino don't have the same...the same aura as most people who come here. I asked around. I hope that's not strange."

"I don't think it is. The Camino is open. It is a path to discovery. To perhaps answer questions. What would that be without meeting a person or two?"

"*Vale.* Why all black? Is there a dress code?" I ask, immediately feeling that I've pried too deep, too fast. She looks up from the notebook. Her eyes like damp shimmering glass. "I'm sorry. I shouldn't have asked."

"No please. It is fine. No one ever asks. You came to me with curiosity. I ask that you only return the favor when it is my chance to ask something."

"Agreed."

"It is my father. I have many issues with his death."

"Was it recent?"

"No, no. Many years ago, now," she says. She wipes away a single tear. Just one. One that she's learned to cry. "I suppose I have not made peace with it. Problems. Issues. I just think many things in my life I am not happy with come from losing him and I can't move on to those new things without dealing with this."

"Working with children perhaps?"

"Yes, in many ways. They give me so much life. They're so precious to me, Teo. I want to be happy in my heart so I can be the best for them...Does that make sense?"

"That makes life, Sara. That's life."

"Well, that is a way to see it. I think I like this idea," she says forcing a smile. Her eyes are no longer glass. "And you? What is life for you? What do you do here?"

I laugh ridiculously loud grabbing at my hair, rubbing my face in pleasant agony.

"What?! What is funny?"

"We're going to need some wine for this. Red ok?"

"*Vale. Vale.*"

After returning from the bar I start at the beginning; at least what I think I can remember being a true beginning. I tell her of my first travels, and how those lead to new ones. I tell her how I wrote a book. How I broke one particular heart to continue traveling and writing and how that all lead to many hearts including my own stranded along the roads of my past. When I think she's becoming bored, I tell her I'll stop. She asks me to keep going. So, I do. She listens like it's a saga. Her eyes are damp again when I talk about my uncle, but are alive with humorous fervor when I tell her about Hermann's influence and the likes of the Full Reda. I tell her how I'd known so many lovers since Derlenzistda, and how I spent last summer learning to accept who and where I was. She rests her head on her fist when I tell her about everything that's happened this summer and seems deeply concerned with my search for definition. Soon the sun sets. We're still on the terrace. I'm wrapping up my story, while she continues doing what I'm not sure I've given someone the chance to do before: listen.

"So now what, Teo? You're at the end of this season, and the end of a bottle of wine. What happens next?"

"I'll probably meet a nice woman named Sara, and tell her too much about myself because she asks. She'll question what's next. I'll tell her I have no idea."

"Tell me something. Well, that is if I am not asking something to personal," she begins. "Why all of these women? You said you cared for this girl in the U.S., so why spend time with so many other women?

"A year ago I wouldn't have had an answer for you, and I probably would think you were asking something too personal. However, I don't think it's too much to ask. Before her, travelling and my work were all I cared about. They consumed me, inspired me. When I came to France it was for those reasons, but I didn't expect to actually miss her. I didn't know that I was even capable of caring about someone like that," I say. I pause and stare at my empty wine glass. I refill it, take a sip and continue. "I'd never felt that way before, Sara. I didn't know how to deal with missing her, and searching for that answer began to consume me. I suppose I did the things I did to try to make that feeling for her go away, but none of that worked. It wasn't until I became accepting of myself that I found some semblance of peace. I can truthfully say that. However, I still feel on the edge. I've made peace with past, and understand that I have to navigate the present. It's the future that I worry about."

"I see. Well, I may have some ideas for you."

"Please. Tell me."

"It seems like you have placed yourself in this box. This small room. On the wall is written your past, even the words of what others have said you are. You read them so much that you do not write anymore. You do not dream. You started talking about travelling and being inspired by adventure, but then with all of these situations with women and parties you have stopped mentioning your journeys. Travel was your dream, was it not?"

"It was all I thought of."

"And now, at least from what you tell me, all you can think of are those things that happened in your travels. You are blinded," she says enthusiastically like she's had some revelation. She feels around the table with her eyes closed until her hand lands on her glasses. She places them on her face and opens her eyes. "You think only of what you have seen and not what you are going to do. You started looking at things for what they were instead of for what they can be."

I look at her. She sits smiling waiting for my response. I crack a crippled smile, but it's at least a true one. My eyes water a bit and I wipe away the only tear I've got left before it can roll down my cheek. She's right. Perhaps it's what Hermann and anyone else who tried to give me advice has been trying to say for a long time. She makes it so simple.

"So then what?" I begin in a timid tone, and wide open heart. "It's perfect, what you say. They're the truest words I've heard in a long time. But how?

"Do you believe in God, Teo?"

"It's been awhile since someone has asked me that...Yes. Why?"

"I had stopped for years, but this journey reminded me of some things. Faith. It is faith. Perhaps, the way I feel about helping children is the same as you do for adventures. We feel that way for a reason and if we ignore it we cannot have the happiness. Our pasts and the pains, they keep us from exploring these passions of ours."

"And we must explore these passions to go into our future?"

"*Si.* We must have faith that on the other side of our pain and confusion is a promise. A promise of not just better days, but better versions of ourselves."

In that moment. With those words. I understand. I drink. Even wine takes time to ferment, and even longer to age into finery. Why should we be any different? Humans ferment. We cause trouble where there was none, whether through malice or ignorance, and then wonder how things become so sour. But with time we become savory. Once crushed grapes under the weight of our indiscretions, we can arrive in a new form. We become like liquid flowing around obstacles. With a little time, if we can keep our shit together in a bottle of wisdom, we may even become worth something. I drink again, before locking eyes with Sara.

"You have to work with children. The world will be a better place if you do."

"Oh my! Thank you," she says as she brushes back her hair with her left hand. "I don't know. I am just speaking what comes to mind. I have had a lot of time to think during *el Camino*."

"Well, don't stop thinking...I guess you will be back on the road tomorrow?"

"Yes. This is my only night here," she says. "But hey! I was going to pass it alone, and now I have met you! We both can go into the future now! That is something, right?"

"It is! It needs to be nothing more."

We're interrupted by a group exiting the bar doors. The night is cool and official. I hear them say they're going to go for another round, so I offer to buy it with my staff pricing. They join our table; Emiel, from Holland, Manon, from Germany, and Jardena, from New Zealand. They're touristic enthusiasm and conversation is much welcomed, especially now that Sara and I seem to be looking to more positive pastures. Sara doesn't say much. She just listens, smiles, and every now and then writes something in her notebook.

"You want some more wine?" I ask her

"No, no. I shouldn't. I have to be up early tomorrow to continue. I will go to sleep now."

"That's probably the best idea. In another life, if we had more time, I would have loved to take you for a coffee."

"In that life, I would have been happy to join you," she says. She scribbles again in her notebook and tears off a piece to hand to me. It has her e-mail. "Until then I will just have to say you owe me a coffee. Agreed?"

"Agreed."

Chapter 14: The Amorous Conquistador

This hostel has become a home. I have my room, an office, and a kitchen. Hermann is like the grandfather who drops in as I look out for my sisters, Katia and Adriana. Our cousins, Hamza, Gil, Augustine, Aude, and Julie might as well live with us, and Uncle Bernard is never too far away. The perfect thing about this home is that it's fit to entertain and at any moment we can have a visitor from any place in the world. It's beautiful. It's chaos. It's crazy. I love it.

It'd be a lie to say that talking with Sara had turned me into some eunuch monk, as my libido is still quite intact and in a league of its own. However, at the very least, it inspired me to think in a way that I'd long forgotten. So, enthralled in the valleys of my life, I'd forgotten how many stories waited behind a friendly smile or gesture. Furthermore, I'd forgotten what it was like to interact with someone without the intention of them being a potential hero to my issue or a defining factor to the almost four months I've basked in Biarritz. I don't care about any of that.

I'm only occupied with these days are the stories of strangers. Where they're coming from, and the reasons why they bothered to visit at all, arouses me. I admire everyone; from the clueless American interrail-goer, to the well bronzed vagabond, who if the moment fancied would be just as fine camping under a tree near the lake.

With a significantly dwindled clientele and more than enough staff, it's safe to say we've got the easy life. Every night, I'm sitting down with different travelers. Some of them invite me to their country saying that I'll have a place to stay during my impending vacation. Others just want some advice on where to go in the city. Everyone who drinks with me gets the benefits of my staff pricing which is a cheap way to make friends. Emiel, Manon, and Jardena have kept me good company since my encounter with Sara. We've been drinking the last couple of night at the hostel bar and I'm content to past the last nights of my summer getting to know them.

"So none of you knew each other before coming to Biarritz?" I ask.

"Well, we do now, Teo. Jardena and I have been sharing a twin room, but we only met the day we met you," says Manon.

"I arrived the day before them," begins Emiel. "I met them that same day and showed them a bit of the city."

"Yeah, it seemed like a good idea," says Manon sarcastically. "It was all fine until we tried to take a trip to the city center. After thirty minutes, we realized that we had passed through all of Biarritz and Anglet and were in the heart of Bayonne!"

"What, what?" he says. "I knew where we were going. I just was, uh, giving a grand tour."

"Oh this is brilliant," I say taking a sip of my wine.

"What is?" asks Manon.

"I don't know. The hostel life perhaps? I mean, think about it. You three have just met after a couple of days. I've been here for almost two months now and was already here last summer."

"Perfect! So, you have to tell us everything. You can be our expert guide to all things Biarritz," says Jardena.

"Ha! I could tell you a lot of things, but I'm quite tired from this whole summer. Let's keep it simple. These days I'm just a guy who likes wine, and in my *expertise*, I'd say it's time for another bottle."

"Best. Guide. Ever!" yells Emiel as the others laugh. These are my kind of people.

I like to think that there is some new beginning, but where is the end? What if something you thought was over was really just in waiting? The volcano which historically destroyed an entire city and has been inactive suddenly roars to life. You can't sweep Vesuvius under a rug. Nope. You just gotta deal with it. The next day I am sitting in the office when a voice rings out from behind the door. It takes me a second to take my eyes off the screen and even longer to respond.

"Iza…," I say as she enters the office smiling with her arms open. I forget that I have legs, and reach my arms out before standing to greet her. It's not until her hands grab mine that my knees spring me unto my feet. I hug her tightly and plant a kiss on each cheek. We stand in silence. Those sandy nights come rushing into my mind. Those green eyes followed me back home, brought messages, and postcards telling of this moment. Now it's upon me.

"I made it!"

"I can see that. Please take a seat," I say. She pulls up a chair. I again forget that I have legs as I remain standing. "I thought that you weren't coming."

"I thought so too. Biarritz is such an expensive city, and there are really so many other places I hadn't seen yet. I met some carpoolers who were on their way to St. Jean de Luz, so I had them drop me off here! Um. Why are you standing?"

"Oh, sorry. I suppose I'm just shocked to see you," I respond as I finally take a seat.

"A good shock?"

"Yeah. I think so. Tell me everything."

She tells me about her studies, about her family. She talks about all of the places she's seen in her travels while waving her hands and laughing. I want to take it for what it's worth; I want to immerse myself in her thoughts and words. But all I can think about is the past. Those nights in the sand. Those messages we exchanged during the last year about what it would be like to see each other again. I was almost relieved by the idea that she hadn't showed up. In the scope of everything that happened this summer where would an old flame fit in? Upon arriving, it seemed to be the most ideal situation, because it was familiar. However, this familiarity was almost forgotten as the days passed to the point where I didn't think it would happen.

"...and then I made it back home, and spent some time with my family. I've been traveling for a bit now going to some music festivals. *Phew.* And you?" she asks.

"Huh? Oh. Well it's the same, but not. I suppose. It's been a long summer but soon I will have holidays, so I can't really complain about that. Are you just stopping in? Were you able to get a room?"

"Yes, I've taken one for a night or two. I'm not sure how long I will stay," she says looking off into the evening's possibilities. We go silent and lock eyes. In that moment, it's no stretch of the imagination that we could revisit last summer's festivities on the spot, but Hermann comes walking in.

200

"Salut Program Manager, are you ready?"

"Oh. Yes. Iza, this is Hermann."

"Sure. I remember him from last summer," she says as he greets her with kisses.

"Sorry young lady, but I need to steal the Program Manager for a moment. He actually needs to do some work today!"

"Op la! Hermann, I've been working all day!"

"On what?"

"You know...My administration."

"Ha. Administration. What salad. We have almost no clients, but somehow you still have your *administratif.* Let's go."

I tell Iza that I will be around tonight and that we will be showing a movie in the bar if she's around. She says it's fine and that she had some surfing courses to do. She gives me two slow kisses on the cheeks, leaving me with an evening of possible scenarios in my head.

"Are you fucking joking?"

"No, Reda! She's here, man!" I say on my phone as I sit by the lake. Normally, sitting by the lake calms me down, but today it's not working. Talking to him isn't helping too much either. "I didn't see this coming."

"Shit, neither did I, boss...Ok. So, what you gonna do? You gonna fuck her?"

"I don't know. I don't know."

"Teo, you two talked about it on and off for almost a year. Get this woman anywhere near the sand, and you're screwed. Well, she will be too!"

"You're not helping."

"I don't know why you call me about these things. You know how I am. In any case, I'm too busy these days."

"Oh? Don't have time for your old Program Manager?"

"How can I when I am the Program Manager for the largest program in the company?"

"They promoted you again?"

"Fuck yeah. It happened a few days ago. Other person couldn't cut it."

"And you're still going to Paris on weekends?"

"I'm Program Manager of a 25-person staff with a salary that I negotiated, and yes I still spend my weekends in Paris. I make more than you now."

"If they don't look out you'll be running the company next year, Reda. Or should I call you 'The Phoenix?'"

"Fuck that! This is the last summer for 'The Phoenix'. Maybe it's over for 'The Amorous Conquistador' as well."

"The what? No, no, no, that name doesn't work at all."

"T. You spent over the last two years trying to conquer lust, love, and all of the above. You fucking flew across Atlantic Ocean for it. What about that name doesn't describe you?"

"Damn. When you're right. You're *really* right. Did you just come up with that?"

"Nah. I've been saving it for the right time," he says. We share a good, solid laugh.

"Thanks for listening."

"Anytime" he says changing the tone of his voice. "Hey man. Thanks for everything. I mean even last year hooking me up with this gig, and being supportive with all that bullshit at the beginning of the summer. It worked itself out. I just had to keep living I guess. I don't really know what to tell you about Iza. She's a nice girl, with a great body. You know what I'd do, but maybe it's just like everything else. Keep moving. Whatever happens will happen."

"Will do, my friend. *A la proche.*"

"*A plus, mon ami.*

That actually helped in some way, and perhaps in the only way that could be helped. She came here to see me, this much is for sure, and is the only certainty. I take a moment to sit by the lake. *Lac Mouriscot* never lost its incredible serenity. Even with rain clouds moving in from the coast, it's still calm. It's still beautiful.

The movie hour comes and goes. I sit behind the bar drinking with Julie. There is no sign of Iza, but my new buddies, Manon, Emiel, and Jardena, seem to be sticking it out for the night. It's pretty bizarre, and I don't know why we planned a movie night when the majority of our clients are surfers who spent their nights in the city center at New Quay dancing and drinking. Adriana and Katia have the night off for a girl's night, and they deserve it for having braved a long summer. However, nights at the hostel bar have become fun and simple, and with my trio of travelers around I'll at least have some company.

After the movie, I grab two bottles of wine from the bar and place them on a table telling Manon and the gang to come over. Emiel insists that he adds something to the occasion this time, and I can hardly refuse a man who is trying to render services. He makes an anticipatory order for a bottle of rosé at the bar, most likely planning for the likely event that the four of us finish the first two.

"Have you done this every day this summer, Teo?" asks Jardena.

"Yes."

"And you still work?"

"Well. Things are done a bit differently here. That and it is the summer," I say.

"To the summer!" proclaims Emiel sticking out his glass for a toast. We meet in the middle of table. "To doing things differently."

We all take hefty sips of our wine. For a moment, a strange sensation washes over me. I remember the first time a strange place became familiar; La Roche-Sur-Yon. I learned how things functioned there, but I've never felt that way about Biarritz until now. It takes me back to those first adventures, to maybe even that joy which Sara hopes that I find again.

"*Bonsoir,*" rings a pleasant voice. We all look to see Iza enter with a bag of food and a bottle of wine. "Mind if I join?"

"The more the merrier!" shouts Emiel, which gives me the sneaking suspicion that if he's not drunk already he's certainly on his way. I take a chair for Iza and a glass from the bar. After some brief introductions, the five of us embark down a wine laden path. Four bottles turn into eight as the calmness of the bar deceives us into feelings of sobriety.

"Teo, are you drunk?" asks Manon.

"I don't remember the last time I was drunk."

"Is it because you have a great tolerance?"

"No. It's because I am drunk when it happens. Haha!" I say. We laugh uncontrollably. You would think that it was a proper party with the amount of noise we make and by now even Julie has been drawn into our revelry.

"Is it true that you two know each other?" asks Emiel to Iza.

"Yes. Actually, I met Teo here last summer."

"Yes! Finally," begins Emiel. "Teo has been holding out on us. He won't tell us his crazy stories. You have to know something. Was Teo Vaga the same?"

"Hmmm," she begins looking at me pensively and stroking her chin. "He seems more relaxed now. The Teo I remember was a man about town, so I'm surprised to see him here at the hostel. He used to prefer trips to the beaches with pretty women."

"I knew it!" shouts Emiel triumphantly. "Was he a 'barman' last year too?"

"*Bah, oui!*" shouts Julie. "I can say that is for sure!"

"I deny nothing! I've done the things I've done, and I'll do the things I'll do," I say giving myself a toast. I polish off the last of my wine. Iza looks at me with a smile.

It's as if she knows what she's doing when she asks me to join her for a cigarette. We step outside. The rain clouds, which once hovered above Mouriscot, have found their way to the hostel and released their tears. With a half full, or half empty, bottle of rosé we sit under the canopy side by side. She lights up a cigarette. Funny. I don't remember her smoking last summer. She lights up one for me. I don't remember me smoking either.

"It is really nice to see you again, Teo," she says calmly. "I wasn't sure if you would still be here."

"It's nice to see you too, Iza. I admit. I didn't think to see you either. I'm glad things have gone well for you," I say. "Do you have plans for the rest of the summer?"

"No...I'm just going with the flow," she says running her finger along the rim of her glass before looking up to me. "What about you?"

"I have some things to do back in the U.S., but not before some more adventures. I need to go back to Portugal, and I have some business in Bordeaux. I've been debating about Berlin all summer it seems. Anyways, I'll travel for a month and then I'll see what will become of me," I say looking into the dark sky.

It is in that moment, that meaningful passing tick of time, where I realize we've run out of things to say. There is nothing to utter. We've caught up with each other's comings and goings so much that we've skipped the present and began talking about the future. There are no more words that can be said, unless of course they are to occupy the minutes it would take us to go from the terrace to my room.

"Do you hear it?" I ask still looking into the dark sky. "The rain. It's so calm. It's like music."

"It is wonderful. Peaceful," she says. "I can't believe no one is enjoying it with us."

"Yeah. Me too."

I finally turn to her. It seems she's inched closer to me during my pondering of the weather. Her eyes have been on me the entire time. At first I could feel them, but now I am looking into their green brilliance. It's as if emeralds shine their greenest through the dark pressures which formed them. I remember those eyes. I've thought of her eyes.

I can feel her breath on my face. It's warm and slow. Anticipating all anew what they've known before. I release a puff of air. It seems I'd forgotten to breathe, and as my breath lands upon her lips she smiles. In the musical silence, we sit. I can't even hear the others now, as sounds have no place anymore, just as words have run dry on rainy nights. There is only one thing to do. Kiss. Touch. Rekindle. A flinch of either of our bodies would bring our lips together. There is only room for action, and that action is one I've thought about for year. I even dreamt of it. I rest in front of her silently, motionlessly, void. It's time. She subtly licks her lips landing breaths upon me once more, but I freeze.

I don't kiss her.

There is no force driving me. There is no unction to take her into my arms. It's inexplicably and calmly enraging. Why am I not making the move I've thought to make? What's keeping me from doing what I've said I would do if I saw her again? There is no Russian grandma in my room, no Camille to coax me into sainthood. There is no pressing obligation or noticeable hindrance keeping me from being with her again. Is it because we're not at the beach? My mind is full of questions too fresh to answer now, so I go with the simplest one.

"Do you want some more wine?"

"Huh?" she responds perplexed.

"We're out of wine."

"Oh...Umm. I'm fine."

"Ok. I'm gonna go take some more," I say as I stand to my feet. I toss the empty bottle in the recycling bin and walk inside.

205

"There he is," says Manon. "Teo, I can't possibly finish this bottle. Come. Sit."

"You must have read my mind," I say filling the glass to the brim. Iza walks in. Her countenance has fallen and she does her best not to look at me. If I knew the answers to the questions asked by her expression, I would express them. But I don't.

"Do you want some wine? We've got plenty," says Emiel chuckling as he pours fills glasses for himself and whoever else wants it.

"Yeah. I guess I do." says Iza. She forces a smile and takes a seat next to him.

Julie is the only one who seems to notice that something's changed, and looks at me inquisitively. I look at her and shake my head quickly, 'no'.

"Why do you shake your head?" asks Manon. "Trouble keeping your eyes open at this hour?"

"No," I say to her. "I think they're open wider than they've ever been.

"Crazy American," she says as she brushes her long blond hair back.

"You have no idea."

"Damn! Is being in Biarritz for two summers driving you crazy?" asks Jardena

"No. I was already out of my mind before I got here. I'm not sure if any of this has helped though," I say standing to my feet. "But it hasn't hurt. Ha! Another bottle?"

"Make it two, Teo." says Emiel reaching into his pocket.

"No, no. It's on me. You're like guests in my home," I say as I walk through the storage room and into the bar.

"Do you even work for the hostel, Teo?" asks Jardena.

"No. He doesn't," says Julie shaking her head. "He just drinks here."

"Aww c'mon. There have got to be some stories other than just drinking. Well, those are the best kinds, but still you've got to let us in on the real deal," interjects Manon.

"Yeah, dude! Tell us some about some wild stuff that's happened," adds Emiel.

"Ok, ok. What do you want to know about? The night life? The food?" I ask as I return from behind the bar.

"No, no, no. That's too easy," says Emiel whose drunken slur has noticeably progressively intensified over the last few bottles. "We can figure all that stuffs together on our own. Give us the 'Teo Experience'. Two summers here. What does it mean?"

Such an earnest question from the drunken Dutchman. My eyebrows arch as memories run through my mind. I remember when trying to reflect on life was reduced to thoughts of Derlenzistda, which were always overtaken by the faces of my folly, the sadness in my soul, and the emptiness of my person. However, I don't feel any of that now. I don't know if I've found some new version of myself, but I smile wider the more I think of these two summers.

"I don't know what it means, but maybe I'm not supposed to know. Basque is beautiful. To be honest, there are very few things about this place that I have an issue with, and so many more interesting things left unknown. I could probably work here every summer for years to come and still have something left to experience, and I say that feeling like I've really tried to let this place inspire me and to make some great memories," I say feeling that my face has reached its limits for expressing happiness. I take hefty sip of my wine. "This place is amazing. I've visited the beaches and cities of the region, and participated in traditions of food, wine, and festival. I've had fun in the night time, and learned some things about myself and life. I don't think I'm supposed to know what any of it means though. Not now, at least."

"Huh?" says Emiel. It seems that wasn't the response he'd hoped for. "You said everyone went to New Quay tonight? We should go."

"Really, Emiel?!" speaks up Manon, a little bit less slurry that him. "He was saying some interesting stuff, and you just want to go to the city center?"

"He said he's had some fun nights. I want to have some fun nights too!"

"It's ok, Manon. He's right," I say laughing. "Do you know how to get there?"

He mumbles something about a bus for a few moments before I finally cut him off and explain that he just needs to take the night bus to the city center. I even go as far as to send a text to see if Katia and Adriana are still there, which they are, and give them heads up to expect some lively company. It seems that the momentum is shifting towards the city center, but I'm good. They'll have a night I've had several times, and will make some summer stories of their own. Emiel on a recruiting campaign convinces Julie to go with them, and I gladly offer to close the bar.

"You sure?" asks Julie.

"Hey, you've put up with me all summer. I'll close things down when I'm done."

"Will you stay up late?" asks Iza who's been uncommonly silent this entire time.

"No. I doubt it. There's a glass worth of rosé left. After that I'm gonna call it a night."

"You sure? Are you feeling ok?" she asks. On the surface, it seems like a final shot at recruiting me for the evening's adventures, but I know what she's asking. It'd be nice to think of a deeply metaphorical response, but I'm just as a confused as to why I didn't make move. I keep it simple, once again.

"I feel great. It's just that I'm tired. The work season is long and even more difficult when you're an amorous conquistador."

"A what?"

"Nevermind," I say chuckling a bit. "After two summers I think I'm ready for some new work and adventures. I've got nothing left to give here. That, and I have a lot of sleep to catch up on."

"I think I understand, Teo," she says with a faint smile. "Sleep well."

"*Bonne nuit*"

Chapter 15: C'est l'Heure

We want answers to questions that we probably shouldn't ask in the first place. We paid for acceptance, only to see that being among the comers and goers has its own unique pains just as any circle does. We jump the gun and make a mess of love and life, when prudence was the most patient virtue. We wait too late, hesitating at the sight of our ideal mate on the other side of the cafe, only to see them a month later in the arms of another. Too little too late, Early birds get the spurn, and time just seems to be a bit too unimpressed with our plans, faults, follies, dreams, goals, and lusts.

The next morning, I began to think a lot about time. What if Iza had come during high season, when I was arguably at my most confused and fragile? Would I have taken her to my room? Should I have taken her into my arms, like I said I would? Even when I said I that, that I wanted to taste such passion again, it was a different time. In any case, it's still too fresh, and I don't fully understand why I didn't take the plunge last night. Our eclectic group spends the next evening drinking together on the hostel's terrace, but Iza is noticeably different. Last summer she would linger around my office just to see me. Now she hardly looks in my direction. She had come here for me. It was her only reason for returning to Biarritz, and when she realized that I would not be her lover she had no more business in Basque Country. She left for Pau the next morning.

I coast through the next couple of days. Katia and Adriana spend most of their time at the beach or shopping, while I linger around the office making plans for my approaching vacation during the day. I have some drinks at night, but not at much as usual. I might as well be a tourist because I spend all of my free time with Emiel, Manon, and Jardena, but eventually their brief Basque experience has to end. We exchange contacts and they're off to live their lives.

Today is the last day. This season is just about over, but there is still time for one more summer treat. I can't think of a better way to end the summer than a quick trip to San Sebastian. Francois and Jean-Henri arrive at the hostel around noon. I'd told them so much about how wonderful *Donostia* is and they insisted that we make a visit together before I leave. It doesn't strike me until we're crossing the frontier into Spain that the return to Biarritz will be a completely different scene than I've come to know. My room is cleaner than usual. In fact, it's almost empty because my bags are packed and in the office. There is hardly any administrative work to do and very few excuses to take advantage of staff pricing because soon I will be unemployed. The last sane semblance of summer lies in the heart of San Sebastian. Its beauty and richness were almost enough to provoke me back to the Basque Country. Now, on the brink of departure, I've already begun to wonder when I will walk its streets again.

As we arrive, I direct Jean-Henri to the underground parking garage entrance near the Maria Cristina. It's funny to think how many times Hermann and I have come here and that now I am at the helm of guiding a leisurely day in *Donostia*. We walk up the steps and into the welcoming sunlight. We see a group of children play with bubbles in the *De Okendo Plaza* as we walk along *Okenda Kalea.* We cut diagonally across the bustling traffic, both pedestrian and vehicular, on Boulevard *Zumardia* until we reach *San Juan Kalea.* We continue past the open markets of fresh produce until we finally arrive at Bar Gorriti.

"Is this the place, Teo?" asks Francois.

"It's the place, my friends."

The barman at Bar Gorriti throws his hands up upon seeing us enter. He begins pouring me a beer, while shaking his head.

"Moreno. I see you've brought more of your friends with you?"

"My friend, I had to. It will be my last time here for a while. I don't know when I'll be back. I had to show my friends the best tapas."

"Well in that case, eat all the food you want. First drinks are on me, yeah?!"

I tell him thank you and shake my head with a grin as the barman hands me the beer and takes the other's orders. We all begin to select from the mouthwatering assortment. The scent of spices ignites my senses. Fish, chorizo, ham, eggs, peppers abound. Francois and Jean-Henri look on in amazement as the barman pours their glasses of wine without looking. He chuckles at them and shoots a wink at me direction. With our plates full and palates ready, we step outside to one of the tall tables. They dive in immediately, while I stand there looking into the distance feeling a very satisfied grin come to my face.

"Teo, are you not going to eat?" asks Jean-Henri.

"What? Oh. Yes of course!" I say as I come to my senses. "I was just thinking."

"What about?" adds Francois.

"It's the service. I love it. It doesn't matter how many times I've come here they remember and greet us like we are locals as though we're here every day. I remember the first time I came back this summer. It's nice to go somewhere where you know someone. Anyways. *Bon appetit,*" I say. I quickly gobble my first tapa and throw the paper to the stone ground. I take a gulp of my beer, feeling pretty content with myself. I'd like to think that Hermann would approve of the entire scene.

We go back for second and third helpings before finally admitting satisfaction. Keeping with custom, I suggest we take a stroll. It was a worthy meal and well deserved after what seems to be a satisfying summer. As we make our way along the seawall admiring the views of *La Concha* beach, Francois and Jean steadily take photos. I am in another zone. I feel fulfillment all around. Hermann is ending his long tenure as Program Director and Bernard will take his place. It's nice to think that even with all my issues during these summers that I was able to keep things afloat for a new chapter in their lives and seemingly mine as well.

"Phew. It's hot. It's hot and I'm thirsty," says Francois.

"Well. You should maybe drink something. Maybe we all should. This sun has a way of making one thirsty," I respond. "We shouldn't resist."

Twelve minutes later we're seated at *Bar Ambrosio* nestled strategically under a large yellow umbrella's shade. I look around *Plaza de la Constitución*. The terrace life is brimming with conversation as the tourists continually pass through in front of our sights. Some stop to watch a trio of musicians and delight in their gypsy tunes. Others are content with the sun simply hitting their faces as they stroll. Everyone seems full of so much energy, but despite our 'thirst' we've slowed down. Jean-Henri takes only half a pint, which is passable because he's driving. However, I can find no excuse for Francois who declines taking a full pint. I destroy my first round to prove a point but slow down quite a bit for my second one. All this drinking and eating has made me tired.

"Yikes, I need a siesta," says Francois.

"Me too," I respond.

"Do you guys want to head back after these drinks?" asks Jean-Henri.

"I don't think so," I begin. "It's the end of the summer for all of us and it's such a pretty damn day. Let's see where it takes us."

"Agreed. I have to be back in Paris to work on Monday, so I need all the relaxing I can get," says Francois. "Anyways, Teo. It was great to see you this summer. How did everything go for you after we left?"

"They went very well. At least, I think so. I had an interesting run in or two, but I think it's all working out."

"So you confessed your love for Camille?" asks Jean-Henri.

"Ha. Not exactly. In fact, I didn't say anything like that. When the time came, I realized there was nothing to say. There was so much going on. There were a few other girls who found their way into the mix."

"Ohhhh yes!" begins Jean-Henri excitedly. "You got laid?"

"Actually, it's the opposite. I think I turned down sex a couple of times to be honest. I haven't had sex this entire summer," I respond. I begin to chuckle hilariously.

"What?! You're kidding, yeah?" asks Jean-Henri

"Nope," I add still chuckling.

"I don't know why you're laughing. This is not funny," continues Jean-Henri. "Some of us haven't been laid all summer, and you are just throwing it away."

"What?"

"He was striking out with every girl in Nice. He couldn't even get a phone number," says Francois laughingly. "It was a pretty impressive streak."

"Screw you, Francois. Why, Teo? Why would you do this when some people are suffering a summer of sexual famine?"

"Honestly...I don't know. I can't put my finger on it. Even one of the girls from last summer showed up. We had talked about making things happen again, but when she was there I just couldn't do it. It's difficult to explain."

"Well, where is she? I'll do it," says Jean nodding his head. "There's no need for everyone to go hungry."

Francois and I look at him, shaking our heads. I order another round of beers, just for the sake of it. Jean-Henri continues for several minutes about his sexual misfortunes. His misery gives us a new energy, and we sit for a while more talking about plans for the rest of the year. I'm pondering on it all. The beginnings. The in-betweens. I look down at my glass. It perspires, dripping cool drops of water. It begs me to relieve it of its slow condensation. I oblige, taking a large gulp. As I do a familiar figure comes walking through the plaza.

"Mariska?"

"Who?" asks Francois.

"Mariska. Umm. She's a Dutch girl I met at the end of last summer during my holiday over a year ago. We met on a walking tour of Florence and ended up playing billiards and drinking together all night. We played on teams and lost every game that night."

"Wait! Is this another girl you turned down?" asks Jean.

"No. It wasn't like that. We only met that night. We kept in loose contact, but that's all."

"Well what are you sitting here for?!" he exclaims throwing his hands up. "Go say something!"

"Oh! Right!" I say. I stand up from the chair and once clear of the terrace, I break into a jog after her and her group. "Mariska! Mariska!"

Everyone but her turns looking perplexed as I approach, and it's not until she finally spins around that I realize it's indeed her.

"Teo?!" she yells rushing to hug me. "I can't believe it's you!"

"I know!" I say breathing heavily and smiling. We stand in shock for a few seconds. She drops her backpack to the floor and hugs me again. "I didn't know you'd be here. I mean, I remember you saying you'd be traveling along the coast, but I never thought you'd come walking past me."

"This is incredible...We've just decided to come here for a day," she begins. We're going to the market to buy some food and then the beach. Then hopefully tonight a disco. You have to come!"

"I can't," I say. "It's my last night in Biarritz. I'm supposed to take my co-workers out to dinner."

"Well. Damn."

"Damn it all," I say laughing and shaking my head. "Maybe they'd want to come here for the night?"

213

"Find out and let me know if anything changes! Maybe we could actually win a round of billiards this time."

"I'll do that and if I can't make it back...I guess I'll just have to run into you next year somewhere in Europe."

"I like the sound of that!" she hugs me for a third time, this time longer than the others.

The group walks off leaving me as I stand in the street for several seconds. I turn and walk back slowly to Francois and Jean-Henri who'd had been waiting for me.

"So was it her?" asks Francois.

"Yeah. It was."

"And? What happened?" asks Jean-Henri.

"She hugged me. Three times."

"And then? I mean what are the odds of you seeing her here?" asks Francois seemingly very interested in the occasion.

"Maybe I can stop by Holland during my holiday and say hello or maybe I'll just have to see if we can continue our trend of seeing each other at the end of summer. In any case, they're just maybes. I can deal with maybes."

"Wouldn't it be nice? It would be pretty cool if you did meet her again at some point a year from now," says Francois.

"It'd be a story worth telling. I suppose I'll just have to wait until then. We will see."

You seem different, Teo," begins Francois. "Last time we saw you, you were ready to burn down the city over Camille. Now you seem almost..."

"Happy?"

"Oui. C'est ça," responds Jean-Henri with a smile coming to his face.

"Yeah. Maybe. Maybe I am."

Hermann pulls his blue Volkswagen onto the grasses by the office window, just like he has for the last two summers and just as I hope to always remember. He steps into the office at 11:00am checking to see that Katia, Adriana, and I have packed all the equipment. Bernard shows up a few minutes later waving from the parking lot while lighting a cigarette. There is the calmest joy among us as we realize that the season is over. It's difficult to grasp at first, especially while caught up in the turmoil of high season. However, this hostel life is temporary, and it's time to say our goodbyes.

"Ok, Team. Are we ready?" begins Hermann as he stands in the middle of the office with his hands poised prominently on his hips.

"Wait, wait. I have a little more *administratif* work to do," I say with a smirk.

"You and your *administratif*. What a Program Manager. You manage everything."

"Ah gawd, Teo. We have a few more things to pack up, Hermann. Perhaps, we'll be done in ten minutes," says Katia.

"That makes more sense," says Hermann. He, Bernard, and I begin taking what we can to his car. Once it's finished he stands in the office once more with a satisfied expression. *"Alors. Je crois que c'est l'heure."*

He walks to his car, lifts the hatchback, and opens the cooler. He pulls out a cold bottle of rosé, which means it must be for special occasion since he normally carries a cube. I continue watching as he smiles at me through the window and shuffles inside the building.

"Do you have a time to break from your administrative tasks for a glass?" he asks. He knows the response and is already pouring some.

"Funny you should ask. I've just finished."

"Opp la! Imagine that!" he says clapping his hands together. Bernard enters from his second cigarette and also agrees it is the hour for a cold drink. Even Katia and Adriana, who normally stay away from our opportune thirst, join in, making it five adults drinking before noon. Augustine walks in with Gil and Hamza during our toast.

"Oh la la! Is it not too early for this?" she says jokingly.

"It seems every time we're in the middle of a toast you decide to visit," I say.

"I suppose the staff pricing was just for show then?" she asks.

"I don't know," I respond. "Never used it."

"Pfttt, Teo. Anyways. I just wanted to say thank you all for the summer. It was a long one and despite a couple of bumps it was a pleasure to have you here. Will anyone be back next summer?"

Katia and Adriana respond promptly with a collective 'no', while obviously, Bernard will be here as the new director with Hermann in the shadows.

215

"I don't think so," I respond.

"You said that last summer, Mr. Program Manager," says Hermann laughingly.

"Yes, yes. I know. However, I suppose that four months is enough for me. At least I don't want to work here again. I'll have to come for a visit though, and make sure the new team is doing their job."

"Yes, of course, and for *les ferias*," says Gil. He winks at me. "There still may be a thing or two we need to teach you about Basque summer life."

"Yes, and it'd be a shame to leave Julien waiting," adds Hamza. Everyone laughs.

"Absolutely," I respond sarcastically having almost forgotten that the whole debacle even took place. "I'd hate to leave an old man waiting."

"Well then stop making me wait to take this drink," says Hermann. Everyone agrees and even Augustine, Gil, and Hamza take small cups to join us. "To a summer well worked, and a life well lived."

Hermann, Katia, Bernard, Adriana and I stop at the *La Station* restaurant just across from the Biarritz Gare, one last time. Adriana takes a train to Irun as soon as we arrive, leaving the rest of us to stand at the bar with our espressos in hand. It's bittersweet. The four of us have spent four months working together, and though everyone tosses around 'maybes' about next summer we all know how fragile that can be. I think we all know that our professional connections have come to an end, leaving only room for creativity about how in the hell we could ever see each other again.

"*C'est l'heure*," begins Hermann. "That is unless you want to miss your train, ex-Program Manager."

"Yeah. I guess it is the hour. *Babushka,* will you miss me?"

"*Vnuk!* Don't be silly! I'll be moving back to Paris in a couple of days, so try not to get in trouble before I arrive."

"Of course, of course," I say as I give her kisses on each cheek and a large hug. I turn to Bernard. "You know, I have some photos from *La Fête de Bernard.*"

"*La quoi?*" he responds.

216

"Don't worry! You will see," I say. His mouth drops once he realized what I'm referring to.

"Oh, *putain*. Ok, ok. I can't wait to see them. Good times, Teo," he says. He gives me a kiss to each cheek.

"Oh la la!" shouts Hermann. "Are you going to give me a kiss too?"

"Do you want one?"

"Not at all. Let's go. I'll walk you to the station," he says. He grabs my bag and we dart across the street stopping just in front of the station's entrance. "Here we go."

"Yeah. Here we go," I say nodding my head. I know Hermann is not big on emotional displays and it takes everything in me to respect that. No, I won't kiss him and a hug still seems a bit much. I settle again for a handshake. "It was a pleasure to work with you again. I hope it's not the last time we meet."

"The feeling is mutual, Teo. Thank you for coming back and sticking it out this summer. You're welcome any time here," he sticks his hand out and crushes my hand the hardest he ever has. I don't let him see the pain. We both tighten our lips and nod in silence. "Did you find what you were looking for?"

"You know," I begin. My eyes almost water, but I take a deep breath to keep composed in front of him. "Yeah. I think so."

"Good. That is good to hear. What will you do after your holiday?"

"I'll go back to U.S., but I don't think for a long. I've got to keep traveling and meeting new people. These summers were an adventure...This life is an adventure."

"Hopefully, your adventures bring you back this way for some rosé," he says. He smiles that grizzled smile of his. "If you need anything at all, you have my contact. *A la prochaine*."

"*A la prochaine, chef*," I respond.

I grab my bag and adjust the guitar hanging off my back. My train leaves in two minutes, so I rush to the platform. It's nearly empty, but I know how these things go. By the time it arrives in Paris it will be full with French folks from various coastal cities. I think to look into my bag for something to read and laugh when I realize there is no book there. With nothing to read, I take out my notebook. I begin to write.

Epilogue: Somewhere
Three Months after Summer 2

The computer screen is bright and only gets brighter as the sun takes its slumber. No worry. Something's got to keep the light shining into the night hours for those of us who thrive in twilight. The jukebox's music has got to keep playing to balance out the roar from the lively cafe clientele. A community. The service. Comers and goers pass through the doors as freely as the espressos pour from the machines behind the bar. The hissing is sweet meditation, calming and reflective. I sit at said bar, and have been for several hours now. It's funny to think that scribbles I began on a train to Paris three months ago are now being put to some use.

"Teo, you look tired," says Alima from behind the bar. "Can I get you a cortado?"

"Huh? Hey. Yes, please. I've been writing for a while now. I've got work these pages out."

"What about some music too? What song do you want?"

"How about Françoise Hardy? *"Comment tu dire adieu?""* I respond.

"Ok, sure. What does that mean again?"

"How do you say goodbye?"

"Agh! It's beautiful. I'll get it down one of these days," she says as she finishes making the cortado. She hands it to me over the bottles of wine. "Missing France?"

"Haha. Something like that. I've left, but it hasn't left me. You know? People thought I was a completely different person when I came back last year. Now, they're always pointing out how much I've changed; from the way I speak, down to the way a dress. I guess the people in France wouldn't recognize me here."

"How so?"

"I sit in the deepest corner at the bar in a cafe glued to a computer screen and prefer not to talk to anyone except regulars. It's almost like I used to be all those years ago."

"I can see that. That's not a bad thing. Those old days were good ones."

"True. I'm happy. This is where I am and is part of where I want to go in my life. I guess that I just think about more and more about how where I am now will take me back."

"To Basque Country?"

"Of course. To there. San Sebastian. Somewhere! I crave adventure, Alima. I need a new one."

"I know the feeling, Teo. Haha. Come to Mexico with us next month!"

"We will see."

"That's what you always say. Maybe you can find some things other than sitting here in front of your computer every night to keep you inspired while you're here. That could be a good change of pace."

"True."

"Anyways. Do you know the number of that song on the jukebox?"

"Yes. It's 9507," I say. I drop the sugar cube my coffee and stir with the small spoon, while she goes to put the song on.

I am terribly scrutinizing of the last lines I've written. I wonder if I can ever capture anything I've lived. Biarritz was just a small part of it all. So many adventures. So many cities, places, sites, friends, and family. I'm happy to have had them, and even more joyful that it wasn't all hangovers and cold beds.

I could certainly use a break and am happy when Kevin walks in through the back entrance. He motions to me if I want a drink and I shoot him a look as if to say, "Really? Do you need to ask?" I'm a bit surprised when I see that he's taken 4 glasses and a bottle of wine, and even more intrigued by the determined look on his face.

"Stop," he says.

"Stop what?"

"Stop working. You've been sitting at this cafe for two months, and while I admire your work ethic, even you need to take a break," he says closing the computer screen.

"Ok, ok," I say. I take the break a step further. I unplug the cord and wrap it up, before placing it in my bag. "What's the plan, my man?"

"Wine."

"I think I can get on board with this. Why four glasses?"

"Aj is coming by."

"So she's drinking two glasses at once?"

"She's bringing a friend."

"Really? Cute?"

"Calm down, T. She's just a friend of hers from out of town," he says laughingly.

"How can you tell me to calm down? I was in a corner when you found me."

"You're so dramatic. Look, let's take this big table. That group is leaving," he says. As they get up, he places the glassware down. We take our seats. "And yes. She's pretty cute."

"I don't know why I asked. I'm not going to do anything about it. I've been in a very committed relationship with my work and wouldn't want to make it jealous."

"Editor is still on your ass for new copy?"

"Yeah, but no worry. I've got a joker up my sleeve," I say. I flinch my hands as if I am wearing a long-sleeved shirt and point to my left wrist. I chuckle joyfully.

"There it is again."

"What?"

"These expressions. 'The joker', 'the service'. The list goes on. Maybe you don't notice it, but you say them all the time. You're smiling from ear-to-ear. The most I can get out of you these days is a smirk without you having a few drinks ahead of time, but you start talking about Biarritz and it's like you tasted tapas for the first time."

"I miss it, Kev. There I said it! I've seen a lot of places, but it seems France has become something else to me. In that same way, Biarritz, San Sebastian, Bayonne...They've made a home in every part of my being. I see them everywhere. I feel it in my taste buds, in my culture."

He asks about the Basque aftermath. I tell him everything I know. How Hermann keeps in touch from his countryside home, now addressing me as 'ex-Program Manager', while Katia has happily made a home in Paris. Reda is doing a masters degree and calls me from time to time and I even keep in touch with *Les Quatre Fantastiques* during their senior year of high school. He pours wine into two glasses and passes one to me.

"It shows. I mean, I know everything you've told me and it's just...It's interesting to see how it reflects in you as a person," he says. He pauses to take a sip. "Did you find what you hoped for?"

"In a way. Yeah. I'd lost myself in pleasure and pain. I was just thinking how sitting here every day focusing on my projects and planning for the next adventures reminds me of...well, me. But something's different," I say. I pause. I take a thoughtful sip and continue. "I did find something. However, I didn't know I was searching for it."

"So what was it?"

"A better version of myself."

"Cheers to that. To a better you and to a better life," he says as we touch glasses. We each take a sip. "And what of your proclaimed 'indiscretions'? Are they a part of this version?"

"Absolutely. I learned and saw a lot during these adventures and my romantic comings and goings are included. Some people get it immediately. They have one bad relationship and something clicks in them. Not me. No. I had to go to another continent to understand that it takes one, to make one. We're all guilty in lust, life and love; whether victims or victors," I say, somehow finally making sense of it all. I have his attention so I continue. "I keep in touch with all of them, some more frequently than others. I may see Manon when she visits New York next month, and Mara finally moved to Italy. I'm still welcomed in Berlin at any time. I have no news from Sara. I wish I did. In just a few hours she helped me make sense of it all. It began with her, and I knew that things had come full circle that last night with Iza."

"Teo 2.0," he says with a smirk on his face. "So there is no plan. You're back in the zone with a mound of experiences to show for."

"I think so, yeah. I'm going to keep getting better. That seems like a good idea to me and honestly it's all I can do. Work at being a better version of myself. Hopefully, that version is capable enough.

"I think it will be, my friend. Everything happens for a reason. I've listened to your story, you know? In acceptance, true acceptance, you consider all things no matter their truth, and then life goes on. It's not some declaration, some empty expression. It's an evolution."

"2.0," I say with a smirk and raise of my glass.

"2.0," he responds as we cheer once more.

We empty the glasses. He nods his head and pours some more wine, emptying the last of the bottle just as Aj walks through the front door. Close behind her is a woman with long wavy black hair. She looks around the full cafe with wondrous eyes. I can tell she's never been here before.

"Hello, boys," says Aj as she gives Kevin a large kiss on the lips. I exchange a kiss to each cheek just before she looks at the table in shock. "Really? You've already finished a bottle?!"

"Um. Of course. We wanted to make sure the wine was of good quality for you and your friend," I say.

"Yeah, babe. It's her first time in town, so we wanted to make a good impression by picking the perfect wine."

"Aren't you just the perfect gentlemen," she says laughing. "Anyways, this is my good friend Kontxesi. She's from Spain, and will be and out of town for a while for work."

Kevin greets her with a kiss to the cheek. I do the same.

"I'm Teo. What was your name again?"

"Kontxesi," she says. She smiles subtly through them revealing a slight gap between her teeth.

"So, what are we going to do about this wine situation?" asks Aj. "Did you wine aficionados find anything good?"

"Perhaps. Teo, why don't you show Kontxesi the wine selection," adds Kevin with a strange smirk on his face.

"Um. Ok. I guess it is my round after all," I say. Kontxesi places her purse on the chair and I lead her to the wines which are lined up along the bar.

"What type of wine do you like?" I ask.

"All types really. I hear you're the expert. Is there something here that you'd suggest?" she says.

"Ha. I'm no expert, just a guy who's had a few long nights," I say. "I don't know why I even look at the choices. I always take the same one."

"Ah. Ok. What is it?"

"It's a rosé *txakoli.* I drank it pretty often during the last two summers. Have you had it before?"

"Oh, of course! We always had this wine at my family's home. I am from where it's made. The region is called..."

"*Euskadi,*" I say.

"You speak Basque?"

"No. Not at all. I spent four months or so there," I say trying not to smile too widely.

"What a coincidence! Of course, we should drink it. Let's take two bottles," she says with a delightful smile.

Kontxesi returns to the table. I wait a few moments in line to get the bottles and return to the table where Kevin sits quite casually with his arm around Aj. I have a sneaking suspicion that he, knowing my comings and goings, has orchestrated this whole deal.

"What did you end up choosing?" asks Aj.

"It is quite amazing. He chose a wine that comes from just near where I grew up. It is such a great coincidence. Yeah?" says Kontxesi

"Oh yeah," begins Kevin as he slaps his hand to his forehead. "I completely forgot that you were from Basque Country! Did he tell you that he used to live there?"

"Only briefly," she responds.

"Well he should tell you all about it," says Aj. I look at the happy couple. It seems they're even happier having seen their plan come to life. Aj continues. "I'm quite busy with work this week, but perhaps you could show her around the city?"

"Yeah? I think it could be good. Also, you could tell me about your time in Basque Country," Kontxesi says enthusiastically.

By now I have already opened a bottle of *txakoli* and have poured it in our glasses, all the while resisting the huge sense of happiness that I feel tugging at the sides of my mouth.

"Sure. Why not?" I say.

Nothing can truly end, when we don't know where to begin. If we know don't where to start, that's ok too. Live until you die. Until then, don't panic. *Ouais*. It's a good way to live, I think.

The End

ABOUT THE AUTHOR

Bradley Basker is a writer, entrepreneur, and musician from Houston, Texas. His other titles include *The Meeting Place (2014)* and *It's Particular (2013)*. He is also the creator of the Shameless Vagabond blog, which shares stories and photos from his world travels. He is the guitarist and lead singer for the Brad Basker Band, and is founder of Griffin Collective, a literary, media, and entertainment services business.

Bradley holds a Bachelor of Public Relations from Sam Houston State University, a Master of International Studies from the University of St. Thomas, and a Course Sequence in Intercultural Communication and International Media from Gonzaga University. He is currently doing a PhD in Social Communication at the University of the Basque Country in Bilbao, Spain.

Www.BradBasker.com
Brad@BradBasker.com
Www.GriffinCollective.com
Www.ShamelessVagabond.com
Instagram: @BradBasker
Instagram: @shamelessvagabond
Twitter: @BradBasker
Www.Facebook.com/BaskerBrad